"I see the

It was so simple, real...
kindness.

What was she doing? Gage wasn't for her, but the beauty of this meadow was. Wonder surrounded her in a pool of delicate flowers.

She ran her fingers through the leaves and petals, softer than silk to touch, and breathed deeply. "This is what hope smells like."

"You could be right." He knelt too.

Gage stared at her, his gloved hand settling at the small of her back, his other reaching toward her face.

There was no panic or outrage or shock as he eased close. So close their breaths mingled and their lips met in a soft, luscious caress.

Eyes fluttering shut, she surrendered. Dying a little bit as he caught her bottom lip between his and sucked just right. The sensation was the single best thing she'd ever felt. *Ever!*

Praise for JILLIAN HART'S recent works

Bluebonnet Bride
"Ms. Hart expertly weaves a fine tale of the heart's
ability to find love after tragedy. Pure reading pleasure!"
—*Romantic Times*

Montana Man
"…a great read!"
—*Rendezvous*

Cooper's Wife
"…a wonderfully written romance
full of love and laughter."
—*Rendezvous*

Last Chance Bride
"The warm and gentle humanity of *Last Chance Bride*
is a welcome dose of sunshine…"
—*Romantic Times*

JILLIAN HART

MONTANA LEGEND

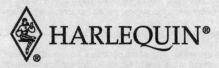

HARLEQUIN®

TORONTO • NEW YORK • LONDON
AMSTERDAM • PARIS • SYDNEY • HAMBURG
STOCKHOLM • ATHENS • TOKYO • MILAN • MADRID
PRAGUE • WARSAW • BUDAPEST • AUCKLAND

ISBN 0-373-29224-4

MONTANA LEGEND

This edition published by arrangement with Harlequin Books S.A.

® and TM are trademarks of the publisher. Trademarks indicated with
® are registered in the United States Patent and Trademark Office, the
Canadian Trade Marks Office and in other countries.

Visit us at www.eHarlequin.com

Printed in U.S.A.

Please address questions and book requests to:
Harlequin Reader Service
U.S.: 3010 Walden Ave., P.O. Box 1325, Buffalo, NY 14269
Canadian: P.O. Box 609, Fort Erie, Ont. L2A 5X3

Chapter One

Montana, 1884

Looking up from her early morning chores, Sarah Redding watched the distant horse and rider against the vast expanse of the eastern horizon. The newly rising sun peered over the edge of the world, casting the mounted man in silhouette, limning him with light. Morning came soft as a whisper to the land, but it seemed as if the daylight did not touch him. The stranger rode in darkness.

He's like a myth, all power and steel, she thought as the rider grew nearer on the road from town. Then closer still until she could see the angle of his Stetson, the glint of silver at his belt and the blue of his denim trousers.

"What kept you? I've been waiting on the milk," a sharp voice scolded from inside the weather-beaten shanty.

"I've got the full pail right here."

"Then hand it through the door. You're running late with your chores again." Aunt Pearl, a babe balanced on her hip, rammed open the screen door and seized the tin bucket. "I'll strain this. Hurry and go, before Milt comes in from the fields wanting his breakfast."

There would be trouble to pay if that happened, Sarah knew. As a widow with an ill child, she could not risk angering her uncle, not when she was down on her luck.

She plucked the egg basket from the porch, determined to waste no more time daydreaming about the lone rider with the fancy Stetson.

Still, she wondered about him. He didn't look to be from around here. Strangers were few and far between on this forgotten spot on the Montana prairie. Who was he and why was he here? Sarah resisted the urge to turn toward the horizon as she unlatched the chicken house door.

High, angry squawks filled the air as chickens hurled toward her, flapping their wings. Yellow beaks pecked at her ankles and she shooed the mean birds away.

I'm grateful to be here, she reminded herself. She wiped a few specks of blood away with her skirt hem before scaling up the wooden ramp and into the dark cramped coop.

If Aunt Pearl hadn't convinced her husband to let Sarah live with them, there was no telling what would have happened to her or to her daughter. She might not be happy living here, but at least they had a roof over their heads. A place to stay while Ella recovered her health.

Already, the little girl was growing stronger. Staying here was only a temporary situation. One day, she would be able to work full-time again. There would be no more Aunt Pearl, no more hardship and no more chickens.

For all Sarah knew, happiness could be waiting just around the corner.

"Shoo, bird." She waved her apron at the wiry old hen wisely guarding her nest.

The hen didn't move, so Sarah flapped her apron harder.

With an insulted screech, the chicken dove at her. Feathers flew everywhere, choking the air.

"Hello? Miss?" a man's voice called from outside the henhouse. "Thought you should know there's a hole in the fence. Your birds are out."

That wasn't Uncle Milt's voice. Then who could it be? Surely not one of the neighbors.

She remembered the dark rider she'd spotted on the horizon's edge, and she plucked a feather from her hair. *No. It can't be him.*

She peered through the small door. Her jaw dropped at the sight of the mounted man in her uncle's yard. With his black hat tipped low over his face, she could only see the cut of his square jaw, dark with several days' growth. His mouth was an unrelenting line that did not flicker.

The dark rider stood in the yard, so handsome she could not breathe. She brushed a feather from her patched apron before stepping into the sunlight. "Thank you for mentioning it. Goodness, the hens are everywhere."

"My pleasure, ma'am." He touched the brim of his Stetson. He looked like man and might, like a legend on horseback, as he stared at her without saying more.

She'd never been so aware of the dress she wore, thin and faded from wear. Her fingers found another feather in her hair and she tugged it free. "We had a hungry coyote last night."

"There are tracks. Two sets of them." His voice was magnificent, too, as he gestured toward the hole in the fence.

Here she was, standing before a dream, and what was she wearing? The ugliest dress in the county. It was clear he was not about to be carried away by the sight of her.

Well, life never promised to be fair or love easy to find.

She brushed at the straw clinging to her hem and knelt in front of the fence.

"Need help?"

"No."

Leather creaked as the stranger dismounted. He was as tall as he looked. He approached with a slow confident gait, strolling right past her as if she wasn't there.

Her skin tingled at his nearness. A zing of sensation skipped down her spine, making her aware of this man, so strong and silent. Far too aware. Her blood felt warm in her veins, and she stared intently at the hole in the earth. Could he guess that she was attracted to him?

"I don't suppose this is the Buchanan spread?"

"No."

"That's the way my luck's been running lately." He tipped his black hat lower over his eyes. "I'll need a shovel."

"A shovel? Oh, I can't let you fix this." The sooner he rode away, the faster her reaction to him would fade. She took off her apron and stuffed it into the small hole. "There, this will do for now."

"Don't want my help?"

"I don't know you, sir."

"Last name's Gatlin." His hard mouth softened into a small grin at the corners. "My friends call me Gage. You look alone here. Is this your place?"

"No, this is my aunt's husband's farm. She's busy in the house, and Uncle Milt is out early in the fields."

She climbed to her feet only to realize there was a dirt stain across the front of her bodice from preparing the garden spot yesterday. She looked like the poor relation she was.

Well, nothing could be done about it now. "What are you doing riding this way, Mr. Gatlin?"

"Looking for my next job."

She spotted a stray chicken and dashed after it. Mr. Gatlin's fine-blooded mare snorted in surprise as she whisked past. Out of the corner of her eye, Sarah noticed the polished leather of the quality saddle, and the expensive rifle cover strapped beneath the right stirrup. "Your next job? You don't look like a drifter."

"And you look like you need some help." The grin in the corners of his mouth widened a little more as he stood, all power and masculinity.

Making her feel small and plain.

She scooped a hen from the grass at the roadside. When she turned around, he was gone. So, he thought he'd help her, would he? Judging by the quality of his horse and saddle, he didn't need to trade work for a meal.

So what did he want? Or was he merely being a gentleman? She marched past his horse and deposited the hen in the coop, not sure what to do if Mr. Gatlin was only being kind. She hadn't been around a kind man in so long—since her husband died—that she'd *almost* forgotten they truly existed.

By the time she'd caught her third escaped chicken, Gage Gatlin ambled out of the barn carrying a battered shovel.

"Might as well make myself useful. I'm rusty at helping maidens in distress, but I'll get better with practice."

"You're out of practice at shoveling? Or helping a woman?"

"I'll never tell."

"Why's that?" She held the squawking chicken against her chest with one hand as she reached for the door latch. "Is there a wife you're running away from?"

He was at her side in an instant, radiating heat and strength as he opened the door for her. "There's no wife."

"I see." She brushed past him to release the bird.

He nodded toward the south, where the rolling prairie stretched endlessly. "I'm looking for a fellow who's got a place not far from here. I thought this was the place, but I must have taken the wrong road."

"You did." She brushed dirt and chicken feathers from her worn skirt. "I happen to know where that ranch is."

"Is that so? Then maybe we can make a deal."

"Why did I know you were going to say that?"

"Because I'm bound and determined to help you out, ma'am."

"Fine. You fix my chicken fence and I'll give you the best directions you've ever had. Is that what you want?"

"I say it's a satisfactory deal. I'd best get to work."

"I have eggs to gather." She grabbed a basket and hurried through the little chicken yard toward the snug henhouse. Her skirts rustled with her gait, her long braids snapping.

Gage watched her go. She moved like May across the prairie, light and easy on the eyes. And because she wasn't wearing a petticoat beneath that threadbare dress, he could make out the shape of her legs as she ran. Long, lean, but not skinny. And her hair, as bright as gold, made him glad to be a man. It trailed down her back as rich as sunlight.

There were times he missed having a woman to pull close. Especially a woman like this one.

She disappeared into the coop, and it was too bad. He liked the way she looked, even with the feather stuck in her hair. Her dress was faded and her sunbonnet needed starching, but she was the prettiest female he'd seen in a long while.

He filled in the hole and tamped it down good around the wood post. Without new wire, he couldn't do better, but it would hold for now. As he climbed to his feet, he couldn't help but hear angry voices coming from the weather-beaten shanty.

Lived with her relatives, did she? He felt sorry for her as he carried the shovel to the barn and stowed it in the same dirty corner where he'd found it. He knew something about families and anger.

Not that he had much family to call his own anymore. Aside from his little girl, his parents were buried and his brothers and sisters were spread across the West like seeds on the wind. Considering the house he'd grown up in and the marriage he'd had, being alone wasn't so bad.

The horse shied as he came near.

"Easy girl, I'm not the one who's angry." Gage patted the mare's warm neck. "I told you, you're safe with me."

The horse's ears swiveled. Her skin twitched nervously and not even his touch could soothe her.

Gage's gaze followed the sounds of anger. In a glance he noticed the shanty's front steps were loose and the porch boards uneven. The screen door sagged on tired hinges. Before he could decide to step up to the house to try to intercede, the shrill woman's voice faded into silence.

Troubled, he waited. He could hear a faint humming from inside the chicken coop and soon, there she was, breezing down the ramp, swinging her basket of well-packed eggs. Her worn gray dress swirled around her ankles like music.

Spotting him, she wove around the chickens and through the small gate. "I see you kept your end of the bargain."

"It's the best I can do without new wire." Gage shrugged, snapping clods of dirt from the crumpled garment he'd rescued from the earth. "Here's your apron. I guess it's your turn to help me out."

"With the directions. I had better take a look at the repair you did to the fence. If it isn't good enough, I just may give you bad directions."

"I expect good directions as I did a remarkable job."

"We'll just see about that."

He chuckled, shaking his head. Couldn't remember the last time he laughed, but this little slip of a woman made his burdens seem to disappear, if only for a moment.

She knelt to inspect his work, a small smile on her

soft lips as if she were holding back more laughter. As if she were taking pleasure in teasing him.

"All right. I guess that will do. It's the Buchanan land you're looking for?"

"That's right, ma'am. I'm expected to arrive this morning. I gave my word."

"A man of his word, are you? I thought those didn't exist anymore." She swept close to snatch the balled-up apron.

For an instant she was near enough for him to see the soft threads of gold in her hair. To smell the warmth of her skin and the faint scent of wood smoke, crisp and clean. She'd lit the morning cooking fire, he'd wager, noticing her delicate hands chapped red from hard work. He felt sorry for her, living in that anger-filled house.

She shook the dirt from her apron in a smooth snap, breaking through his thoughts and calling his attention back to watch her fold the length of calico over her lean forearm.

"You'll want to head back the way you came," she said in that gentle way of hers. "Stay left at the first fork you come to in the road. Buchanan's place is about the fifth ranch you come to. Keep our barn in your sight, and you'll be fine."

"I'm indebted to you, ma'am."

"Stop calling me 'ma'am.' It makes me feel too old. I'm not stoop-shouldered yet."

Old? She looked young—not too young—and easy to look at as she shaded her eyes with one hand. "My name is Sarah Redding."

He tipped his hat. "Well, Miss Sarah Redding, I'll round up your chickens and be on my way."

Sarah couldn't help the pull of disappointment in

her chest. "Miss," he'd called her. It was a common enough mistake, she supposed, thinking of the several bachelors and widowers who'd been by to call when she'd first arrived at Aunt Pearl's house last spring.

As soon they'd learned she was not as young as they figured *and* she had a daughter, they nearly tripped over their feet to leave in a hurry and never returned. And if it hurt, she wasn't about to admit it or to expect that this man, as appealing as he may seem, would be any different.

And if that were true, she didn't want him gathering up her aunt's escaped chickens. "I can catch the hens on my own," she called after him. "They're my responsibility and besides, didn't you give your word? You have places to be."

"It won't take more than a few minutes to help."

"Go on, cowboy. It's my work to do."

A chicken squawked, flapping to keep out of his reach. He hesitated, straightening to figure out the best thing to do. Didn't seem right to leave her like this, but she looked determined to be rid of him. Maybe she was one of those independent types, never settling for a husband and marriage.

Or maybe it was him she didn't want hanging around for too long.

"I'll be on my way, if that's what you want, ma'am." He gathered his mare's reins, taking comfort in the familiar feel of worn leather against his skin. Something made him hesitate, maybe because she was the most decent woman he'd come across in some time.

Maybe he had no right taking an interest, but it didn't stop him. "If you don't mind my asking, why are you living with relatives? A pretty lady like you ought to be married.''

"The truth is, I haven't found the right man. Only inferior ones wind up traveling down my road.'' Her eyes sparkled as she teased him—not coy or enticing, but gentle and honest. She tilted her head to one side, scattering the gold wisps that had escaped her braid.

And revealing a small white downy feather stuck in the hair above her left ear. The breeze lifted and made it flutter. "Good luck to you, cowboy. I appreciate your help.''

"My pleasure, miss.'' He tipped his hat and mounted. The creak of the saddle was the only sound between them and he waited, trying to think of something more to say.

But the truth was, he'd never had much desire to charm the ladies. He was more practiced in keeping his distance from them, not in figuring out how to talk with them. When was the last time he'd been interesting in keeping up a conversation with a woman?

He couldn't rightly say. Just as he couldn't rightly explain why his heart ached with her sweetness as the breeze ruffled her skirt and the wisps of hair that escaped from her braids.

He liked the sight of her, faded dress and all.

"By the way, you missed a feather.'' He said it kindly as he nudged the mare with his knees and guided the animal with an expert's ease. "Just thought you'd like to know.''

"*What?*'' Sarah's hand flew to her head and her fingertips bumped into the feather's stiff spine. She tugged it out of her hair, but he was already riding away.

Oh, had it been sticking out straight like that the entire time?

Probably. Heat swept across her face. There he goes, the most handsome man who had ever wandered down her road, and what kind of impression did she make? Certainly not one that charmed him to the depths of his soul.

Sarah brushed at the skirt that had been her mother's. So old, the dyes had faded from the cotton, leaving only light gray. Her hair wasn't even up yet, she realized, a long braid sticking her mid-back as she rescued an escaped hen. A terrible feeling settled into her stomach. Had she made a fool of herself? Most likely.

Well, *today* wouldn't be the day she fell in love with a wonderful man.

She'd long since stopped expecting love to happen twice in her lifetime, but the tiny hope inside her remained.

Maybe tomorrow. A woman could always hope there would be another man riding her way, tall and strong, with eyes the color of the wind.

Over the last rise the Buchanan ranch came into view, or what he figured had to be the Buchanan spread. Because the split-rail fence alongside the road went from well-maintained to tumbling-down.

He ought to have expected it, the way his luck had always been. Still, this was a fair piece of prairie that went on as far as he could see. A slice of heaven for sale right here on the vast Montana prairie.

Gage reined the mare to a stop and looked. Just looked. What a sight. The sun was drifting over the horizon, gaining in brightness, chasing away the last of the night shadows. He couldn't get enough of these wide-open spaces and it filled him with hope.

Real, honest-to-goodness hope, and that was a hard thing for a practical man like him. A man who'd seen too much of the bad life had in it. But that life seemed a lifetime away as the warmth of the morning seeped through his clothes and into his skin. He didn't believe that dreams existed. But maybe here he had a chance. To make a permanent home for his daughter's sake. To find some peace for his.

Maybe.

Looking from left to right, he remembered the description in Buchanan's letter.

Two whole sections. Two square miles of his own land. Larger than any he'd yet come across. It was something to consider even if neglect hung on the crooked fence posts that leaned one way, then another. How they stood up at all was a wonder.

Gage nudged his mare onto the dirt path and considered the desolate fields surrounding him, fields grazed down to earth and stone. Cattle dotted the pasture and lifted their heads at his approach. Several bawled at him, their ribs visible, suffering from hunger. Good animals, too, and valuable enough—

He swore. Whoever Buchanan was, he was a damn fool.

Turn around, his instincts told him. *You've looked at better property and kept on riding.* Gage knew what he wanted, and this rundown homestead wasn't it. Yep, he ought to turn around and head south. Look at the land for sale near Great Falls. There had to be a better deal for his hard-earned cash.

He touched his knee against the mare's flank, turning her toward the main road, but a niggling doubt coiled tight in his chest. Something deep within made him hesitate against his better judgment. Maybe it was the haunting beauty of the plains. Or the vast meadows that didn't hem him in.

Maybe he was just tired of roaming. Gage couldn't explain it. He simply let the high prairie winds turn him around. He guided the mare down the rutted and weed-choked path while hungry cattle bellowed pitifully as he passed by.

After riding a spell up a slight incline that hid the lay of the land ahead, the road leveled out and Gage stood in his stirrups eager for the first sight of what could be his home. As the ever-present wind battered his Stetson's brim, he spotted a structure on the crest of the rise, silhouetted by the sun, shaded by a thick mat of trees.

"Get up, girl," he urged, heels nudging into the mare's sides, sending her into an easy lope.

The structure grew closer and, as the road curved 'round, it became a tiny claim shanty listing to the south, as if the strong winter winds had nearly succeeded in blowing it over. One entire corner of the roof was missing.

That's it. Turn around. There was no sense in talking it over with Buchanan. The place was a wreck. The cattle were starving. For all he knew, they might never regain their health.

A wise man would keep on moving.

Now normally he was a wise man, but for some reason the reins felt heavy in his right hand, too heavy to fight them. So, he let the mare continue along the path and reined her to a halt in front of the ramshackle excuse for a house.

The door squeaked open, sagging on old leather

hinges. A stooped, grizzled man wearing a faded red cotton shirt and wrinkled trousers limped into sight, leaning heavily on a thick wooden cane. "You Gage Gatlin?"

"Yes, sir, I am." Gage dismounted and extended his hand. "Good to meet you, Mr. Buchanan."

The old man braced his weight on his good leg, leaned his cane against his hip and accepted Gage's hand. His handshake was surprisingly solid for a man so infirm, and Gage felt some sympathy for the man who'd grown too weak and old to care for his land and livestock.

"Pleased to meet you, stranger. You can call me Zeb." Buchanan repositioned his cane and the hard look in his watery eyes was unflinching. "Now that you've seen my place, are you still figurin' to buy?"

"Don't know. Trying to decide that for myself."

Gage studied the shanty. It didn't look good. The unpainted boards were weathered to black and where boards were missing, Buchanan had used tarred paper as a patch. "I've gotta be honest. This place is going to take hard work and a lot of it."

"It's rundown, I didn't lie to you about that." Shame flushed the man's aged face. "The land's good, you keep that in mind, and my herds are fine stock. Don't look like it, I know, but it was a long winter and I had to make the hay last. Others had the same trouble 'round here. I'll give you a fair price, that's for sure."

A fair price was always something to consider. But still. The house was a disappointment. Barely livable. Gage took a step back, studying the size of it. "This looks like a one-room shanty. The stove stays?"

"I'd throw it in for free." Zeb perked up, leaning

heavily on his cane as he pointed around the battered corner of the house. "Been looking for the right man to come along. The neighbor has pushing me to sell my good animals to him, but he is a rough son-of-a-gun. You—" Zeb paused. "You have horseman's hands."

Gage nodded slowly, knowing well what Zeb meant and didn't say. "Maybe I'll take a look at your herd."

"Out yonder. Go ahead and take your time. Reckon seein' my horses'll make up your mind one way or the other."

There was a glint in the old man's eye, like a promise of good things to come, and it felt infectious. A lightning bolt of hope zagged through Gage as he crunched through tall, dead grass. Couldn't help expecting to find a good herd of horses to work with. Horses to call his own.

Each step he took through dry thistles made him more certain. He could feel it in his bones as he looked beyond the falling-down fences, sad-eyed Herefords and the remains of a barn, rafters broken in the middle, sagging sadly to the ground. Hope beat within him as he hiked past a gnarled orchard and then froze dead in his tracks.

He was looking at heaven, or the closet part of it he was likely to see.

The brown prairie spread out like an endless table below him, breathtaking and free, in all directions. Unbroken except for the faint line of fallen split-rail fencing and grazing horses, stretching all the way to rugged mountains a haze of purple and pure, glistening white, and close enough to touch. The sun gleamed so bright, it made his eyes water.

He wanted this land. This dream.

A gentle neigh shot through the morning's stillness. Gage looked over his shoulder and lost his breath at the sight of a little bay filly trotting up to the fence, head held high, mane flying, ears pricked forward.

"Howdy, girl." He held out a hand so she could scent him and see there was no danger. "You're a pretty one."

As she reached her nose over the top rung of the listing fence, he gazed out across the endless meadows to watch heads lift from grazing and long manes flutter in the breeze. He picked out the arched necks of Arabians, the sturdy-lined Clydesdales and hardworking quarter horses. There had to be a hundred of them. Maybe more.

Dozens of breeding mares, he realized, their sides heavy with foal. Most of the herd stayed at a far distance, but several animals trotted close and warily approached, ears pricked, nostrils flaring as they scented him, determining if he was friend or foe.

Negligence hung on them like the dirt on their coats. The filly at the fence nickered for attention. Her sad eyes implored him, as if she were hoping he had food. Her ribs showed plainly through the thick mat of her dirty coat.

Gage took a minute to study her. Good lines, no doubt about it. Underneath all the mud, she'd clean up real nice. He rubbed her nose, and she was trusting enough to lean into his touch. She hadn't been abused. A damn good sign.

Gage crawled through the fence and ambled close enough to the small group of mares before they bolted, galloping to safety, their tails sailing behind them. Pleasure filled him like the sweet prairie air. They looked like a fine group. There wasn't a swayback in the lot of them.

You've struck pay dirt, cowboy. Gage leaned against the fence and watched the stallion pace around his mares. Watched the mares calm down and return to foraging for food. He felt the old hunger rise in his blood.

A man didn't get luckier than this.

He stood there for what felt like hours. Soaking in the sunshine and the freedom. He could feel his old life slip from his shoulders like a coat no longer wanted. A new start. Fresh possibilities. Oh, it'd take work—and a lot of it. He wasn't fooling himself about that—

A sharp chicken squawk interrupted his thoughts. He remembered the pretty country woman and how her simple dress had skimmed her slim hips. Thinking of Sarah Redding made a different hunger rise in his blood, one of longing, one he hadn't felt in a long time.

He'd surely have to return that chicken. Only because it was the *neighborly* thing to do.

Chapter Two

Sarah mopped her brow and clods of dirt tumbled from her fingers. Her back burned from hoeing for an hour straight, and she'd only turned one row of the acre patch. She loved gardening, but this was her least favorite part. Her back agreed as she sank the edge of the hoe into the stubborn ground and her spine burned.

The drum of steeled horseshoes rang on the road behind her, growing steadily louder, and she didn't bother to look up. It was probably Aunt Pearl and the children back from shopping in town. Sarah's stomach tightened because her cherished peace was about to end.

Well, at least she was ready for them. The noon meal was cooked and ready, the table set, the floors swept and the beds made—and all ahead of time. Not even Milt could find fault with her today. Satisfied, she wrestled the hoe from the stubborn ground.

"Hello again," a man's voice called from behind her, as rich and deep as a midnight sky.

Could it be? Sarah dropped the hoe, squinting against the bright sun to see the man silhouetted, tall on his horse, his Stetson tipped at a friendly angle.

"Mr. Gatlin. I'm surprised to see you again."

"Look what I found." His horse stepped forward, bringing him out of the sun's glare, and he gestured toward the white chicken tucked in the crook of his left arm. "I assume this is yours."

"One went missing this morning." She bounded forward, eager to relieve him of his burden, and found herself standing in his shadow, close enough to see the texture of his unshaven jaw. A shiver passed through her, wondering what it would be like to lay her hand there.

He leaned forward in his saddle and bent close to hand her the hen. And as she reached up, their fingers brushed. He was like sun-warmed rock and she went up on tiptoes, her wrist brushing the soft downy hair on his forearm.

"Do you have her good and tight?" he asked, the rumble of his voice wrapping around her, moving through her.

Breathless, she managed to nod. The bird flapped and squawked as Sarah tucked it snugly against her apron, but she was hardly aware of anything as her heart tumbled, a strange falling sensation she'd never felt before.

Gage straightened in his saddle, adjusting his hat with ease. "She was scratching in the grass near the property line fencing. Since your hens escaped this morning, I figured she had to be yours."

"I thought that hungry coyote got her." Sarah took a step back. "I can't thank you enough, Mr. Gatlin."

"My pleasure. Least I can do for your help this morning. I found Buchanan's spread just fine. Fact is, it's my land now."

"You *purchased* it? I can't believe he finally sold

it. He's been trying to for as long as I've lived here.''
Feathers flew as the chicken in her arms struggled.
''Excuse me. I'd better put her in the pen with the others.''

Gage tipped his hat in answer, struck again by the sight of her. Sarah Redding was a good-looking woman, sure as rain, and made a pleasing sight as she dashed through the shade of the house. Feathers flew in her wake, and her dress snapped around her slim ankles. Her sunbonnet hung down her back, drawing his gaze to the dip of her small waist.

No doubt about it—a darn pretty sight.

What was a woman as fine as her doing here on this sorry-looking spread? He had to wonder. Living with relatives barely etching out a living, by the looks of things. And working damn hard herself, judging by the abandoned hoe at the end of one long overturned row. Dismounting, he considered the long acre of unturned dirt. That just wasn't right for one woman to do all that hard work by hand.

He lifted the hoe and felt the handle worn smooth by time and use. The hairs on the back of his neck pricked at the pad of her feet in the earth behind him. ''This is a mighty big piece to furrow by hand.''

''I know, since I tilled it last spring, too.'' She took the garden tool from him as if the thought of all that backbreaking work didn't trouble her. ''If you've purchased Mr. Buchanan's land, then that makes you our neighbor.''

''It sure does.''

''Did Buchanan tell you about the water problem?'' She wiped a stray chicken feather from her skirt with the sweep of her hand.

It was hard not to notice the delicate shape of her

fingers as she pulled at her sunbonnet strings, tugging the calico bonnet up her back and over her head, covering her golden hair.

He returned his thoughts to the matter at hand. "I checked the wells myself. They're deep enough not to run dry in summer."

"That's true." She leaned on the hoe. "I thought you were seeing Mr. Buchanan for a job. Had I known you were buying the place, I would have said something."

"What's the problem? Has it got something to do with the creek?"

"So you noticed that?"

"Hard to get anything by me." He tipped his hat to her, his lopsided grin dizzying. "They don't call me the toughest horseman this side of the Rockies for nothing."

"You're going to take back the creek?"

"It's mine, and the law is the law." Gage considered the garden patch again and the pretty slip of a woman standing beside it. "What's wrong with your uncle that he won't plow for you?"

"I've got to earn my keep, and he only has one set of workhorses. They're for the fields, not for working the garden."

"We'll see about that. I'll be right back." He led his mare away by the bit, striding as easy as you please, kicking up dust with every step he took.

He disappeared around the side of the house, and Sarah released a pent-up breath she hadn't realized she was holding. The toughest horseman this side of the Rockies, was he? He sure looked it. He was powerful enough to make her pulse skip crazily. Man enough to make her wish. Just wish.

See there? There she went again, hoping for what was as rare as hen's teeth.

He's not interested in you. How could he be? She was a widow with a stack of medical bills and a child to provide for. A woman down on her luck and with little to offer a man. Gage Gatlin was handsome enough. He could probably have any woman he wanted. A woman of means and beauty. There were surely enough of those types of ladies in town, and Sarah knew she couldn't hold a candle to the lot of them.

She dusted a streak of dirt from her skirt. No, a man like Gage Gatlin wouldn't be interested in a woman like her.

Time to get back to work. She gripped her hoe, the smooth wooden handle warm from the sun, and lifted it high. Down it went, striking into the earth. Metal clinked as it hit a rock and the impact recoiled up her arms. As she worked the hoe deep into the dirt, the blister on her thumb ached.

"Whoa, there. What do you think you're doin'?" Gage returned, leading his mare hitched to Milt's small plow. "I figure this won't take long, so just step back and rest a spell."

"But—"

His back was to her as he looped the long thick reins around his neck and dug the plow's metal tooth into the ground.

He was no stranger to work, and she had to admire the way his muslin shirt stretched over his broad shoulders as he handled the plow. The wind battered the shock of dark hair tangling below his collar— longer than was proper, but it seemed to fit the rough, raw image he made, a lone man against the endless prairie and sparkling sky.

And what was she doing? Wasting time standing idle while he worked? Goodness, he'd already completed one long row. Swiping off his hat, he tunneled his fingers through his dark locks, then glanced at her, his smile slow and easy.

"Does it meet with your approval, ma'am?"

Oh, his Western drawl was honey-sweet and made her chest flutter. She did her best to hide it and to answer politely, not like a woman interested. "Just fine, Mr. Gatlin. How can I thank you?"

"There's no need, as we're neighbors now. I might be needing a favor in return one day." He repositioned the plow, making a second row. Muscles bunched beneath his cotton shirt, and sweat beaded his brow as he worked.

A favor, huh? She couldn't imagine what. Plowing was hard work, so how was she ever going to help him in return? She wasn't used to being beholden to a neighbor—and a handsome stranger at that.

Well, there was work always waiting to be done. She'd best get to it. After one last look over her shoulder at the man with the dark Stetson shading his face, she hurried into the kitchen. She truly shouldn't be watching him so much, it's just that her eyes kept finding him if he was in sight.

You wish too much, Sarah, for things that cannot be. Was it sadness or regret that lingered heavy and familiar in her chest? She didn't know which as she pumped water until it ran cool and she discovered she could see Gage through the open kitchen window. Hat tilted at a jaunty angle, he was speaking low and easy to his mare. His big hands held the plow with ease.

What kind of man was he, at heart? she wondered. There was an untamed toughness to him, rugged like the very land itself. Yet he handled the mare with kind words when other men would use the reins as a whip.

Oh, well, it wasn't her concern, anyway, was it? she reminded herself and turned her back on the kitchen window, winding through the dim, cramped shanty to the back bedroom. The door creaked on its hinges as she peered into the room far enough to see Ella, asleep in her bed. Fierce love burned in Sarah's heart for her child, who lay lost in dreams, her blond locks curling across the snowy pillowslip like finely spun gold.

Unable to stop herself, Sarah smoothed the crocheted afghan tucked beneath the girl's chin, remembering a time when Ella had been a baby asleep in her crib and a man had been plowing their first garden patch—her husband.

It was so long ago now that her grief at his death had healed. One day she knew there would be another man in her life she thought to herself as she walked to the kitchen. A man who had enough love in his heart for a woman with a child and responsibilities.

Looking out the kitchen window as she mixed sweet ginger water, Sarah watched Gage Gatlin finish furrowing another row of her garden. The rich earthy scent of freshly turned dirt filled the air as he managed the plow with easy skill. He gripped the handles and clucked to his mare to send her plodding forward. He looked hot beneath the noontime sun.

She had to figure out something to repay him, something a neighbor would do for a neighbor. The thought heartened her as she searched the pantry for sugar and spice, and a jar of winter preserves caught her gaze.

That's what she'd do. She would bake him a cherry pie in exchange for his kindness to her.

Feeling lighter, Sarah rescued the best cup from the top shelf in the kitchen and filled it with cool water. The curtains snapped in the breeze to give her brief glimpses of the man hard at work. She tried not to think about how masculine he looked as she measured sugar and ginger into the cool water.

By the time she swept down the steps and into the side yard, Gage was pulling his lathered mare to a halt. He was breathing hard with exertion. He whipped off his hat and raked his fingers through his dark locks.

"You're done already?" She handed him the glass.

"I don't let grass grow under these boots." He drank all the water in one long draught, the cords in his strong neck working with each swallow. He gave a well-satisfied sigh and held out the glass. "Sweet and cold. Sure hits the spot. Like what I've done to your garden?"

"It's wonderful. I can't begin to tell you the time and the blisters you have saved me." She took the empty cup, the glass warm against her fingertips from the breadth of his hand. "I suppose you'll want to wait for my uncle after this."

"If you think I plowed your garden to get on your uncle's good side, then you'd be wrong." He scanned the fields, the wind tousling his dark hair, looking pirate-tough and lawman-strong. "It seemed the right thing to do is all."

"So the truth is out. You're an honest-to-goodness gentleman." Sarah's heart fluttered. She couldn't help the pull of warmth and attraction deep in her stomach. "I didn't know they still existed."

"I guess there's a few of us good guys still roaming

the earth.'' He winked, and the fine smile lines around
his eyes crinkled handsomely. Taking a step back and
away from her, he tipped his hat so he could scan the
sky. ''The sun is nearly straight up. I'd best be on my
way. I have business in town.''

''My uncle and his family should be returning soon.
Would you like to stay for the noon meal?''

''Nothing against you, Sarah, but your uncle and I
are not going to be friendly, be it over a dinner table
or not.'' He gathered the reins and his mare sidestepped and turned neatly, hauling the disengaged
plow to the barn.

Every step he took was a powerful one. The way
he walked sure could affect a woman. The straight line
of his shoulders and the breadth of his back, his lean
hips and long trim legs. He had just enough muscle to
make a woman feel tingly all the way to her toes. And
yet not too brawny so there was an inborn grace to
him, like a cougar prowling his territory.

Sarah dragged in a deep breath, but it didn't chase
away the flutter of attraction in her chest or drain the
heat from her face. Besides, Gage Gatlin didn't have
the look of a courting man. He was friendly and polite,
that was true enough, but he didn't catch her gaze and
hold it with interest like others had done—before
they'd met Ella.

And it wasn't as if she would attract any man's
attention dressed in her work clothes. This morning
battling the chickens and finding their feathers
snagged in her braid. And now in the often-patched
dress she wore only for messy work, a man would
have to have extremely poor eyesight to find her the
least bit attractive.

Looking down, Sarah brushed a streak on the front

of her skirt. She sat on the steps, working at the dirt stain on her dress. It was vanity, and she knew it, but she couldn't help the embarrassment heating her face.

Twice now Gage Gatlin had seen her at practically her worst. Goodness, there was more dirt on the other side of her skirt. She looked as if she'd been rolling in the garden patch instead of hoeing it.

Land sakes, she did have bigger problems to face than how she looked to a complete stranger. And that it mattered just a little—all right, maybe a whole lot—bothered her. She was a country girl and always would be.

Anyone could see by simply looking that Gage Gatlin was a man of means. Not that he wore a coat and tie like the men in town with fine jobs and hired servants in their large brick homes, but Sarah could see it all the same. It was in the steel of his spine and the controlled confidence that shone in him like a winter sun.

Ready to go, Gage Gatlin returned, mounted on his fine mare. "I'll see you around, ma'am."

"Good luck with my uncle."

He tipped his hat like a man out of a legend. Her heart flip-flopped once—just a little bit—as she watched him ride away. All myth and dream, disappearing into the vast prairie.

And he was far too fine for her.

Sarah looked after him, although there was nothing but brown prairie and a dust plume where his horse had walked. She'd learned long ago that a person often didn't get what they wanted. So it wasn't too hard to let the air out of her chest and her wishes with it.

So, what did it matter if Gage Gatlin was not the man for her? There *was* someone destined for her, someone kind and caring who could look past the five-year-old dress with the streaks of dirt on it and see the real her. He was out there somewhere, and he'd be worth the wait.

What she'd better do now was get back to the house and check on her daughter. Sarah stood and noticed ten naked toes peeking from beneath her hem.

No, it couldn't be. She blinked, but her bare feet were still there. She wasn't wearing her shoes. The whole time Gage Gatlin was here, she'd been exposing her bare feet like some sort of strumpet.

Embarrassment burned through her like a grass fire, and she started to laugh. Gee, he had to notice. Laughing harder, she covered her mouth with her hand to keep from waking Ella. See? That's what she got for being prideful and fretting about her appearance.

A floorboard squeaked behind her. "Ma, is it dinner yet? I'm awful hungry."

Ella appeared, thin and pale, in the shadowed hallway. Sarah forgot everything, even a man as handsome as Gage Gatlin, as love for her daughter filled her up. She folded the spindly little girl into her arms and held her tight. It hadn't been that long ago when she'd feared her daughter would not live. "Are you feeling better, sweetie?"

"Yeah, but I wish I didn't get so tired all the time." Ella rubbed a fist over her forehead as if her head still hurt.

Sarah pressed a kiss to her child's brow. "You'll feel better after you eat. Come, let me get you some dinner."

"I wanna drumstick." Ella collapsed in a chair and propped her elbows on the table edge, her blond hair escaping from her braids in a sleepy tangle. "It's nice with the cousins gone. *Real* nice."

There was no denying how difficult times had been staying in this house, but it wasn't as if they'd had another choice. Sarah slipped the platter from the warming oven. "We're grateful to them for letting us stay, remember?"

"I know, I know. But do you have to stay here forever?"

"Not forever, baby, but it is hard to say when we can leave." Sarah kept her voice light, knowing her girl couldn't understand how tough the world was for a woman alone.

"As soon as our medical bills are paid off, we'll get our own place. I promise." Sarah set the plumpest drumstick on a blue enamel plate alongside two big potatoes. "There's carrot sticks in the covered bowl in front of you."

Ella found one and crunched into it. "Ma, could it be a house painted white and pretty?"

"We'll see." She set the plate in front of her daughter. "Clean your plate, or I'll have to string you up by your toes from the maple tree."

Ella rolled her eyes. "I know, I know, and I'd better drink every drop of my milk or you'll flog me."

"I'm glad you know how things run around here." Sarah reached for the pitcher. "Do you feel up to helping me plant the garden this afternoon?"

"Sure," Ella said around a mouthful of potato.

"Don't forget the bread." Sarah set the glass of milk on the table and nudged the covered basket closer.

A clatter rose in the yard outside. A second later two small boys charged into the house. Pearl followed, carrying squalling Baby Davie on one hip. His twin was silent but red-faced, balanced across Pearl's other arm.

Sarah hurried to help. "Here, let me take Davie—"

"You'd better take him because I'm worn out." Pearl thrust the year-old child into Sarah's arms as if eager to be rid of him. "At least you got the garden turned while I was gone."

Remember to be grateful. Remember how no other relatives had offered to take you in. "I have lunch ready to set on the table. All you have to do is sit and rest."

"We ate in town." Without an apology, Pearl headed back outside to shout at the children to come in and get started on their chores.

Sarah adjusted Baby Davie on her hip and patted his back, trying to comfort him.

With any luck, Pearl had brought the newspaper back from town and it was full of job advertisements.

Sarah might be down on her luck, but that only meant there was no place to go but up.

Good luck *had* to be around the corner. Right?

Gage climbed the Buffalo Inn's carpeted staircase to the third floor where he knew his daughter would be waiting. Gentle spring sunshine streamed through windows and cast a golden glow onto the bed where his little girl sat, her nose in a book.

"Pa!" Lucy leaped off the mattress, her book tumbling to the quilt. "Did you buy this one? Do we got a new home?"

He laughed as she wrapped her arms around his

waist. "Hold on now, that's no way for a little lady to behave."

"I ain't no lady, Pa. Did you buy it?" Her eyes searched his and she clapped her hands together. "You did! I *know* you did."

"Yep. We got ourselves a home. Now don't go getting your hopes up too high. The place needs a lot of work. Did you behave for Mrs. McCullough?"

"Sorta." The seven-year-old shrugged her narrow shoulders. "I tried. Honest."

"She didn't try hard enough," Mrs. McCullough reported from the chair in the corner, where she gathered her embroidery things. "I must say I'm disappointed in you, Mr. Gatlin. You charmed me into agreeing to watch this child and I have come to regret it."

What did Lucy do now? he wondered, but did his best to look apologetic. He might need Mrs. McCullough's help again. "I'm sorry, ma'am. I'll pay you extra for your trouble."

"Indeed." Mrs. McCullough's gaze narrowed as he placed dollar bills on her outstretched palm. A small pile accumulated, and she nodded. "I suppose it's not her fault, the poor motherless thing. You find a mother for that girl. Just my piece of advice."

"Yes, ma'am." He didn't think much of her advice, but he held his tongue and closed the door behind her.

"Pa, I'm dyin'!" In agony, Lucy hopped up and down, her twin braids bouncing. "Tell me. I gotta know."

She had a knack for changing the subject but luckily he wasn't easily distracted from the problem. "I expect you to do better next time I leave you with Mrs. McCullough."

"I'll do my best, Pa, you know that. But sometimes it's just hard." Lucy sighed, full of burdens. "I'm only a little girl."

"You aren't foolin' me one bit, darlin'." He tugged on one end of her twin braids. "Find your hat and I'll take you out to our new place. It's tumbling down, but I can fix that."

"I know, 'cuz you can fix anything." She dashed to the bureau. "I got my sunbonnet, but I can't do the ribbons."

"Then it's a darn good thing you have me around." He caught the blue straps of her sunbonnet and made a bow beneath her chin. "You're the prettiest girl this side of the Rockies. I'm proud to be seen with you."

"You have to say that. You're my pa." Lucy beamed at him anyway and slipped her small hand in his.

In the livery, he saddled Lucy's little mare while she pulled sugar cubes from her pocket for the horse. When he had the cinch nice and tight, he gave her a hand up.

"Do you know what, Pa? I'm sure glad I got this new saddle." Lucy settled into the leather like a natural-born horseman. "It's got a good horn. Know what I need now? A rope."

"We'll see."

"That's what you say when you mean no."

"I mean, let me think about it." He mounted and led the way toward the main street. "Come on. We'll take the long way through town so you can see the sights."

Lucy reined the mare into step beside his. Her ruffled skirt hem caught the breeze and the matching blue sunbonnet shaded her face.

Would she be happy here? He watched her study the storefronts and shoppers scurrying along the boardwalk. A frown dug into her forehead. Her mouth twisted.

Finally she nodded, her inspection complete. "This don't look like a bad place to live."

"That's what I figured." Gage tipped his hat to keep the high sun out of his eyes.

"Know what, Pa? I don't see a school. There's gotta be a school."

"And so there is, that way." He gestured down the street that cut between the hardware store and the shoemaker's. "We'll get you enrolled Monday morning."

"I can see it." Lucy stood in her stirrups, straining to see the whitewashed building down the street. "Oh, Pa, a real school. It's got a bell and everything."

"It sure looks fine." Gage nodded toward a neat little storefront. "There's a seamstress shop. I figure we can get you fit for new school dresses with the way you're growing."

"I keep gettin' bigger." Lucy hitched up the brim of her sunbonnet as she gazed on the woman-filled boardwalk just outside the mercantile. "Do you know what, Pa? There sure are a lot of pretty ladies in this town."

Gage kept riding.

"*Awful* pretty ladies, Pa."

"I heard you the first time."

"I just had to be sure."

He chuckled, not one bit fooled by her sly innocence. "You know I'm not the marrying kind."

"You married my ma."

"And I could marry some other woman, is that what you think?"

"Sure. A girl needs a ma. Mrs. McCullough just said so. What if she's right? I reckon she could be."

There was too much hope in those sparkling eyes, and it troubled him. "Lucky for you I'm an exceptional father."

She shook her head. "Yeah, but you can't sew."

"What if I learn?"

That earned a giggle and effectively ended the conversation. He breathed a sigh of relief. Settling down was the right step to take for Lucy's sake, but that didn't mean he had to find her a mother. The thought of taking a wife again—

He shuddered all the way to his soul. Once he'd been carried away by what he thought was love. But in time it had crumbled to dust.

The ride was a pleasant one across a prairie awakening to spring. Birds fluttered about, gathering makings for nests. And a few fat jackrabbits darted across the road, daring to escape their warm warrens. Lucy remained quiet during the ride to their land that spread out for miles.

He showed her all the horses, hungry and half wild, that dotted the fallow fields, unable to hold back his excitement. His dreams were so close he could taste them.

"These are all ours?" Lucy hopped down to poke her hand through the fence and rub a filly's velvet nose. "Every single one?"

"Hard to believe, isn't it?"

"Sure is!" Lucy gazed with wonder at the large herd. "They look so sad."

"They've got us now. We'll feed them and make

them happy again. It will be a big job. Do you think we can do it?''

Lucy tilted her head to one side, pursing her mouth as she considered. ''I'm glad we live here, Pa. Because I think these horses needed us to take care of them.''

''That's the way I see it, too.''

So far, so good. His dream for Lucy was taking shape. He'd put in corrals, leave the far fields for grazing, build stables all along the rise—

''Pa? *That's* our house? Are we gonna *live* there?''

''I figure I can have a new house up in a bit.'' Gage knuckled back his hat and watched her carefully. ''One that's good and strong with enough room for the two of us. Would that be all right with you?''

''As long as it has a veranda. 'Cuz ladies like to sit on them.''

''If that's important to you, then it's a deal. In a month I'll have us a new little house with a nice wide porch.''

''With a swinging bench. The kind ladies like. And we gotta have flowers. Lots and lots of them. We won't get anybody nice if all we got is weeds.''

''If you have your way, this place will be so fancy, women will come from miles away, flocking around us, proposing and fainting and all sorts of nonsense.''

''Oh, Pa.'' Lucy flicked one braid behind her thin shoulder, done arguing.

Thank heaven.

She tiptoed up the front steps, the aged boards groaning beneath her weight. ''Are we gonna sleep in here? It looks dirty.''

''I figure we'll stay a few more nights at the inn. Mr. Buchanan is busy packing up and needs a day to move out. First thing tomorrow we can start fixing this place.''

''It's gonna take a lot of fixin'.'' She slipped her hand in his—so much trust. ''You're gonna make it real nice, aren't ya, Pa?''

''You bet.''

''Good. Can I go pet the horses again?''

''Sure thing.''

It was a pleasure to watch her traipse down the weed-strewn path. Little and reed-slim, filled with such important hopes.

He was all she had in the world, and he didn't want to let her down.

Maybe on these high Montana plains, things would fall their way.

Chapter Three

"It's gonna be trouble, that I can guarantee you." Seated at the kitchen table, Milt slurped the last of the coffee from his cup. "Heard in the saloon last night that Buchanan sold his land to some drifter. For nothin' more than a song."

Sarah heard Pearl exhale in frustration. She didn't know what had gone on with old Buchanan, but she knew her uncle. Milt wasn't a man of high moral fiber.

Half listening, she finished wiping dry the last of the baking dishes and cracked the oven door to check on the pies. Golden and bubbling. *Perfect.* She donned the oven mitts and carried the pie plates to the windowsill to cool.

"Surely not to a drifter!" Aunt Pearl was beside herself. "We can't have someone like that for a neighbor. What was the old man thinking?"

"Hard to say, and after all I done for him. All I know is that no drifter is gonna take what's mine." Milt's chair screeched against the wood floor as he pushed away from the table. "Sarah, you bring me out a slice of that pie when it's cool enough to cut."

She nodded, turning her back as she put away the

mixing bowl. A chill curled around her spine and she shivered. What did Milt mean? Would he cause trouble for Gage Gatlin?

Gage's image filled her thoughts—tough, capable, everything a Western man should be. By the look of him, he could handle Milt.

Then again, it never hurt to have a little warning just in case. Sarah considered the four pies cooling on the sill of the now open window.

"Ma, I'm ready." Ella deposited Baby Davie into his settle. "Got my shoes on and everything."

"Good. Help me pick which pie looks the best."

"That one." Ella pointed. "Oops. I gotta find my sunbonnet."

"Quick, before Aunt Pearl discovers something else she wants done." Sarah slipped the chosen pie into the prepared basket. Why was she so jumpy? Surely not over the prospect of seeing Gage Gatlin again. And where had the pie cutter gone to?

She yanked open the top drawer. There. She cut Milt a generous piece of still steaming pastry and set that in the basket, too.

"It's a waste to welcome a drifter as a neighbor." Pearl appeared with the ironing basket on her hip. "I hope you're not taking that extra pie to him."

"He's a horseman, not a drifter."

"A horseman? You mean a wrangler? Or one of them hired men paid to clean out barns?" Pearl wrinkled her nose. "Either way, he won't be here long. Not if Milt has anything to say about it."

Sarah held her tongue and headed for the door. "Do you need anything from town?"

"A spool of brown thread. Milt tore the knee in his

trousers again. Don't dawdle too long. I need you to get supper tonight."

"I'll be back in time. Ella, are you ready?"

"I found it." The little girl breezed through the small, cramped front room dragging her sunbonnet by the strings. "Are we gonna cut through the fields?"

"It's nicer that way." Sarah let the screen door bang closed behind them, grabbed a spare shawl, and tied on her bonnet. The brim shaded her eyes as she headed out into the sunny fields.

The earth stretched brown for as far as she could see, but there at her feet were new green shoots struggling up through last summer's tangled stalks. Like hope. She wished the same for her life. For new opportunities to come her way.

Surely this spot of bad luck she'd been caught in for the past year couldn't last. At least it was easy to think she might be in for a turn of fortune with the sweet breezes snapping in her skirts and the robins swooping through the fields.

After giving her uncle his slice of pie from her basket, she let Ella skip ahead. Prairie dogs popped out of their dens to scold them, their sharp chatter blending with the music of the plains.

A creek gurgled through the fields. A white-tailed deer bolted from the bank as Ella hopped from one rock to the other.

"Look at me, Ma!" Her twin braids flew as she leaped. "We don't have to get mud on our shoes."

"You usually like getting mud on your shoes." It was easy to laugh when the sun was shining and her worries felt so far away.

Midstream, Ella continued to jump from rock to rock. Then her arms shot out as she fought for balance on a slippery-looking rock. Her skirt swirled around her knees. "Look! I didn't fall."

"You're doing great, sugar." Sarah held her breath as her little girl made one mighty jump and landed safely on the grassy bank.

It was like a gift, seeing her like this. A year ago Ella had been bedridden, suffering from illness, her future uncertain.

Now she was skipping across the field like any healthy little girl.

Every sacrifice, the long work hours and everyday hardship had been worth it.

"That wind is still a little cool." Sarah took the shawl hung across her arm and laid it over her daughter's too thin shoulders. "I don't want you to pay any mind to what Aunt Pearl said about Mr. Gatlin. He's no drifter. Look, there's his wagon."

"Maybe he's got kids?"

"He didn't tell me if he does. And if he doesn't, then you'll make friends when you start back to school."

"*Oh.*"

How one single word could hold so much sadness, Sarah didn't know. She ached for her little girl. "Remember how much you loved school?"

Ella nodded slowly, her braids bobbing. "I wasn't behind then. A whole year, Ma."

"It won't take long for you to catch up."

"Yeah." But the fear remained.

Sarah wrapped her arm around Ella's shoulders and pulled her close. "We won't be stuck living with Uncle Milt forever. Things are changing, even though you might not know it. Pretty soon we'll be living somewhere else, and all these worries about school will be behind you.''

"And maybe I could get my own horse?''

"In the grand scheme of things, maybe.''

"Look, someone's comin'.''

Sure enough, there were two riders—Gage Gatlin, strong-shouldered and tall, and at his side a little girl, her face hidden by the brim of her sunbonnet. Her twin braids bounced in time with the small mare's gait. Could it be? Was Gage Gatlin a father?

"Hello, Miss Redding.'' He tipped his hat. "Don't tell me you brought baked goods. I can smell that cherry pie from here.''

"I thought it might be the neighborly thing to do. And it's 'Mrs.''' She lifted the basket lid to show off the pie's golden crust. "Fresh from the oven.''

"Yum.'' The girl rode closer. She was button-cute and lean, her neat braids as black as ink. She had Gage's sparkling eyes and his quick smile. "You brought a whole pie just for us?''

"That's right. To welcome you as our neighbors. We live on the other side of the creek.'' Sarah lifted the basket so the girl could see. "I'm told I'm not a bad baker, so I hope you enjoy it.''

"I bet it's real good. Thank you, ma'am.''

"Call me Sarah. And this is my daughter, Ella. When I met your father earlier, I didn't know he had a little girl. That's a very pretty mare you have.''

"Thanks, I'm Lucy and I'm a great horseman like my pa.''

"I'm pleased to meet you, Lucy.'' Sarah held the handle so the girl could grasp the basket—it wasn't too big or heavy for the child to carry.

Ella took a step closer, unable to take her eyes off the mare. "What do you call your horse?"

"Her name is Scout and she's an Arabian. Wanna take this to the shanty with me? Pa says it's a real eyesore."

Ella nodded, and Lucy dismounted. The girls headed off across the prairie, side by side. Sarah felt warm clear through watching them.

"So you're a missus *and* a mother."

"Are you surprised?"

"Considering you told me you weren't married." Leather creaked as he dismounted.

"I'm not anymore." She steeled her heart, but it still made her sad to remember.

He looked sad, too. "Lucy's mother died when she was three. Scarlet fever."

"I'm sorry. Ella and I have been through a tough bout with diphtheria, so I can only imagine."

He fell into stride beside her. "I suppose that's why you're living with your uncle."

"For now. I had to give up my housekeeping job when Ella became ill. In these hard times, it was difficult finding relatives who would take us in." She fell silent, feeling his gaze intent on her, and she blushed. She'd said too much. "Now that Ella is stronger, we'll be moving on soon."

"Is that so? Where to?"

"I have no idea, but I'm certain the right opportunity is waiting for me. I only need to find it." Sarah swept a grasshopper from her skirt and noticed Gage's jaw tighten.

His mouth became a hard frown. "Opportunity?"

"Don't worry. I wasn't talking about marriage."

"You got me nervous." He winked, knuckling back his hat. "A man can't be too careful."

"You're safe from me." She liked the way his mouth curved in the corners, not quite a grin, but enough to make the laugh lines in the corners of his eyes crinkle. "I'm looking for love. That's an entirely different thing."

"You'll be lookin' a long time."

"You don't believe in love?"

"Let's just say I believe in something more practical."

The shanty came into sight over the rise, and Gage could see Lucy's mare standing in the shade. The two girls burst through the shadowed doorway and into the sun. Gage's daughter held the reins while her new friend petted the mare.

Sarah looked happy watching them, lit up from within. "Our girls seem to be getting along."

"Sure do, with their heads together." He was glad to see that.

Lucy was quick to make friends; she had to be, always moving from place to place, always the new girl. Now was her chance to make lasting friendships like other kids her age. That was one of the reasons he was here.

Marriage wasn't one of them. He couldn't deny his great relief to know the pretty woman at his side was only being neighborly. "It was thoughtful of you to bring the pie."

"That isn't the only reason I'm here." The gray brim of her sunbonnet shaded her soft face, and she blushed as she kicked at the bunch grass at her feet. "There's something you should know. Milt isn't happy you bought the place."

"He's about to lose his stolen water supply." Gage hadn't met Mr. Owens, but he'd asked around enough to know the kind of man he was. "I can handle your uncle."

"I know you can. But it's always better to be prepared. He said something about making sure you weren't here long."

"Then I'll have to show him how wrong he is."

"Good." Her chin came up and it was easy to see the strength in her. The steel.

He could imagine how well she'd cared for her daughter, all alone, and endured hardship to do it. And yet it hadn't embittered her. He admired that about her and something else—the way she walked. She was all gentle beauty. He couldn't help noticing how her pale cotton dress skimmed her slim, very attractive curves—and that troubled him.

Of all the women he'd come across over the years, why was he noticing this one?

Just lonely, he figured. Last night in his bed at the inn, he'd felt alone. Endlessly alone. Maybe it was simply being in town—he hadn't stayed in one for years—where all those houses were spread out in orderly rows, windows glowing cozily in the dark.

Memories of better times had sailed over him. Of how good it felt to come home to find baby Lucy crawling across the polished floor and his wife smiling a welcome.

For one instant it was easy to want that again. The comfortable companionship after the supper dishes were done, joining his wife to read in front of the fire until bedtime.

Nice memories, but they came hand in hand with the bad. The evenings that hadn't been pleasant. The woman who'd looked at him with hurt in her eyes, with anger and resentment. Remembering how hard he'd tried to make things right and failed, put to an end any wishing.

Loneliness ached hollow and cold, but it was a better state than marriage.

As they neared the house they could hear the girls's happy chatter, bringing him back to the present. To the woman standing before him.

"If there is some trouble between me and your uncle, will it cause problems for you?"

"No. I'll be fine." Her problems weren't his, after all.

They'd reached the shade of the shanty, where stacks of new lumber glowed like honey against the earth. A handsaw was tucked safely in the back of a battered wagon.

He was an industrious man, by the looks of it. He'd probably been up at dawn working to accomplish so much. "You plan to repair the shanty?"

"Repair it? More like demolish it and start from the ground up. It's likely to tumble over any minute." He tossed her a wink that made her miss a step.

His hand shot out to steady her. His fingers seared her skin. Even though she was upright and both feet were square on the ground, she still felt as if she were falling. There had to be something wrong with her—and now she knew why she'd been jumpy earlier.

Attraction for Gage Gatlin tingled through her like a fever.

"I'd best collect Ella and be on my way," she said as an excuse. "I can see you're busy, and we have errands to run."

"You're walking to town? It's a long way. If you'd

care to wait, I'll be heading back in a couple of hours."

His offer was kindly spoken, neighbor to neighbor, but he'd done enough for her. "I can't wait that long, thank you just the same."

Behind her, she heard steeled horseshoes clomping on the earth. She turned around in time to see a sleek black mare, neck arched and mane flying in the breeze, pulling a polished buggy along the rutted driveway. Sarah recognized the two young women perched on the shaded seat. The banker's daughter and the daughter of a well-to-do neighbor.

"Good morning, Mr. Gatlin." The young woman holding the reins set the brake and held out her gloved hand. "I'm Susan Lockwood. My father owns the bank in town. He told me that you purchased this charming piece of land."

Gage tipped his hat and took a slow step forward. "Yes, miss. Is there some problem? Did your father send you?"

"Oh, no. We only wanted to welcome you." Susan pressed her hand on his and allowed him to help her from the buggy. "This is my dearest friend, Louisa. Louisa, hand me the welcome basket."

"It's good to meet you, Mr. Gatlin," Louisa said with a rare pleasantness, giving her new lawn skirt a flick. "I hope meeting our poor Widow Redding hasn't given you the wrong impression of our community. Why, I'm practically your neighbor."

"How lucky for me." Gage quirked one brow.

Sarah felt out of place and took a backward step, thinking of her home-baked pie as she spotted the fancy tins piled at the top of Susan Lockwood's fine basket.

She didn't belong here. Next to the well-appointed banker's daughter, she felt as plain as the earth beneath her feet. Better to leave before she embarrassed herself, so she took one last glance at Gage, standing bold as the sun. He tossed her a look as if to say "Help!"

She shook her head. There would be no rescue for him. It served him right for being so handsome—and for not believing in love. What had he said? He believed in something more practical.

She *did* feel sorry for him.

"Come on, Ella, it's time to go."

Huddled close to Lucy, Ella gave the mare one last pat. How wistful she looked, just wishing. Her eyes were so big in her pale face. There was so much Ella deserved. So much Sarah wanted to give her.

The first chance I'm able, I'm going to buy her a horse. New towns were cropping up all over the West as the open prairies became more settled. There had to be a job for her somewhere out there. She was sure of it.

"Sarah?" Lucy dashed over to her and peered around the corner of the shanty. "Who are those women?"

"The blond one lives down the road."

"So she lives real close?"

"Yes. The other lady is her friend from town."

"Ladies come up to my pa all the time."

"I'm sure they do." Sarah felt foolish—at least she knew she wasn't alone in her attraction to the handsome horseman. She was lonely, after all, and wishing for a better life. For someone to love. It never hurt a woman to dream.

"Can Ella come to play sometime?"

"Anytime." Sarah took her daughter's hand. "If you need anything, Lucy, our house is just over the creek and down the rise. It's the first shanty you see."

"I'll tell my pa that you said that." Lucy squinted in the direction of the fancy buggy gleaming in the sunshine.

A movement caught Gage's eye. Sarah was leaving? She couldn't leave him here with these girls. He tried to call out to her, but Sarah was too far away, waving goodbye. Her skirt snapped around her shoe tops, and he remembered her small pale feet, bare and smudged with soft dirt.

Louisa cleared her throat to grab his attention, but nothing was likely to do that.

"Excuse me, ladies. My daughter will enjoy your gifts." He tipped his hat, taking the basket only because handing it back would be rude. He didn't want to offend the banker's daughter—at least, not too damn much. Yet.

He left them standing there, turning his back on their huffs of disapproval as they left. That had been a waste of his time, but at least he knew the banker couldn't be trusted.

He'd bet the only reason those girls were here with their fancy basket and simpering smiles was because Mr. Lockwood had revealed the size of Gage's bank account.

"I see the welcomes have started." Sarah didn't hesitate on her way down the road as he caught up with her. "Remember what I said about my uncle."

There was something about her. As he let her go on her way, Gage felt a thud in his chest, a foolish thud, because he knew darn well where listening to his heart led.

"Ella's ma is really nice." Lucy's hand slipped into his, her fingers warm and small. Trust glittered in her dark eyes and something else.

Longing.

"Mrs. Redding told me she isn't looking for marriage. In case you have any ideas."

"Aw, Pa. I already got ideas." She leaned her cheek against his arm, all innocence and dreams.

She'd been too young to remember how it had been, so he didn't blame her for wishing, but he had to be honest with her. Maybe in time she'd understand.

He wouldn't be walking down the aisle a second time.

Lucy took the basket from him and lugged it into the shanty. Her footsteps faded away, and he was alone on the windblown prairie, staring after a woman in a simple checked dress.

She grew smaller with distance and still he watched. Her blue skirt became nothing more than a dot on the brown plains, and he could not turn away.

One thing was sure. When it came to Mrs. Sarah Redding, he'd be wise to keep his distance.

Chapter Four

Late-night weariness tugged at Sarah like a cold north wind as she wrung water from the mop. Droplets tinkled in the bucket and the soap sudsed, sending up tiny bubbles to pop in the candlelight.

Over the past year she'd washed this floor so many times, she didn't make a sound or need more than the single flickering light as she bent to her work. A board squeaked beneath her foot, the only sound in the silent hotel.

Earning her keep at her aunt and uncle's homestead left her little time to earn the money she needed. There was always an expensive new medicine to pay for or new shoes to buy, for Ella was always growing. What was left of her salary went to pay the doctor.

It was times like these when she was exhausted from a long week of working days and half the nights and when living with her aunt and uncle seemed unbearable, she didn't know how she could keep going.

Her small weekly payments seemed to make no difference; the debt she was in seemed insurmountable. When she was falling asleep on her feet and her hands bled from lye soap, it seemed her life was never going to improve.

She was simply tired, and she knew it. Tomorrow, when the sun was rising and the breeze brought with it the sweetness of the morning prairie, she would feel differently. She always did. She took heart in that. Today had been an especially difficult one.

Uncle Milt's mood had not improved by supper-time, and he grew into a rage when told of the latest gossip concerning their new neighbor, Gage Gatlin. Sarah shivered, remembering the look in her uncle's eyes when he spoke of the man he believed to be a drifter, the man who'd taken cattle that Milt had decided were his.

A shivery sense of foreboding that sat deep in the pit of her stomach stung worse than her hands as she dunked the mop into the pail and wrung the excess water. She had a bad feeling about this. Milt wasn't the most kind or honest of men. How far would he go? Would he steal those animals? Or worse?

Sarah's chest felt tight with worry as she gripped the mop handle more tightly and accidentally banged the side of the bucket.

A metallic clank shot through the silence like a gun-shot. She froze, listening to the echo fade in the long corridor. Wincing, she gently eased the mop back into the water, hoping beyond hope that she hadn't startled anyone awake.

The door in the shadowed hallway flew open and a man's broad shape emerged as dark as the night, only a silhouette against the pitch-black room behind him.

Sarah felt a sinking feeling in the pit of her stomach. With water dripping onto the floor, she carried her mop with her as she dared to step toward him. "I'm truly sorry I woke you, sir. I—"

There was a metallic click that echoed eerily through the night. Sarah froze when she realized it was the sound of a revolver being uncocked and lowered. The man was armed. She didn't know what to say as he jammed the Colt into the leather holster he carried and wiped his brow with his sleeve.

"Sorry about that, ma'am. I guess that sounded too much like a gunshot to a man sound asleep." He lifted one sculpted shoulder in a shrug.

Gage Gatlin. The mop handle slipped from her grip and clattered on the wet floor. She jumped when the noise bounced down the hallway like cannon fire. Oops. That wasn't helping her job any. "I suppose that sounded like a band of road agents taking over the hotel."

Before she could kneel to rescue her mop, he was there, bending down and into the light, his dark hair tousled handsomely, his jaw rough and his eyes weary.

So very weary. Sarah could only stare, mesmerized, as he straightened, only wearing his trousers, un-snapped and unbuckled, the faint lamplight caressing the span of his bare chest and abdomen.

A very fine chest and abdomen. Sarah swallowed hard, feeling heat burn her throat and sear her face. It was entirely indecent to notice the light dusting of fine dark hair that splayed across his chest and arrowed down his firm, toned abdomen to where his silver belt buckle winked in the shadowed light from downstairs.

"I didn't know you worked here." He held out the dripping mop, his stance open, a crook of curiosity arching his brows. "Your uncle and aunt don't keep you busy enough?"

She blushed harder, but for a different reason. He'd said his words kindly enough, although it didn't stop the shame from creeping through her.

Remembering how lovely the banker's daughter had looked this morning when she'd visited Mr. Gatlin, Sarah felt plain indeed. Small and mousy and as dull as the patched dress she wore.

She didn't want to be attracted to Mr. Gage Gatlin anyway, so it didn't matter what she looked like. Gathering her pride, she straightened her spine, looked him in the eye and took possession of her mop. "Living on the homestead has become rather dull, so I spend my nights in town seeking one thrill after the next."

"You strike me as that sort of woman. Far too bold for propriety's sake."

"That's what everyone always tells me." As if to prove her point, she dunked the mop in the bucket and knelt, her soft skirts swirling around her, and wrung the excess water with a twist of her small, delicate hands.

Gage swallowed. "And you spend your free time roaming the halls of this hotel, I take it. Causing trouble wherever you go."

"That's right. I've even been known to be so brash as to scrub pots in the kitchen, if it's been a late night for the cook."

"Ma'am, with your reputation I'd best stay clear of you."

That made her laugh, light and quiet, and how that made his pulse surge through his veins. Fast and thick and hot enough to make him take notice of the way her apron clung to her shape as she swished the mop across the floor between them. He was a man and couldn't help noticing the soft nip of her waist and the gentle sway of her breasts as she worked.

Gage tamped down a hotter, more primal response. He was tired, that was all, and troubled by the nightmare that had torn him awake tonight. By the remnants of a dream that had been shattered when he'd heard the pop of metal in the corridor.

Memory was a strange thing, making the past so real he could taste it, smell it. He wondered if there would ever come a time or a place where he felt safe. Had he come far enough? Would he find peace in this small Montana town? On these high, desolate plains?

Sarah Redding wiped at the floor with determined strokes, leaving tiny soap bubbles popping in the air above his bare toes. She was looking awfully hard at the floor, and now that his head was clear and the nightmare gone, he could see why.

Half naked, with a holstered gun in one hand. Now, didn't that beat all? "Guess I'd best apologize. Next time I hear a commotion in the hallway, I'd better pull on a shirt first. If you come here often, that is."

"Five nights every week."

He reached into his room and found his shirt hanging on a peg by feel. "It's two in the morning. When does your wild night on the town end?"

"When I reach the end of the hall." Her mop dove playfully at his feet.

Being a wise man, he backed into the threshold. "So, you work half the night, and then you're up before dawn to feed the chickens."

"Sure. It keeps me busy. Out of trouble."

He heard what she didn't say. When you have a child, you do what it takes to provide for her. He knew all about that. And he'd had his share of seeing what happened when parents didn't. Or worse, for that matter.

He closed his mind against the memories he didn't want. From a time when he'd worn a silver badge on his chest.

"As you can see, I get into my fair share of trouble." Her mop bumped the wall, scrubbing the last of the floor. "Banging my bucket in the hall, waking up paying guests. I hope you're not angry with me."

"I would have woken anyhow."

"A light sleeper?"

"A troubled one." It surprised him to admit the truth, but the low-spoken words escaped from his tongue and he shrugged, bashful at revealing so much.

"The life of a widow. Or widower." Her voice softened and she straightened, turning to gaze up at him with understanding alight in her gentle blue eyes.

It had been a long time since he could look on the world and see goodness in the people in it. And it touched him right in the center of his chest, in the place where his heart used to be.

Where he hoped it still was.

"Don't tell me you ride home alone this time of night," he said as he lifted the bucket for her.

"All right, I won't tell you." She lifted her chin a notch as she stole the pail from his grip. "Now that I know you're a light sleeper, I shall try harder tomorrow night not to wake you."

A frown furrowed a disapproving line across his brow. "Your uncle thinks so little of your protection that he would allow this?"

"The countryside is safe."

"No countryside is that safe." He passed a hand

over his eyes, looking troubled, looking weary. "Let me grab my boots and I will see you home."

"No, that's not necessary—"

"I'm not going to sleep at all if I let you go alone."

"I have done so hundreds of times," she reassured him, touched that he—nearly a perfect stranger—would care for her welfare when her kin cared so little.

Still, she was not his responsibility and she'd been independent far too long to lean on a man now. "Go back to your room, Gage Gatlin, and rest well. I'll be fine on my own, and besides, what are you going to do? See me home every night?"

"Well, now, I admit I haven't thought that far." He flashed that grin at her, softened by sleep, edged by the dark shadow of a day's growth.

He *was* a charming man. "You've got a child to look after," she reminded him, because it was the practical thing to do. It wasn't as if he was attracted to her, the way she was to him. He was simply being neighborly. Gentlemanly. Polite. That was all.

She clutched her mop close as she headed down the hall. "Good night to you, Mr. Gatlin."

He didn't answer as she swished down the stairs and into the lamplight of the lobby.

Someday, she thought wistfully as she stowed the broom in the back hall closet and carried the bucket out the side door and into the alley. One day she would no longer be alone. Someday she would have the warm embrace of a man holding her close through the night. Know the welcome comfort of a good man's love.

"Done for the night, then?" Mrs. McCullough asked from the front desk, her knitting needles pausing as she looked up, squinting through her spectacles.

"You sure do look tired, Sarah. These late nights are too much for you. I can get you a morning shift in the kitchen—"

"I wish I could." Sarah sighed, trying not to think of the work that awaited her each day at her aunt's shanty. "See you tomorrow evening."

Sarah stowed the empty bucket in the small closet and her coat sleeve brushed her shoulder. As she lifted the garment from the hook, she tried not to think of the long walk ahead. Weariness weighed down her muscles as she tripped down the crooked board steps and hurried down the dark, narrow alley.

Piano music from the nearby saloon rang sharp and tinny on the icy wind. Random snowflakes drifted through the shadows and clung to her eyelashes and the front of her cloak as she shivered, walking fast past the lit windows where rough men drank inside.

For the ten thousandth time she felt the old anger rise up, anger at the injustice of David's death. It wasn't his fault, Lord knew, but nights like this when exhaustion closed over her like a sickness and even her soul felt weary, she longed for the way her life had been. For her own humble home, a cozy log cabin in the Idaho mountains, where Baby Ella had banged pots and pans on the polished puncheon floors and David's laughter rang as he made a story over the events of his day at the logging camp, where he'd worked.

She longed for that gentle peace she'd known cuddling him in their bed at night, listening to his quiet breathing and feeling the beat of his heart beneath her hand. Of how when he stirred in his sleep, he reached for her, pulling her against his warm strong body, holding her close.

And although she'd grieved him long and well, she missed all he had given her. She knew she couldn't go back, couldn't live for the past and try to resurrect it. But she ached to know that kind of happiness again, the kind of love David had taught her a man and woman could find, if they were honest and loving enough.

Remembering made the night colder and more desolate as she left the town behind her. Walking quickly and steadily down the road as dark as despair.

Perched in his stirrups, Gage could barely make out the shadow of Sarah Redding as she walked the deserted road. The prairie winds moaned, making the landscape seem alive. Dried grasses rasped, an owl glided low, startling the mare. Coyotes howled, close enough to make the skin prickle at the back of his neck.

Old instincts reared up, ones that had once served him well. He'd vowed to keep away from Sarah, and here he was, looking out for her, making sure she was safe in the night.

But from a distance of half a mile. That was keeping away from her, right? Thanks to the long, flat prairie, he could see the road for a good mile and the lonely woman on it, walking with a tired hobble that was almost a limp.

He told himself it was sympathy he felt—not attraction—for the woman with the circles beneath her eyes and the worn dresses. For the widow with a daughter who'd been ill. He knew what it was like to be alone in the world with the sole responsibility of a child. And it was the former lawman in him that made him uncomfortable with the thought of any woman walking alone, in a peaceable countryside or not, because cruelty could dwell anywhere.

The road rolled down a gentle incline, stealing Sarah from his sight. He waited as a distant cow's moo carried on the breeze until she reemerged, a slim shadow of grace against the endless prairie.

Sarah slipped from his sight completely, and he nudged the mare forward, searching for her in the dark.

There she was. Outlined against the empty road and rolling prairie. Looks like she was right all along. Maybe Buffalo County was as safe as it appeared. No danger in any direction.

Feeling foolish, he circled the mare around, nosing her north toward town. Keeping the reins taut, he hesitated, not sure what it was that made him pause. He felt unsettled, and it wasn't the coyotes's call or the restless winds that made him hesitate and gaze out over the plains.

Loneliness did. A loneliness that felt as bleak as a night without dawn.

Gage waited until he could see Sarah's faint shadow at her front door before he turned, riding the mare hard. He knew from experience that it would take many miles to drive the demons from his mind and the nightmares from his heart.

Maybe there'd come a day when he could outrun them forever.

"Know what, Pa?" Lucy tromped through the tall thistles, casting a long shadow across the timber he was sawing. She paused, hand on one hip as she waited for his undivided attention.

"What?" he said for the tenth time that morning.

"At breakfast, Mrs. McCullough told me the schoolteacher was real nice."

"So I heard." He'd been there, too, blurry-eyed from a night of hard riding and, when he'd returned to the inn, hours filled with troubled dreams.

"Do you know what?" This time she didn't pause but went right on talking over the sound of the saw. "Her name is Miss Fitzpatrick. Guess that means she ain't married."

"Guess so." The saw's teeth caught in the stubborn wood and the metal screeched in protest. He held back a curse as he worked the damn thing loose.

"Know what, Pa?"

"What?"

"I sure hope Miss Fitzpatrick likes me. Not that I want to be her favorite or nothin', 'cuz I get to be the favorite a lot."

Gage leaned on the saw and studied his daughter. Sparkling and excited. This new teacher was apparently a big worry, but as much as he loved Lucy, he had to get this house built. There was a whole lot of work to do before the mares started to foal.

"I reckon Scout is wondering why you aren't showing her the new spread." He set back to work. "Why don't you go ride her around so she can get to know the place?"

"Sure. Know what, Pa?"

"What, Lucy?"

"'Suppose there's lots of girls and boys my age at that school?"

"I reckon so. Now go ride your mare."

"Oh, all right." Lucy sparkled. "Do you know what, Pa?"

"*Lucy.*"

She giggled, not the least bit perturbed by his mood. "I'm gonna go ride, but I want some of Sarah's pie for lunch."

"Go." Gage bit the inside of his cheek to keep from chuckling.

There went his little girl, dashing through the weeds. Lucy flourished wherever they'd landed, but she looked lighter somehow, as if this place suited her. She hopped over the rail fence and unwound Scout's reins from the post. With a whoop, she leaped onto Scout's withers and the two of them were off, streaking out of sight.

Just how long would she be able to stay out of trouble? He didn't know. Lucy was a mystery to him, but he loved her. He shook his head, sank his saw into the cut and worked, sweat dripping down his face as the sun strengthened.

This was happiness. A beautiful morning. Hard work to occupy him. A day spread out before him without a single problem he couldn't handle. He'd been needing this for a long time. Wandering from job to job, trying to put the past behind him hadn't worked. Maybe the peace of this great land would be the balm he needed.

The timber broke apart and he wiped his brow with his shirt. He straightened, taking a breather. He could see Lucy loping Scout through the fields and into the creek. Water splashed everywhere.

The squeak of a buggy wheel spun him around. Was it Sarah? He didn't know why his thoughts turned to her, maybe it was because he knew she lived close. When he spied the tasseled surrey drawn by a pair of matching gray Arabians, he couldn't explain the disappointment that whipped through him. It wasn't Sarah.

What was wrong with him? He needed his head checked, that's what it was. A man opposed to marriage knew better than to start pining after a woman looking for matrimony.

"Mr. Gatlin, I presume?" The surrey squealed to a halt.

There, looking at him from beneath a fancy bonnet, was a beautiful redhead with a fetching smile. He knew the look of hope, having seen it a time or two before, and panic kicked through him like a cantankerous mule.

Being a brave man, he straightened his shoulders, told himself to buck up, and managed what he hoped was a cordial smile. "Howdy, ma'am. What can I do for you?"

"Then you *are* Mr. Gatlin." Her smile widened, and there was something artificial about it, as if she'd practiced just that same striking curve of mouth and sparkle of eye in a mirror.

"I hate to say I am." Resigned, he knelt to heft the timber off the sawhorse.

"Then I'm so pleased I was able to find you at home." She climbed down from the surrey. "I wanted to welcome you to our little corner of Montana. I baked a cake for you."

"That's mighty kind of you, ma'am—"

"Call me Marilyn." She gazed up at him through long lashes, a coy look, just this side of proper, but her message was clear.

How many more women were going to be stopping by to measure up the new bachelor? He dropped the timber, letting it thud to the ground. "That was mighty kind of you, ma'am, but I'm already stocked up on baked goods.''

"I'm sure your daughter will help you eat it." Marilyn pranced closer on her dainty slippers, arms extended with a glass cake plate.

Angel food. Lucy's favorite. It wasn't as if he could be impolite and send her away. He wasn't a man who could hurt a woman's feelings, but he didn't feel right about taking the cake. Or the delicate plate it was on.

"My daughter and I thank you, ma'am." He wasn't about to use her first name. He'd learned long ago that would only encourage a marriage-minded woman.

There was only one thing to do. He heaved another timber onto the sawhorse. "It was kind of you to stop by." He grabbed his saw and set to work.

He figured Miss Marilyn had a few prying questions for him, and after she'd batted her eyes a few more times and walked with a sway of her curvy hips meaning to give him something to think about, she'd be gone.

But not soon enough.

Gage set his jaw, watched the saw bite into the raw lumber, and cursed. All he wanted was to be left alone. Was that too much to ask?

At the sound of a knock at the door Sarah looked up from her kneading. There, on the other side of the pink mesh screen door, stood little Lucy Gatlin.

Her freckled face was shaded by her sunbonnet and sparkled with a grin as she pressed against the mesh. "Howdy, Sarah. Whatcha doin'?"

"I'm making bread. What are you up to?"

"Nothin'." Lucy pulled open the screen door and

leaned one reed-thin shoulder on the frame. "That looks sticky."

"That's why I use flour." Sarah dug the heel of her hand into the dough ball. What was that look on Lucy's face? Her eyes were pinched, her mouth pursed tight. "I wager your father buys bread in town."

"Yep." Lucy took one step forward, watching intently. "That pie you made was *real* good. We had big slices after supper last night."

"I'm glad you liked it."

Lucy stalked closer. "I bet your bread is real good."

"I can bring over a loaf when it's done cooling."

"Could you?" Lucy's dark eyes sparkled like Gage's, full of something extraordinary.

Sarah couldn't help being charmed. "You can help yourself to a roll if you'd like." She nodded toward the wire racks on the other side of the kitchen.

"Gee, thanks!"

Sarah pinched the ends of the rolled dough and popped it into a waiting pan. The last one. The back of her neck ached as she straightened. She'd been bending over the breadboard since dawn, but at least the hardest work of the day was over.

Sarah opened the oven door, ignored the blast of heat and slipped her hand inside to test the temperature. "Do you want a glass of milk to go with that?"

"Nope. Can Ella come play?"

"So that's why you came to raid my kitchen." Sarah slipped the half dozen-bread pans into the oven and eased the door shut. "Ella's in her room—"

Footsteps knelled in the front room as Ella burst into sight. "Can I, Ma? Can I *please?*"

Breathless, Ella clasped her hands together and

pleaded. It had been a long time since there had been anyone Ella's age to play with.

"Take your sweater." Sarah tried to keep a firm look so there would be no argument. "And you girls don't go far."

"We won't!"

The screen door slammed shut. Laughing to herself, Sarah watched the girls dash into the yard. Ella tugged on her sweater while Lucy untied Scout from the porch post. The bell-like cheer of their voices rang through the kitchen. What luck that a girl Ella's age had moved in next door.

"Going to take Mr. Gatlin a loaf of your bread, are you?" Cousin Lark, a young girl of sixteen, swept into the kitchen. "I don't know, Sarah. It sounds like a wasted effort to me."

"A kind act is never wasted." Knowing full well what Lark meant, Sarah swept the caked flour and bits of dough into the garbage bucket. "Would you like to take some fresh rolls to your meeting in town?"

"As if I would bring something homemade." Lark wrinkled her dainty nose as she lifted her best cloak from the peg at the door. "Although I'm sure your baking leaves a certain impression with a man like Mr. Gatlin."

Sarah had grown used to her stepcousin's biting remarks, and she was old enough to know the girl was spoiled and sheltered. Life would teach her differently soon enough. But what truly cut to the quick was the derisive look that said, "poor relation."

That was a sore point. Sarah felt her face flame and she turned her squared back, grinding her mouth shut and keeping it that way. She could not risk losing her temper and being tossed out of the house, a house Ella still needed.

Sarah's gaze shot to the window where her little girl was stroking Scout's silky-looking neck. Ella glowed with happiness, standing beside her new friend, but she remained wan and thin. No amount of food and care seemed to make a difference. Ella's health was still frail, the doctor had told her. It was likely to remain that way for a while longer.

"Everyone in town will get a chuckle out of your baking for Mr. Gatlin." Lark shot out the door, apparently delighted to have the last word.

Sarah leaned her forehead against the upper cupboard door and tried not to let the words take root, but how could she help it? Especially when Lark was right.

The laughter of little girls called Sarah to the window. Seeing Ella on the back of Scout, holding tight to Lucy's waist, steadied her. Made her remember what truly mattered. Her daughter's life, health and happiness.

Cousin Lark or Susan Lockwood or Louisa Montgomery could have Gage Gatlin, the man who didn't believe in love.

Because *she* did believe.

Chapter Five

"I sure hope they got something besides frilly dresses." Lucy skipped beside him on the busy board-walk, braids bobbing, as happy as a lark in a field. "I don't wanna show up at school in some ruffly dress and everyone'll think I don't know nothin' important."

She'd been talking his ear off all morning. When he couldn't take it anymore, he'd agreed to take her into town. Instead of causing her to quiet down, it only made her talk more. Gage tried his best to follow her, but listening wasn't a man's strong suit and his head was starting to hurt. "We wouldn't want that, darlin'."

"That's right. 'Cuz I know all about riding and horses and building up a house good and tight. Ain't that right, Pa?"

"That's right, Luce." He nearly fell to his knees in thanks—and he wasn't a church-going man, when he saw the frilly sign overhead: Millie's Dresses & Hats.

"They got ruffles, Pa." Lucy froze stock-still in the doorway. "And lace."

He tugged on her sunbonnet, which hung down her

back, to get her moving. "Maybe a little lace wouldn't be so bad."

"Cowgirls don't wear lace, but you know what, Pa?" She darted to a rack of children's dresses. "This is buckskin. Real buckskin."

He was in trouble now. "We're here for school dresses."

"Maybe I can be of service." A sweet-faced woman without a wedding ring on her hand waltzed into sight, her well-tailored dress swirling around her like a soft rosy cloud. "Did I hear you right? You're looking for school dresses?"

Gage could see Lucy was charmed at once. She put on her best smile, the one with the dimples, and used her nicest manners. "Yes, ma'am. My pa doesn't know nothin' about dresses so maybe you could please help us?"

"Us," she said. Gage wasn't lost on that. The lovely woman flashed him a gentle smile, she was really quite attractive.

"You came to the right place. I'm sure we can find something your girl will like and if not, I can sew up whatever she wants."

Lucy's eyes sparkled, her mouth opened—

"No buckskin," he commanded before she could say it.

"Certainly not for school," the seamstress agreed. "You have such a lovely complexion and those dark eyes. Let's start with a red calico. Do you like red?"

"I like blue better."

"I'll see what I have." The shopkeeper's smile was genuine. Before she hurried into the back to fetch the promised dresses, she tossed Gage a demure look that let him know she was interested.

What was a man to do? He swept off his hat and tried not to panic.

"You're 'supposed to talk nice to her, Pa." Lucy looked thoroughly happy. "You gotta stop scarin' the nice ones off."

"I like scaring them all off," he mumbled, retreating to the far end of the shop where there were more women who looked up at him.

"Aren't you the fellow who bought the Buchanan place?" A matronly woman looked down the bridge of her nose at him as she turned a glossy page in a pattern book. "I hear you're a widower."

"Excuse me." He'd been in town for only a few hours, but it was already too long.

He missed the open plains, his work and his horses. He knew what to do with a lasso in his hand, but not in this woman's domain with its leafy wallpaper and crystal lamps. It even smelled female—like starch, soap and dried flowers.

"Pa, where ya goin'?"

"You're old enough to do this yourself." He didn't know if that was true, but he knew one thing for sure. That pretty seamstress was going to come back and wear her "I'm available" smile and what was he going to do with that? Give him a bronco to break or a colt to gentle and he was happy. But give him a husband-hunting woman, and he ready to head for the hills.

"No more than three dresses. You pick 'em out and I'll say yes or no when I come back." He wrapped his hand around the dainty glass doorknob that felt like a pebble against his wide calloused palm.

The door opened of its own volition and whacked him in the shoulder. On the other side of the threshold

stood Sarah Redding, looking fine. Just fine. Blond
curls peeked out from beneath her plain sunbonnet,
and her so-blue eyes twinkled up at him in a friendly,
neighborly, non-terrifying way.

"Sarah." He held wide the door. "I'm glad to see
you."

"You look pale enough to faint." Sparkling like the
very sun itself, she laid her hand over his, an act of
comfort. "I suppose the toughest horseman this side
of the Rockies is miserable in a lady's dress shop."

"You're darn right about that. I need to escape to
the stockyard and lasso a few steers to feel better.
Maybe just some fresh air on the boardwalk. What are
you doing here?"

"Ella spotted Lucy through the window—" She
tried to explain, but the girls were busy weaving
through the store together, their happy chatter explanation enough. "I was surprised to notice the progress
you've made on the house. I could see it from the
road."

"Got two outside walls framed. Figured I can do
the rest by nightfall if I can drag Lucy back to the
ranch." He noticed the two little girls, heads together
considering the buckskin skirt, and knew there was a
good chance he'd be buying that skirt. "Suppose work
can wait for tomorrow. What are you in town for?"

"I have correspondence to mail." She patted her
bulging reticule slung neatly around her slim wrist and
leaned close, lowering her voice, bringing with her the
scent of sunshine and roses. "Don't tell my relatives,
but I'm beginning to look for work."

"Won't they approve?"

"You would think they'd be glad to be rid of me,
but I seem to have made myself indispensable."

"You mean they like all the work you do for free."

"Like to look on the sunny side of things, do you?"

"Don't see the need to fancy up the plain truth."

"You're a straightforward sort of man, are you, Mr. Gatlin? Then why don't you ask for help when you need it?" She was teasing him now, her mouth drawn up so her bow-shaped top lip was soft and plump, just right for kissing.

Kissing? Why in blazes would he think of kissing her? It was proof enough he was loco.

"Come on, admit the truth." She yanked the door-knob out of his hand with a brush of her small fingers. "Lucy needs new dresses and you don't have the faintest idea where to begin. Maybe you'd like a woman's help. A woman with experience in this, seeing as I have a daughter the same age as yours?"

Why couldn't he concentrate on what she was saying? Gage tried to focus, but his mind was too fuzzy. All he could seem to notice was Sarah's mouth moving as she spoke. Her lips were a gentle pink color, the same shade as summer roses, and probably tasted like passion—

"Mr. Gatlin?" It was the seamstress lady who was talking. "I believe we should go with a generous hem. Something to grow into. Like this cornflower-blue calico for instance—"

She may have well been speaking Greek for all he could understand her.

"Millie, that would do fine." Sarah took charge in a gentle way, clearly taking pity on him, the poor man who had no idea what cornflower-blue was.

Gage watched in amazement as Sarah took a yellow dress from the table and held it up to Lucy's shoulders—a dress with lace and ribbon trim.

Wait a minute, wasn't Lucy opposed to such frills? Why was Lucy nodding earnestly and gazing up at Sarah as if they'd discovered the perfect dress for Lucy's first day of school?

"If you'd like to take a stroll down to the tavern, Mr. Gatlin—" the shopkeeper's mouth was a straight, tight line "—we may be a while."

No glimmer of interest lit her up as she turned her back, carrying a few dresses toward a back room.

Whew. He released a deep breath he didn't know he was holding and felt a hundred times better. Whatever had made Millie the Seamstress decide he wasn't a suitable candidate for a husband, he was grateful. He'd head down to the feed store and escape while he could.

"Isn't that just the cutest thing?" the matronly woman at the pattern books whispered to another, but her words carried all the way to the door. "Who knew those two would take a sparking to one another? A widow and a widower with girls the same ages. A match made in heaven, no doubt."

They were talking about him. About him and Sarah. Gage lost control of the door and it smacked him in the knee. Overhead the tiny bells jangled crazily and pain shot up his leg.

What the blazes were those women thinking? He opened his mouth to deny it, but Sarah was chuckling.

"Is it true, Sarah?" Lucy demanded, tugging on the woman's sleeve. "Are you taking a spark to my pa?"

"Look at him. Too tall, too muscular, too unkempt." Sarah selected another dress from the table with the ease of a woman made to shop. "Do you think I could take interest in a man like that?"

"You see my troubles." Lucy sighed as if she carried overwhelming burdens on her shoulders. "He didn't shave today. I told him to brush his hair."

"There's nothing to be done about that." Sarah looked as though she were enjoying herself, her cheeks pink and mirth lightning her up like a midnight star. "It's called hat hair—"

"Hey, I've taken about all the insults a man can stand." Hat hair. Is that what Sarah really thought about him?

Her eyes glittered with suppressed laughter as he managed to yank the door wide enough for it to smack against the wood wall and those little frail bells sounded like a flock of squawking birds.

He just wanted out of there and fast. "I'll be down the street."

Sarah's hand covered her mouth, probably to hide how hard she was laughing at him. Women, he muttered as he pulled the door shut behind him. See what a good thing it was he knew to stay the heck away from them?

"What should I do about Pa's hat hair?" Lucy asked as the door clicked shut and he was on the outside, looking in.

Sarah was bent over laughing—what a tiny waist she had; why hadn't he noticed that earlier?—and she brushed away Lucy's concern with a gentle hand to the girl's brow. Lucy gazed up at her as if Sarah Redding had hung the moon, and he didn't blame her one bit.

He caught his reflection in the barber's front window and stopped to take a quick look. There was no flat mat of sweaty hair clinging to his head. *I do not have hat hair.* His dark locks were windblown, like always. What was wrong with that woman? One thing was clear, Sarah was going to have to pay for humiliating him. The question was, how?

"Pa, look! I got dresses." Lucy skipped beside Ella down the boardwalk, pointing behind her. Sarah was trailing behind, the prized garments slung over her arm.

"Only one has lace on it, and it ain't too frilly."

Gage froze stock-still in front of the mercantile. His little girl looked the happiest he'd ever seen her. "I guess that means you're ready for your first day of school."

"Yep. Sarah even got me some new shoes, but only if you say so. We picked 'em out just in case. Ella helped."

The pale, thin girl nodded, apparently too shy to add her two cent's worth.

"I was about to take this into the hotel." Sarah lifted her other hand, showing him the shopping bag stuffed full. "We started an account. Millie said it was no problem to bill you. And to return anything you wanted."

"Didn't have trouble spending my money, did you?"

"It's a woman's duty. I think it's written in the Constitution, probably in the Bill of Rights."

"You mean the part about the pursuit of happiness?"

"What else?" She bustled past him, her petticoats rustling and her step light. "Are you going to stand there or help me with these packages?"

"Sorry, I'm overwhelmed by so many lovely ladies in my presence," he said by way of excuse for having been so rude.

He rectified that by lifting the package from Sarah's hand without touching her fingers. Her hair brushed his jaw as he lifted the dresses slung over her forearm.

Her scent of roses clung to the fabric and made it impossible not to think about the woman, and about his reaction to her. She fell into an easy gait at his side.

"I hope you didn't take to heart what Mrs. Walters said in the dress shop." Sarah quirked a slim brow, and he couldn't help noticing the way her light blue sunbonnet framed her face.

"What?"

"You know, about us taking a sparking to one another."

"I do recall that particular comment."

"Then you know how ridiculous it is." The last thing Sarah wanted was for Gage—or anyone else— to think she was harboring romantic notions toward him. "Just because we have children the same age doesn't mean a thing."

"I agree."

"And we're clearly looking for different paths, you and I."

"Absolutely." Gage tugged open the hotel's etched-glass door. "Besides, why would Mrs. Walters or anyone think that you'd lower your standards so far as to be seen with the likes of me?"

"I agree. You *are* a disreputable character."

His baritone chuckle rumbled like midnight. Too bad he was so disillusioned. Too bad he wasn't looking for love. He looked like a fantasy come true. He'd forgone his morning shave, and dark stubble clung to his rugged jaw. Her fingers itched to know the texture and feel of him.

And there she went again, thinking of the impossible. How could she help it when she had such inspiration?

He began speaking with the doorman and handed over the dresses and packages. She wanted to say goodbye to Gage, but since he was busy, she decided to stop staring at him and headed to the front window instead. The girls were outside, swinging on the empty hitching post.

Ella's sunbonnet had slipped down her back, and fine white-blond strands had loosened from her braid to fly around her. She pulled one leg over the post and sat alongside Lucy. Lucy leaned to whisper in Ella's ear, and Ella's hand flew to her mouth as she giggled.

Seeing how happy and healthy her little girl was made Sarah believe anything was possible. Maybe the future was about to change for the best. Perhaps, if heaven smiled upon them, she would have a full-time position by this time next month. It was so much to hope for—

"Why, Sarah Redding, what are you doing here?" Louisa Montgomery emerged from the hotel dining room, parasol in one hand, regal as always in her fashionable bonnet and tailored brocaded-silk dress. "I didn't know you started working during the day."

It had been loud enough for Gage to hear. Sarah watched as he glanced over his shoulder at the lady who waltzed into the lobby, a vision in lilac sateen.

Sarah straightened, hating that many pairs of eyes were looking at her, both through the doorway to the hotel's busy dining room and in the lobby. "How is your mother?"

"Wanting to hire you again to do the canning. What a touch you have with kitchen work."

"Give my regards to her, please." Sarah headed for the door.

"I'm sure she'll be delighted. Why, Mr. Gatlin, have you hired Sarah, too? She's a real help when it comes to tasks such as spring cleaning."

Heavy bootsteps thudded on the floor hard enough to shake the floorboards beneath Sarah's feet as she reached for the brass doorknob. Firm fingers curled around her arm, burning through her cotton sleeve to the skin beneath. Gage caught hold of the door, refusing to let her open it.

"Sarah is my dining companion." His warm baritone rumbled like cello strings. "And a finer one I couldn't have."

He thought he was charming. Or did he think he was doing her a favor? Everyone was looking at her, or at least it seemed everyone was, the poor relation who'd asked at every home in the county and every business in town for extra work, the kind that could be done around a sick child's uncertain schedule and her duties for her demanding relatives.

"Gage, I have to run to the post office."

"The mail doesn't leave for hours."

"My aunt is expecting me—"

"You were detained. It was unavoidable." He leaned close so that his mouth brushed her hair. "Please, save me. That woman is going to talk with me and try to charm me. I don't think I can survive it."

"That's a risk I'm willing to take."

"Heartlessness. I didn't expect that from you, Sarah." His mouth crooked into that grin that took her breath away. "I expect that you'd be nice to me. Think of the damage you brought on me today."

"Damage? You don't mean the bill at the dress shop—"

"No. The harm caused to my feelings. Your criticism cut me to the quick. The least you can do is to let me be seen with a beautiful woman. Repair my wounded pride."

"What are you talking about?" Truly, he amazed her. Was it all men that failed to make sense, even one so finely made?

"The 'hat hair' comment. It pains me deep, Sarah. Rectify your mistake by protecting me from Louisa. She's likely to follow me into the dining room and where will I be?" His hand remained banded around her wrist, solid and scorching. "Please?"

The kindness beneath his lightly spoken words twisted like a vise around her chest. He felt sorry for her! That's why he was doing this. Why he was standing so true and tall, pretending as if *she* would be doing *him* a favor. When the truth was that he was simply being polite to a poor widow.

"Sorry, but I am otherwise engaged." She yanked her hand free and spoke low so that her words would not carry. "I'm certain you're tough enough to handle Louisa on your own."

"Wait—"

She wasn't about to be the center of attention. Sitting in the hotel's fancy dining room and being served with the best of the township's citizens. Alongside the dashing new man in town. In her gray calico work dress? Next, folks would think she'd set her sights for Gage, and she'd had enough humiliation.

"Ma!" Ella hopped from the hitching post. "Can I—"

"Sorry, baby, but we're going home."

"But—"

"You and Lucy can play later." Sarah charged down the boardwalk, not at all surprised to hear the boom of a man's step behind her. "Come, now. We have letters to mail."

"'Bye, Lucy." Long-faced, Ella waved solemnly to her new friend. "You could bring Scout by if you want—"

"Now, Ella." Sarah rushed past, not daring to stop. "I hope you enjoy your dresses, Lucy."

"Hold up there." Gage fell into stride beside her. "What other previous engagement did you have?"

"You think a woman like me doesn't have somewhere else to be?"

"What do you mean? You said you had errands, sure, but you had time to help Lucy—"

"Which I thoroughly enjoyed. You have a very likable child, Mr. Gatlin. She is so unlike you."

He froze, apparently contemplating that remark. "You mean, you don't like me?"

"No, I don't."

He came after her, all power and might. "I thought we were friends."

"You and I can never be friends."

"Why not? What do you have against me?" He knuckled back his hat and flashed her the smile that could melt steel.

"What do I have against you? Why, the list would be too long to discuss. We only have seven hours of daylight left."

"Did I do something and that's why you're angry with me?"

Wasn't that just like a man? Well, the last thing she had time for was to enlighten him. Angry? Of course she was angry. And she was going to stay that way. She marched into the post office, determined to leave him behind.

She wasn't interested in him, anyway. A man who didn't believe in love—he probably wasn't aware of other emotions, either—probably why he was so surprised to hear she was angry.

Perfect. There had to be a line when she was in a hurry. With any luck, she'd left Mr. Gage Gatlin on the sidewalk where he belonged. Maybe providence was smiling on her and he was storming back to the hotel to ask Louisa Montgomery to share a meal with him. Sarah would wager her mother's gold watch that he wouldn't buy Louisa dinner out of a misplaced sense of pity.

She might not have a lot, but one thing she didn't need was Gage Gatlin's pity.

Is that why he'd plowed the garden patch for her? She slipped into the back of the line, surprised by the harsh knell of her heels on the floor. Heads turned to look her up and down. Mrs. O'Malley lifted one curious eyebrow. Mrs. Lockwood's face wreathed with clear disapproval.

Heat stained her face and she dug her correspondence out of her reticule. Had she made a spectacle of herself? She hadn't even considered that other people might have noticed how she'd argued with the handsome widower. Argued. In public. What had she been thinking?

"Saw you in the hotel window with that horseman." Elderly Mr. Lukens turned around in line and winked. "Don't you worry none. You're more than pretty enough to catch the likes of him."

"You know I'm saving my heart for you, Mr. Lukens."

"Don't I know it. All the pretty girls want to court me, but I'm remaining true to my Ann."

"His Ann" had been buried for five years. "There are a lot of broken hearts in this town because of it. Including mine."

He chuckled as he glanced past her shoulder to the door as it flew open. "Looks like I'm about to have more competition than an old goat like me can stand."

Gage. He eased into line behind her.

What should she do? Mrs. O'Malley hid a smirk behind her gloved hand. People were noticing and likely to form the wrong conclusion.

What she had to do was to keep it proper and formal. Act as if she and Gage were nothing more than acquaintances, which was only the truth.

She faced him with as much dignity as she could manage. "Good day, Mr. Gatlin. I was unaware you had business here."

"My business is with you."

Sarah took one look at the tight clamp of his jaw, where muscles quivered beneath the sun-browned skin and rogue's stubble. "We have no more business, Mr. Gatlin."

"Is that right?" His gray eyes glowed as dark as a winter storm and he snatched the envelopes from her grip and handed them to Mr. Luckens along with a five-dollar gold piece. "Would you mind, sir?"

"Never was one to stand in the way of two lovebirds." Mr. Lukens cackled with delight and gave Sarah another wink.

As Gage took her by the arm, she caught sight of

Mrs. O'Malley choking on unladylike laughter and Mrs. Lockwood shaking her head with abject disdain.

"I have to work in this town," she told him the instant the post office door swung closed behind them. "I can't afford to be made a laughingstock. I'm fairly new to town and have had enough trouble getting work when I can—"

"Sarah." His hand brushed the side of her face, rough calluses rasping across her skin.

He was going to kiss her, she realized. The sounds of the world around them faded until there was only the rapid panic of her heart thudding in her ears. And the naked want in Gage's gaze as he leaned a fraction of an inch closer.

Unable to breathe, unable to think, all she could see was him. His shoulders an uncompromising line, his Stetson dark against the thick gray clouds that made the sky. The desire in his eyes deepened, and her lips began to tingle.

What would his kiss feel like? Bold, she had no doubt of that. Intense. Overwhelming. The thought made her knees shake. Anticipation buzzed low in her stomach. As if by magic, she felt the heels of her feet lift upward, putting her in perfect kissing position.

He eased closer, their lips a scant inch apart. He was going to kiss her, there was no doubt about it as he turned his head slightly. His mouth parted just enough to call attention to his lips. His chiseled, hard-looking lips that softened, gentled as he leaned closer. She smelled wind and leather and man, as intoxicating as wine, as exhilarating as dreams. Her own lips responded, eager to feel the heat of his kiss, the taste of him—

Like the crack of a whip, the door behind them

caught the wind and smacked wide open. Sarah jerked away from Gage's impending kiss. Mrs. Lockwood filled the threshold.

"Goodness be!" Nose up, she marched down the boardwalk with amazing speed. Her finely tailored skirt with her quick gait.

Reality crashed into Sarah's mind like a blow to her chin.

What had she been thinking? She hadn't been, that was the problem. She'd let her romantic fancy get the best of her when she should have kept her wits and her principles about her.

They were standing on the boardwalk, six paces from the town square. In plain sight of the street and the shops and the hotel. She was a mother. Mothers didn't behave this way, kissing handsome men in the streets.

Where was Ella? It suddenly occurred to her that she'd lost her child. Well, what could be expected? She'd clearly lost her mind. Gone daft. A total lunatic. What kind of sane, sensible, practical mother lost track of her child?

Gage stared at her, confusion making harsh lines dig deep into his forehead. Maybe common sense was returning to him, too. He jumped back as if finally figuring out what disaster had almost occurred.

"Ella?" Sarah skidded to a halt when she spotted her daughter sitting on a bench with Lucy in front of the barbershop.

At the sound of her name the girl glanced over her shoulder, her cheeks rosy and her smile bright, completely unaware of her mother's behavior.

Thank heavens for that. Sarah cannoned down the boardwalk, relieved to find that Augusta Carpenter greeted her with a pleasant nod, and the barber, coming out to catch a bit of fresh air while he waited for his next customer called howdy to her.

Good. With any luck, she hadn't totally embarrassed herself in front of the whole town. If this luck held, then probably no one had noticed. Look how busy everyone appeared.

"We must hurry home." She caught Ella's hand in hers. "Lucy, good luck to you on Monday. Miss Fitzgerald is a fine teacher."

Gage watched his daughter look far too innocent as she smiled prettily up at Sarah Redding.

"Thank you. Now I shan't be worried at all."

Shan't? Where had Lucy learned that word?

It was too late to call after Sarah. She walked amazingly fast considering a woman's burden of skirts and petticoats. Poor Ella was nearly running to keep up. At the end of the walk, they slowed, looked for traffic, and crossed the busy street.

"Hey, there, young fella." The old man from the post office scampered toward him. "Don't go running off before I can get your change to you."

"You might as well keep it for your trouble." He jammed his hands into his trouser pockets. "I owe you for seeing that Mrs. Reddings's letters were mailed."

"I'll give the coins to your girl then." Winking, as if the man were taking the greatest amusement in Gage's plight, he dropped the coins on Lucy's eager palm. "You take good care of your papa. Bein' lovesick is the greatest affliction there is. Sorry, my boy, but there's only one cure."

"Death?"

The old geezer chuckled. "A sense of humor helps."

Humor? He wasn't trying to be funny. Squinting, he tried to make out the brown of Sarah's coat and the hem of her gray dress in the crowded boardwalk, but he'd lost sight of her.

Just as well. What was he going to do? Apologize? Try to figure out what had made her so damned angry with him? Hell, that would only lead to looking at her. And looking at her would lead to noticing her mouth. And noticing her mouth would only cause him to lose every sense of decency and restraint he possessed. And if he actually succeeded in kissing her...well, wouldn't that bring with it a whole passel of trouble?

Yessir. It was best to keep far away from Sarah Redding. This time, he meant it.

Chapter Six

"Hear you and Mr. Gatlin have taken a sparking to one another." Mrs. McCullough set her knitting basket on the front desk.

"Where did you hear an untrue rumor like that?" Sarah eased the heavy bucket onto the bottom step. "You know better than to believe everything you hear, don't you?"

"Well, at my age I've learned to believe in possibilities." Mrs. McCullough lit the crystal lamp and pulled up a chair. "You and Mr. Gatlin. Now there's a possibility."

"You're just anxious to see me married off." Sarah wrung the mop and for one brief moment imagined it was Gage's neck. "The last man I would ever want is one who won't marry for love."

"What other reason is there? For money?" Mrs. McCullough reached into her basket and produced her knitting needles and a ball of green yarn.

"Mr. Gatlin doesn't believe in love." Sarah swabbed one step, maybe a little too hard, and the mop head rammed into the newel post with a smack loud enough to echo through the sleeping hotel.

"Ain't his girl about the same age as your little one?"

Sarah moved up a step, leaning on the mop. It didn't take a brilliant mind to figure out what Mrs. McCullough was about to say. "Our girls are friends, that's all. Why, the man insulted me terribly today."

"Sure enough sounds like a courting man to me."

"Courting? I hardly know him." She knew enough about him already—and she didn't like him. Not one bit.

He was forward and brash. He was a scoundrel of the very worst sort, charming her, furrowing the garden, returning her chicken and smiling at her as if she were a young and beautiful woman. When she was a widow with more debts than a future, more dreams than money in the bank.

"We don't like each other." That much was true. He'd been pretty mad at her.

So, why had he tried to kiss her?

Troubled, she sudsed her mop, churning it up and down in the bucket. Water splashed and soap bubbles drifted and popped.

She was still so furious at him.

Every time she thought of him, there he was in her mind, more handsome than any man had the right to be, and he was asking her—her, Sarah Redding—to dine with him. In the fanciest dining room in the county. The dining room she'd just finished mopping from corner to corner tonight.

She fetched her bucket and carried it the rest of the way up the stairs, feeling more angry than she had a few moments ago. What was it about Gage Gatlin that affected her? That cut straight to her heart like a double-sided blade?

Because Gage had held out his hand and asked her to dine with him. For one brief moment Sarah had believed he'd meant it.

When he'd been feeling pity—not friendship—for her.

And then he'd hauled her out of the post office, which would be the stuff of which gossip was made for months to come.

He'd probably thought he would kiss her out of pity, too.

Well, she would have no more of it. Gage Gatlin would never do her another good deed. She would never again be beholden to him for a dollar or a plowed garden.

She'd pay him back. They'd be even. And she'd never have another reason to see Mr. Gatlin again.

Unless it was across the fields, as she'd noticed him this afternoon when she'd returned home and gone to the barn to milk the cow.

Was it her fault that if the door was open, she could see Gage's land while she milked? Surely it wasn't her fault that the sight of him at work, shirtless, with the sun burnishing his dark skin, made her forget what she was doing until the cow kicked her?

That was the best way to see Gage Gatlin—from a distance. And that's how it would stay.

Sarah reached into her apron pocket and withdrew two coins. There was no light coming from beneath Gage's door. He was probably asleep, for it was late. The thought of him lying on the other side of the wood wall, sprawled across the big comfortable bed...

A slow shiver zinged down her spine. All in a flash, she imagined him shirtless, his bronzed skin exposed to the night's touch, his strong chest rising and falling slowly in sleep—

Enough of that. How was she ever going to get him out of her head if she kept imagining him like that? She had no idea.

Sarah studied the coins in her hand. She worked hard for that money, and it meant a lot to her. But her pride meant more, so it was easy to slip the coins beneath Gage's door. Easy to find satisfaction in the rasp of silver against polished wood and know that she need never be humiliated by Gage Gatlin again.

As she straightened, smoothing her fraying apron and the patched calico dress, she told herself her heart wasn't hurting.

Really. It wasn't.

Gage bolted awake. Sweat beaded his brow and cooled on his bare flesh as he realized he was already out of bed, standing in the dark silence of his hotel room. Not in the Badlands, but in the prairie town of Buffalo. In the present. Not the past.

Hell, he was shaking as if he had a fever. Hands quaking so hard he couldn't wipe the sweat from his face. Memories taunted him, faint shadowy images of a past he'd put behind him forever. No, damn it. He wasn't going to let those images into his mind, asleep or awake. A man could only take so much.

And he'd had his share.

The wind gusted, driving hard pellets of rain against the window. A mean storm was blowing tonight, and he lit the lamp against the darkness. Wondered if he could get back to sleep.

A flash of light caught his gaze. There, in the shadows by the door. Looked like something metallic. It sure as hell wasn't his. He knelt, recognizing the coins before he touched them.

Two fifty-cent pieces. Why would anyone shove them under his door?

Sarah. Her name drove into his thoughts like a well-aimed bullet. Why had she gone out of her way to reimburse him for a few letters? Did she think he was the kind of man who held a grudge over a dollar?

Guess she'd made her point. She didn't need his help. Which worked out just fine because he didn't need her. He didn't need anyone.

"Ma?" Ella skidded to a stop among the mown thistles and weeds and glanced around. "They aren't here!"

There was no mistaking Ella's disappointment. Sarah deposited the picnic basket in the shade of the tilting old shanty. "It's early yet, baby. School just let out."

"Oh." Ella's head hung. "I can wait."

"It's really good luck that Lucy is going to be living here soon, isn't it?" Sarah eased the hoe she carried to the ground. "Their new house is going up quickly. Look, you can see where the rooms are going to be."

"It's gonna have an upstairs." Ella paced around the building site. "Lucy's gonna have a bedroom all to herself."

Wistful those words, quietly spoken, but Sarah understood the longing beneath. "I know it hasn't been easy in Aunt Pearl's shanty."

"I know, I know. We're grateful." Ella dropped to her knees to search through the growing grasses. "But I'm all better now. Maybe I could get a job to help out. Then we'd get our own house, too."

"Oh, baby." Like a blow to her chest, Sarah felt as if she'd had the wind knocked out of her. She brushed stray wisps of curls from Ella's face, but the worry remained etched deeply in her soft brow. "This isn't your fault."

"I got sick." She spun away and dropped a nail into a pail on a stack of lumber. "I didn't mean to."

"I know that." She was only a little girl, small for her age, frail from a year battling illness. Even now she covered her mouth and coughed, a testimony that her lungs were not as strong as they'd once been.

Aching, Sarah pulled Ella against her, wrapping her arms around her dear child. "You are all that matters to me. Do you know that?"

"I know."

"There isn't one thing I wouldn't do to make you happy. But first, we have to make sure you're well enough for me to work full-time."

"I can help—"

Sarah knelt to brush those glimmers of tears away with her thumb. "You can help best by being a little girl. That's your job. You know I answered all those advertisements. Now we just wait for the answers."

"But it will take *forever*."

"Not quite that long. And if we're lucky, someone will want to hire me. Think about it. Maybe you can have your own room."

"And a horse, too?"

"You just can never tell what's going to happen. Maybe." Sarah tugged Ella's sunbonnet into place and retied the strings. "Why don't you sit on the fence and watch Mr. Gatlin's horses? You might get an idea what kind you'd like to have."

"Sure!" The sadness disappeared as Ella dashed

away, braids flying out behind her as she sailed across the yard.

Please, let there be a good job for me. For us. It mattered so much. In truth, living with the Owenses was wearing her down. And if Ella kept growing stronger, then moving out was a possibility.

As Sarah gripped the hoe's smooth handle and dug it into the gnarled tangle of bean vines and weeds, she couldn't help imagining—just a little.

A little house with a big window in the kitchen, like the one Gage was building. Where she could mix rolls or knead bread and get a good dose of sunshine. Where she'd be able to watch Ella ride her very own pony through the fields.

Dreams. They kept her going. Even when she noticed a dark spot on the awakening prairie—Milt. He was driving the plow, and raised his arm to lash the whip. The horses leaped forward, and her stomach clenched as she realized Milt was watching her. Or rather, keeping an eye on Gage's property.

Feeling uneasy, Sarah cleared the plot of vines, weeds and half-rotted stems. Didn't look as though old man Buchanan had bothered to put in a garden for the last year or so. Frost has pushed a few rocks to the surface and she cleared those, too, whenever her hoe struck them.

That made the work harder, but she didn't mind. She'd get the earth nice and soft and ready for planting. Maybe Lucy would want a long row of carrots planted right here, so she could pluck them sweet and juicy from the ground during the summer. Or a stand of corn—

A jangling harness and the clomp of hooves on hard-packed earth announced Gage's arrival. There he was, looking more fine than any man had the right to, perched on the wagon seat. His hat at a jaunty angle. His spine straight, his jaw set. What a fine man he was.

Too bad he was all wrong for her. Completely, utterly wrong.

"Howdy, there." He didn't sound pleased to see her.

Well, she wasn't pleased to see him. Remembering the hotel, fresh resolve swept over her so it was easy not to look at him as she gouged the blade into the stubborn ground. For Lucy and Ella's sakes, she would not be rude.

She would not let her anger show. "Good afternoon, Mr. Gatlin. How was school today, Lucy?"

"I'm the new girl all over again." There was a thud as she landed nimbly and skipped away from the wagon. "Ella! Wanna help me brush Scout?"

"Sure!" Pure delight in that word.

The girls scampered off together, already talking a mile a minute.

And leaving her alone with Gage. He was unhitching the horse without saying a word. Kept his back to her. Didn't look at her. He had to be remembering their almost-kiss. Did he regret it, too?

Her hoe struck a rock with a *clink,* sending a ricocheting pain up her arm. She could feel Gage's gaze on her, so she kept her back to him as she knelt for the offending rock—

His wide fingers curled around the stone and gave it a toss. "I know why you're doing this. It isn't necessary. It's my land. If I want a garden—"

"Just returning the favor."

"Repaying a debt, you mean. I don't like it."

"I don't care what you like. I'm furrowing your garden and then I'm done with you. For good."

"That's a mighty shame." He straightened, sweeping off his hat so the wind caressed those thick tousled locks and the sun burnished his perfect smile. "I was counting on you for a friend, Sarah. A man like me doesn't get the chance for too many of those."

"Why is that?" She hurled the hoe into the earth, refusing to let his good-natured words whittle away at her fury. "Because you're so incredibly disagreeable?"

"Partly. Moving around hasn't helped." He thought he was so irresistible with the way he agreed so easily.

He didn't fool her for a second.

"Plus, I'm a scoundrel of the worst sort. I ought to know better than to try to kiss a decent and proper widow who was minding her own business at the local post office."

"Darn right I was!"

"Based on my appalling behavior, I ought to be the one doing a favor for you. Not the other way around." He whisked the hoe from her grip with the ease of a seasoned thief.

She'd underestimated him. "It's not the fact that you assumed you could kiss me on the boardwalk, in plain view of our daughters and half the township that has me so furious with you."

"Then tell me. Or I'll be forced to pay you another favor." He narrowed his gaze beneath the Stetson's brim, as if to gauge her reaction.

"I'm not sure you deserve an explanation." She held out her hand, determined to not look at him or his smile that would only remind her of how his mouth

had parted and her own lips had buzzed with anticipation. "Give me back my hoe."

"How about if I hire you to plant me and Lucy a
garden? I'd pay you a fair wage—"

"*Pay* me?" Was he this thickheaded on purpose?
Was he *trying* to aggravate her? "That's enough. Give
me my hoe. I'll return when you're asleep or something and finish this up."

"Because you think you owe me?"

"No. Because I'm no charity case, Mr. Gatlin. I'm
proud to earn my way, and don't you dare forget it."
She yanked the hoe from his steely grip and stormed
past him as fast as she could without tripping on the
mown weeds.

"Charity case? Where in tarnation did you get that
notion? Because I paid for your postage? It was a dollar."

"That's not your only offense." She snatched the
basket from the shade and kept going. One look at
Gage would make the burning behind her eyes worse.
She wanted to forgive him. She wanted him to like
her.

"Wait one minute. I'm not in the habit of letting a
woman toting a food basket walk away from me."

"There is a first time for everything." She *had* to
stay angry with him. She bit her tongue and kept going.

"What's in that basket? Another one of your great-
tasting pies?"

"Wishful thinking. If I had one, I may or may not
share it with you."

"What do you need? Bribery? A horse? Cold hard
cash? I'd do just about anything for a slice of your
pie."

That made her stop and stare. What a sight he was, with that saucy glint in his eyes. He thought he was funny. Thought he was charming her.

He was wrong. She *refused* to be charmed.

"An apology might be in order," she hedged.

"A dumb man may need to know what he's apologizing for."

Astounding. Her chest felt near to cracking in two with the shame. And he didn't know.

"You asked me to dinner in front of Louisa Montgomery." It seemed silly and shallow, but he'd hurt her pride. "You made it seem as if you were doing me a favor. Feeding the poor widow."

"Oh, Sarah." All of his jesting vanished like smoke on the wind. He closed the distance between them, one hand taking the hoe, the other snaking around her waist to rest on the small of her back. "I never meant it that way. You know I was grateful to you."

"There was no need. I enjoyed helping Lucy. That isn't what upset me."

"And that you helped Lucy isn't the only reason why I asked you to dinner." His eyes went black and his gaze swept down her face to land on her mouth.

Her lips tingled. A wild sensation whiplashed through her.

Then he blinked and dropped his hand from her back. "I did it for the girls. Lucy is glad for a friend. I thought she'd like to have Ella stay a little longer that day."

"The girls. Of course." She ought to feel relieved. Be glad Gage Gatlin wasn't looking for a *convenient* woman. Trouble was that the tingle of want remained, she beating rapidly and shivery in her blood.

"The girls are friends," she managed to confirm.

"I suppose we should be, as well. Since being near you seems unavoidable."

"Good. What do you think about my proposal?"

"What proposal?"

"To pay you for—" He paused, glancing past her shoulder. "Who is it this time? Will those women ever stop calling?"

Oh, no. Sarah took one look at the fancy buggy rolling to a stop in the driveway. The banker's daughter. Again.

Susan climbed down from the vehicle, her goal clear. She wanted Gage. Her gaze slid from Sarah's homemade sunbonnet to the tips of her patched shoes. The dismissive look said it all.

Sarah swept the dirt from her skirt, feeling plain.

It shouldn't hurt. It was only vanity. Beauty is as beauty does, but that didn't change her feelings. She didn't need a well-groomed, flawlessly gowned banker's daughter to tell her that her days of youthful beauty were gone.

Looks like I'm stuck with you. Milt's often-spoken words resounded through her thoughts. *With your looks, I'd have to pay someone to marry you and take you off my hands,* he often told her.

Deep down, she feared Milt was right. What if she was never loved again?

Susan carried a fine basket, covered with an embossed lace cloth. "My father told me how you were giving up the hotel room and roughing it out here without hired help."

Gage hardly looked at her. "Don't see that it's your father's business."

"Well, I certainly care that you have a decent meal."

He felt like a rabbit being chased by a pack of hungry wolves, and he didn't like it. Not one bit. He didn't much care for the cold shoulder the banker's daughter was giving Sarah.

"Sarah, we aren't done with our discussion." He thought it best to remind her, because it looked as if she was trying to fade into the scenery.

"We can talk later. It's fine with me."

She moved fast, he had to grant her that. Why was she leaving? When she was the only woman he wanted to stay?

"I'm sorry." He turned to the banker's daughter. "But as you can see, I have what I need."

"I see that you *hired* Sarah to prepare meals for you—" Susan's eyelashes fluttered, sidling closer.

"I didn't hire her." Gage stared at the girl long and hard.

Realization stole over her face. "Fine. I thought you were a man of culture—"

"I'm a horseman, lady." He left it at that. She stormed off, but he paid her no mind. He'd long stopped caring what other people thought.

Now, where had Sarah gone off to? She was almost at the creek when he caught up with her. Swinging her basket in one hand, her hoe with the other, her slender back was perfectly straight. It was hard to miss her elegance, her grace.

She was ten times the lady Susan Lockwood was. Twenty times more beautiful. Not that he should notice. He was running after her because of Lucy. Ella and Lucy were friends. It was important for parents in such a situation to get along. That was all.

"Sarah. Wait up." He was likely to turn an ankle chasing after her. Couldn't believe his eyes when she actually stopped, watching him approach with a frown shaping her pretty mouth.

Not that he ought to notice her mouth was pretty.

"I thought you would prefer Susan's company."

"So you left me alone? I'm not about to forgive you for that, Sarah. Not when I need protecting from misguided young women. The more I ignore them, the worse it gets."

"I suppose you get this all the time, at every ranch you worked at."

"Sometimes, but they accept defeat after a while."

"You must have a lot of money to make all these young women from wealthy families set their caps for you."

"Here I thought it was my charming good looks."

"Hate to tell you, Gage, but that's not it."

"Now I'm a broken man."

"You don't look like it."

"Looks can be deceiving. I'll feel better if you accept my offer. Come on, help a man in need."

"You could have asked Susan Lockwood. She looked eager to do whatever you wanted."

"I'm not interested in her."

Sarah's chin lifted, and she was no longer teasing. "That surprises me. I thought you were interested in something more convenient than love. What could be more convenient than marrying for practical reasons, like social position?"

He winced, recognizing his words. "I didn't mean that. Is that what you think? That I want—"

He blushed and had to look down at his boots. Hell, did he really sound like that? He was sorry he'd given that sort of impression. "I only meant I find it convenient to remain unmarried."

"Oh." She pursed her mouth, that perfect mouth he kept noticing.

That was easily explained. He was a man with long-standing unmet needs, and she was a woman he liked. A lot. Wouldn't mind kissing to find out what it would be like between them.

Which reminded him. He'd decided to stay away from her. Far away. Self-preservation and all that. His willpower seemed a little weaker when she was anywhere in the vicinity. He'd encourage her to go. That's it. He'd be polite, but firm. Because he kept wanting to kiss her. Wanting to know if her satin-soft lips were as captivating as they looked.

"Can you stay for a bit?" Why in blazes had he said that? "We can talk about your fee."

"My fee?" The corners of her mouth smirked.

"I heard loud and clear when you got all mad at me in town that it's possible to hire you for say, canning. Or maybe planting a garden."

"I was only intending to furrow it, and I don't want your money. You've been helping me out of pity, Gage, I know it. You know it. I can't stomach it."

"See what happens when you listen to folks? You might get the wrong outlook on things. If you listened to your own judgment, which was the correct one, you'd know I helped you because you helped me. Because that's the way I am."

"You didn't help Susan Lockwood."

"She doesn't need my help."

"I do?" The fury was back. "I survived just fine before you rode into my life—"

"Sarah." He tugged the bow at her chin. "Let's be friends. Just friends. We have daughters in common.

We've buried loved ones. It would feel good to have someone who understands, and I think you do.''

"I do."

Her sunbonnet slipped from her head and a cascade of blond hair tumbled over her shoulders to caress the enchanting curves of her breasts.

Not that he ought to be noticing that. Not at all.

Gage reached for the basket. "Allow me."

"I'm not sure I should," she teased, and in her smile he saw something he hadn't believed in for what seemed a lifetime. Hope.

Chapter Seven

"**D**id I hear right? Are you moving out of the inn?" Sarah asked as she set the plate of sugar cookies on the step between them.

"Yep." Gage grabbed a cookie and bit into it. "Figured the time has come for me to start keeping an eye on what's mine."

A chill sluiced down the back of her neck. "Are you having any problems?"

"Maybe. Hard to tell." He bit into the cookie. "There's only one way to know for sure. I would appreciate it if you didn't mention this to your uncle."

Milt. She couldn't stop the bad feeling settling into her midsection like a bad batch of oatmeal. "What kind of trouble?"

"I'll let you know when I'm certain." He shoved the final bite of cookie into his mouth and stole another. "These are good."

"It helps to keep the cookie jar full with nine children in one house."

"*Nine?* Suppose that's why Milt let you move in. Don't hold it against me for saying so, but it looks like he demands a lot of work out of you."

She winced. "I told you. I'm grateful."

"A woman alone with a child to raise…" He took the cup she offered him. "How did you do it?"

She closed her thoughts, banning the painful ones as she filled a second cup with sweet, cool cider. "I was lucky, I had a house and land to sell. An extra set of horses and a buggy. I had some savings, and I found a job as a cook at the logging camp where David used to work. I did well enough, between renting a room and paying for another widow to watch Ella."

"I know how hard that had to be." He swallowed, staring across the new-green plains to where Lucy was teaching Ella how to bridle Scout. "When my wife died, it was tough. I had to be away at my job, and Lucy had already lost one parent. I traveled a lot then, and decided to quit. It was a rough time for her."

"I understand. As little as Ella was at the time, she knew she'd lost her papa. She cried through the night, heartbroken, waiting for the gentle man who cuddled her and comforted her and tossed her up at the sky."

"You missed him, too."

"Yes." The day didn't seem as bright or the sun as warm when she thought about it.

"You loved him."

"You sound surprised."

"After meeting you, I shouldn't be." His mouth pulled down into a mix between a smile and a frown. "Maybe I'm too cynical in my old age. Or, it could be that marriage broke my heart in a way it won't ever be fixed again."

He bowed his head. Sarah stared at him. He looked wounded. Lost. What kind of marriage had he had? Is that why he thought love didn't exist?

She laid her hand on his broad back. He felt strong

as a myth, as if nothing could harm him. She knew better.

"I'm sorry, Gage."

"The past is done." He shrugged. "Whatever my regrets, there is one I will never have. Here she comes."

Sarah didn't need to follow his gaze to know what he meant. Lucy and Ella were running, first Lucy in the lead, then Ella, then Lucy again. Their laughter preceded them, sweet on the fresh spring winds, and they tumbled onto the rickety steps.

"I won!"

"No, I did!" they argued, out of breath and giggling.

"Cookies!" Lucy dove into the plate first. "Thanks, Sarah," she added around her bite of cookie. "It's real good, ain't it, Pa?"

"I've had better." He reached for another.

Sarah stole the plate away from him. "Maybe I'll just take these, since you don't appreciate them."

"I suppose I can choke another one down, as rotten as they are. If you'd be kind enough to pass me the plate."

She kept the plate out of his reach. "I'd hate for you to suffer. Maybe I'd better take the cider, too—"

Lucy stole another cookie from the plate. "Sarah, Pa's just sayin' that so I don't get ideas. He liked your pie the best of all."

"Tattletale." Gage winked as he hauled his daughter onto his lap.

Lucy shrieked in delight. "Don't punish me, Pa. I'll be good."

"I doubt that." He gave her a resounding smooch on the forehead before he let her go.

Sarah's heart melted like fresh butter, warming her from the inside out. A father's true love. She hadn't seen it, not up close, since her David died. Since he snuggled little Ella in his arms and blew raspberries until she giggled and giggled.

Ella stood staring, mouth open, cookie forgotten in her hand.

One day, sweetie, she yearned to tell her girl. One day we might have that beauty again. If we're lucky.

There was the crux of it. Luck. She was starting to think she'd run out of it. Began fearing that real love was as rare as everyone kept telling her.

That she'd never find it again. Ever.

It was near midnight, and no sign of trouble. Gage fished for the battered tin coffeepot in the darkness. Lucy was asleep and he didn't want to wake her. Heat radiated from the cookstove he'd dismantled from the shanty and set up in the new house. Or what would be the new house. He'd hung canvas tarps over the framed walls to keep out some of the night air.

They moved as the wind did, like ghosts in the dark, but that wasn't the reason for the odd shiver he felt. Or the sensation that he was being watched.

Yep, no sign of trouble—yet. But he was prepared. He leaned the Winchester against his thigh as he fumbled for the pot and refilled his cup.

The rich scent of strong black coffee perked him up and helped to keep his eyes wide open. His muscles protested, not a lot, but enough to remind him he wasn't twenty years old anymore.

Lucy sighed in her sleep and rolled over. It was too dark to see her, but she would be safe here. He'd make sure of it. He'd made promises to her. Promises he

intended to keep. That's why he was awake tonight
and heading for the fields, with a rifle and a cup of
coffee to keep him company.

Listening to the sounds in the night, he hunkered
down on the knoll, looking out across the prairie—and
the creek where his property ended. Out of the corner
of his eye he could see the skeletal structure of his
new house. All was calm. He propped the Winchester
against his knee and tried not to let the chill of an
early spring night settle into his soul.

The coffee tasted like turpentine—just the way he
was used to it in the old days. Strong enough to strip
the hide off a bear. Bitter enough to sear the bumps
off a tough man's tongue. Likely to keep him up half
the night.

Good thing, since the night prairie had a beauty to
it, reverent and lulling. The sky seemed to whisper,
the grasses sing, and an owl glided low, wide wings
spread, sailing over black fields beneath diamond stars.
Easy to relax, to lose his vigilance.

Up ahead, a doe's head shot up. Ears straight, nose
scenting. In a flash, she was gone, loping with four
others at her side. The deer blurred across the dark
prairie until it swallowed them whole, keeping them
safe.

Gage drained his cup and reached for his rifle.
Cocked it. Waited.

Sure enough, there was movement. Hard to see with
heavy clouds rolling in from the west, and he didn't
dare stand up and expose himself to get a better view.
Then a crack of wood against wood, man-made and
threatening, rang through the stillness. There went a
section of his fence.

Just like he figured. Gage watched, gun ready, anger

growing as Milt Owens and a boy maybe fifteen or sixteen strolled through the pasture, lassos in hand.

A dozen cattle and two Clydesdales passed through the creek and onto the Owenses' property. Gage's anger grew silent and strong. He watched the man and boy replace the rickety fencing with a few blows of a hammer and disappear into the night.

A rasping sound woke Sarah from a deep sleep. Whispers in the kitchen, low and rough, told her it wasn't one of the children searching for a drink of water. Something was wrong.

The mantel clock's tick-tick echoed in the dark front room as she sat up, careful not to roll off the narrow sofa. The door snapped shut, and Milt's harsh "Shh!" didn't sound drunken. But it was hard to tell.

Her stomach tensed into a hard ball. Hearing a cupboard door squeak open, she lay back down and tucked the blankets beneath her chin.

"I'll take care of it first thing," Junior's whisper knifed through the silence.

There was a chime of tin cups clanging together. "Make sure you get a decent price for them horses. If the stockyard won't take 'em, they'll be others—"

What horses? She leaned forward, straining to hear more, but their whispers were masked by the clink of a glass bottle and the splashing glug-glug of pouring whiskey.

It would be impossible for Milt to sell his only team. He needed the big draft horses for fieldwork. *No drifter is gonna take what's mine.* Isn't that what Milt had threatened?

What had he done? Stolen Gage's livestock?

"Sarah? Is that you?" A shadow filled the doorway,

black against black. "What the hell are you doin' home?"

She realized her pillow had tumbled to the floor and retrieved it. "It's not my night to work."

"Damn it! Did you hear anythin'? Did you?"

Her stomach clenched. His anger felt as threatening as a weapon.

"Don't you say nothin'." Milt lumbered closer, towering over her in the dark. "Do you hear me? Not one word against me, or I'll toss you and your daughter out of here so fast it'll make your head spin. Do you hear?"

"Yes." She lied. Let him try to intimidate her all he wanted, because he wasn't going to be successful.

"You just think, missy, where that daughter of yours will be without a roof over her head. Dead, that's what. You owe me—"

His beefy fingers scraped along her chin. How dare he? She struck his arm and leaped off the sofa. "You're drunk and disgusting. Go back in the kitchen."

The fireplace utensils were a step away. She sidled closer and reached for the iron poker.

"You just mind what I said." He retreated, as he always did, to pour more whiskey and drink with his son.

Sarah collapsed onto the sofa before her knees gave out and laid the poker on the floor so it was handy. The room was cool, and her blankets were still warm. Her exhausted body longed to lie down and sleep, but how could she?

The sound of a muffled cough had her off the sofa and opening the door to the girls's bedroom. A series of coughs led Sarah to Ella's side. Tucked in with three of her cousins, she was toasty warm.

"I'm all right, Ma." Ella's whisper was broken by another cough.

"You don't sound all right." Sarah eased onto the edge of the mattress. "Need some water?"

"Yes, please."

Sarah found the cup that was always on the tiny table by the bed and held it for her daughter. Ella drank, and her coughing eased.

"Just thirsty, I guess." Ella curled onto her side.

"You don't feel hot." Sarah took comfort in that. "Does your throat hurt?"

"No, Ma. I'm fine."

"That's all that matters." Sarah tucked the blankets into place, savoring the sweet warmth. "Pleasant dreams, baby."

"'Kay—" Ella was asleep, her breathing steady and clear.

All that mattered was Ella. Sarah thought of Milt out there, drinking with his son. She gathered her courage and left the room, closing the door tight behind her. A faint light shone from the kitchen, but she wasn't afraid. If she had to, she could handle Milt.

A bang on the door shattered the quiet. In Pearl's bedroom, Baby Davie began to cry. Sarah reached for her house robe as the kitchen door flew open.

"What the hell?" Milt boomed. "You can't—"

"Quiet, Owens." Sarah recognized the sheriff's voice as she tied the sash around her waist. "Remove your revolver and lay it on the table for me. You, too, son."

Sarah peered around the corner into the room that held four men. The sheriff, who cocked his revolver, and Gage. He filled the threshold, his hand on his holster, as if to second what the sheriff had to say.

His gaze shot to her. "Sarah, I was hoping you'd look after Lucy for me while your uncle and I sort a few things out. I have her right outside."

"Of course I'll take her." Sarah slipped behind the sheriff, who was watching while Milt and Junior disarmed themselves of guns and knives.

The cool wind wrapped around her ankles and she shivered. Only then did she realize she was barefooted.

Gage didn't seem to notice as he disappeared into the inky-black night. The air held a mist of rain and the board steps felt slick beneath her feet.

Lamplight tumbled through the kitchen window, spilling over Gage as he lifted a drowsy Lucy from his saddle. Wrapped in a blanket, the girl settled against his chest, as relaxed as a rag doll.

"Pa, I can...s-stay...awake," she mumbled, fighting to keep her eyes open. They drifted shut as she snuggled against her father, safe in his arms.

Tenderly, Gage brushed a kiss across the crown of Lucy's head. Sarah swallowed, surprised to find a lump in her throat and a catch in her breath.

I'm in trouble now, she thought as she led the way through the kitchen and into the front room. Trouble because she had a weakness for tenderness in a man. For a man who loved his child.

I'd be foolish to let myself fall in love with him. She pulled back the blankets and exposed the sheet spread out on the sofa. Moved aside so Gage could lay his child on the cushions.

Falling in love with him would be foolish for at least ten reasons she could think of. Sarah stood stalwart, vowing not to watch as Gage tucked the blankets around his sleeping daughter. Refusing to let his gentleness break down the defenses around her heart.

Reason number one: he's wealthy. Reason number two: he wants to stay unmarried forever. Reason number three—

"You sleep, darlin'."

Sarah couldn't move. Couldn't blink. Couldn't breathe. There was just enough light from the kitchen to watch him smooth his big hand over Lucy's brow.

The girl mumbled in her sleep, already lost in the dreams her father had wished for her.

Gage straightened. "I sure appreciate this, Sarah. I intend to pay you—"

"No. This is one neighbor helping another. If what Milt did to you what I think he did, it's the least I can do."

"It's not your fault, Sarah, and I appreciate all you've done for me. It's been a long time since a woman did something for me without an ulterior motive. I'd forgotten there are women like you in the world."

She *really* could fall for this man. "Compliments will get you anything. Now go tend to your business with Milt. I promise I'll keep watch over your daughter."

"I know." His trust felt rare and sincere and it warmed her as he stalked away, leaving her alone in the shadows.

"Ma, is Lucy gonna stay all day?"

"I don't know, baby." Sarah stoked the cooking fire so it was hot enough for the biscuits. "Would you girls set the table for me?"

Ella nodded. "I sure hope she can stay. Did you know we're best friends?"

"I sorta figured that." Sarah tugged the end of one blond braid before Ella scampered off, all smiles and joy to join Lucy setting flatware around the big rectangle table in the center of the room.

"Heard anything?" Pearl bustled into the kitchen, a baby on each hip. Heavy lines drawn into her face spoke of a long night without sleep. "Oh, I don't know what I'm gonna do!"

"Why don't I pour you a cup of tea?"

"At least that would warm my weary bones." Pearl was the youngest of twelve siblings and only ten years older than Sarah, but she looked ancient as she settled into the ladder-back chair at the foot of the long table. "They ain't back yet?"

"No."

Over the clink of flatware and the clank of enamel, Sarah added honey to a cup and poured the tea she had steeping. Out of the corner of her eye she watched the girls work, not talking, sensing the seriousness of the morning.

Lucy had to be worried about her father, Sarah realized. After handing Pearl her tea and waiting until she left the room, Sarah circled the table to give Lucy a reassuring hug.

"That's nice," Lucy sighed as she held on tight. "My pa's been gone a long time. He used to go away when I was little and it was a long, long time before he'd come back. I missed him."

"He's most likely no farther away than town." Sarah took the forks from Lucy's fist and plunked them on the table. "I promise he hasn't gone far, and

I know he'll be back for you soon. He would have told me if he had other plans."

"I know. It's just a worry." Lucy bucked up her chin and went back to work.

What a nice daughter Gage was raising. Sarah knew exactly how hard it was. She caught Ella at the cupboard and gave her a hug.

"Would you girls want pancakes this morning?"

"Yes!" Ella clasped her hands together, for pancakes were her favorite. "With sausages, too?"

"I think I can manage it." She was rewarded with two happy girls as she reached for her favorite mixing bowl.

"I get to help." The table set, Ella raced to the cupboard. "I'm getting the eggs."

"What can I do, Sarah?" Lucy pushed close. "I help my pa all the time."

Bootsteps rapped at the screen door. "She's a darn good helper, too."

"Pa!" Lucy dashed into his arms. Gage lifted her up and swung her around in the fresh morning air.

Ella watched, clutching an egg in each hand.

Sarah lifted them carefully from her daughter's grip, glad to see father and child reunited. "I was about to make my special applesauce pancakes. Would you like to join us?"

"You are an optimist, aren't you?" He leaned one shoulder against the threshold, unshaven and night-rough. "Doubt I'd be welcome."

"Lucy's planning on staying, aren't you, Lucy?"

"Sure. You can stay, can't you, Pa?"

"I've got work to get started on." He tweaked her nose playfully. "You have fun and behave yourself."

"I try."

Sarah laid her hand on Ella's shoulder. "Why don't you take Lucy to the smokehouse and fetch us some sausages."

"Let's go!" Ella and Lucy caught hands and bounded out into the morning.

"They seem happy." Gage swept off his Stetson and studied it instead of looking directly at her. "We found twelve cattle without brands and two Clydesdales in a hay shed on the far edge of Milt's property."

"I wondered. I think I overheard them discussing how to sell the animals last night." Sarah cracked an egg on the edge of the bowl. "Do you want me to tell the sheriff?"

"I don't want to cost you your situation here."

"I know, but what's right is right." Sarah emptied the egg from its shell. "What's going to happen to Milt?"

"It's up to the sheriff. I got my animals back, that's all I wanted. Thanks for being a good friend, Sarah. For watching Lucy for me."

"Sure thing." She snatched the sugar bag from the pantry. "Anytime."

"Don't think I'm too welcome here, so I'd best be on my way. Send Lucy over when she's done so I can get her ready for school, if you don't mind." He tipped his hat to her. "I'll be seein' you around."

It was as if he took the sunshine with him.

Sarah instructed Pearl's children, who came pushing into the kitchen, to sit and mind their manners as she peeled back the curtain.

Gage Gatlin was already gone from her sight.

"Why, Sarah Redding, as I live and breathe, what a surprise running into you like this." Mrs. Luanne

Montgomery pushed aside two shoppers and rounded a new-this-week fabric display. "What a mess it is, with Milt and that wonderful Mr. Gatlin. You must have been in such a fright when the sheriff came knocking on your door in the middle of the night."

"Good day, Mrs. Montgomery," she greeted the woman whose extensive land bordered Milt's on the other side. Not one for gossip, she decided to take charge before the older woman did. "I hear Mr. Montgomery is very pleased with his new bull."

"Shipped in on Monday's train." Luanne lifted her gloved hand in a dismissive wave. "It sure must be something to have such a *respected* man for a neighbor. I hear you two have been spending time together."

"He's paying me to till his garden." Sarah held up a packet of bean seeds.

"So, then the rumors are *not* true. About you and our esteemed Mr. Gatlin? Why, how can they be if he's hired you? You have a good day." Luanne bustled off, apparently pleased with her new piece of news.

Esteemed? It wasn't that long ago folks were calling him a drifter. Sarah snatched a couple corn seed packets from the shelf and added them to her collection. That should be about enough. Gage's garden patch was small—nothing like the one she tended for the Owenses' large family—but Sarah would make sure Lucy had a lot of variety in her first real garden.

"It sure is something, having Mr. Gatlin in our town, isn't it?" Mary Flannery asked as she stepped into line at the front counter. "Of course, you've probably known about him all along, haven't you, Sarah?"

"I met him the first day here." Folks must be impressed with the way Gage stood up to Milt.

"Why, the two of you have been courting all along." Mary winked. "I should have known those rumors I heard were true."

"They *aren't* true—"

"Fine, Sarah. Deny it all you wish." Mary held up one hand. "I know what I know."

With any luck, there would be new, different rumors for the townswomen to pass back and forth over backyard fences—and soon. Rumors that would not involve her and Gage in any way whatsoever.

"Sarah," Clancy Nelson behind the wide, scarred counter greeted her with an old sailor's salute. "Mr. Gatlin stopped by after taking his girl to school and talked to me. Don't you worry about a thing. Said you'd be buying a few things for his ranch."

"What do you mean?" She spread her purchases on the counter.

"You leave your hard-earned money in your reticule. Anything you buy goes on Mr. Gatlin's account." Clancy made a few quick notes. "Will there be anything else today?"

"No, thank you." Puzzled, Sarah waited as the shopkeeper wrapped her purchases.

Surely she'd mentioned to Gage that she would be stopping by for his garden seeds. That was all. Just went to prove what a thoughtful man he was. She sighed, feeling a little tickle of awareness deep inside. It only took the thought of him to make her pulse race.

Well, there was a definite solution to that. She'd do her best *never* to think of Gage Gatlin again.

Thanking Clancy, she tucked the small package into her cloak pocket and hurried to the door.

"Yoo-hoo, Sarah!" Mary Flannery waved goodbye, her voice clear as a bell for every shopper in the back corner to hear. "Be sure and give that wonderful Mr. Gatlin my regards."

"If I see him, I will."

"That's right. You're not *seeing* him. Don't worry, we just want the best for you, deary."

What on earth could she say to that? Aware of a dozen or more shoppers watching her, curious for any sign of confirmation, she steeled her face and walked woodenly to the door.

What was Mary thinking? Anyone could see that Gage wasn't the man for her.

Seven people said hello to her on her way out of town. Not just any ordinary hello, but they added a knowing smile to it, as if they were privy to her deepest secret. It was those rumors!

Last year, as a new widow to town, she'd endured her fair share of them. Too often she'd overhear what a "poor young thing" she was. She'd been able to turn the other cheek then, although her pride took a battering. Why couldn't she do it now?

She could think of several more reasons right off the top of her head why anyone could see Gage Gatlin wasn't the man for her. He'd been a widower a long while, so no doubt he was set in his ways. He never wanted to marry. If he did, it would be to a woman who wore sateen gowns and feathers on her bonnets—

"Hold up there, Sarah." There he was, the very devil himself pulling his wagon to a halt, the reason why she ought to keep her heart under lock and key. He was grinning like a bandit who was up to no good. A bandit who'd let a widow fall in love with him and not have a single affectionate feeling in return.

That's why she ought to keep ten yards away from him at all times. So she couldn't see the flecks of black in his gray eyes, today as warm as melted silver.

"Need a ride?" He hopped from the seat, his big boots kicking up dust as he landed in front of her. "I wouldn't charge you. Much."

"I'm not sure a ride with you would be worth any amount of small change."

"There is the view to consider. High up on this seat, you'll see the mountains much better. You're likely to be free from dust, too. Won't choke when some thoughtless fellow races his wagon right on past you. C'mon, Sarah, I might even let you ride for free."

"Free? Why, surely your company is worth more than that." She dug into her reticule and tossed him a coin.

"A penny?" Considering, he rubbed his knuckles against the dark stubble at his jaw.

She refused to wonder how extraordinary his whiskers might feel against her fingertips. She was *not* attracted to him. Not in the slightest. "Take the penny or leave it."

"I have to say this is a little hard on a man's self-respect. I bet I can get that banker's daughter to pay me at least two bits."

"I don't see her around, do you? You're out of luck. This is my best offer."

"I'll take it. All I really want is your company. I have a weakness for extremely beautiful women."

"You flatterer. No wonder everyone's singing your praises in town."

"Are they? Those poor misguided women. Someone obviously started a false rumor about me."

"That's exactly what I suspected." She climbed

onto the wagon fast, so he couldn't help her. But she wasn't fast enough.

His gloved hand caught her elbow and called every bit of her attention to that one spot on her arm where his touch was firm and hot. So very hot.

Where was her willpower? Her self-control? As he slid onto the board seat beside her, his arm collided with hers and remained, as solid as sun-warmed steel.

She *refused* to be attracted to him. She *wasn't* attracted to him.

"I want to show you something." His voice was low and rough, as if he felt this, too. He gathered the thick leather reins in his gloved hands and gave them a gentle snap.

The team of Clydesdales dropped their heads and pulled. The wagon leaped ahead, the lumber in the bed behind her rattling pleasantly. Out of the corner of her eye, she secretly watched the man seated next to her, his arm flush with her shoulder, his body heat merging with hers. Did he have to be so irresistible?

She had to stop thinking about him as a man. He was a father. She was a mother. That's why they were friendly. "Lucy told me she liked sleeping in the new house."

"Yep. Thought she'd have more fun there than in the old shanty. This is her home, and I want her to be happy here."

"What about you?" The words were out of her mouth, surprising her as she said them. "Are you happy?"

He gazed out at the road ahead. "I've got space, freedom and horses. What more could I need?"

"I understand perfectly."

Contentment could be a rare thing in this world.

She'd learned that the hard way, and she intended to do what it took to find happiness again. She had dreams for her and Ella. Dreams of a peaceful home, of a pony in the backyard, of another child one day.

"Here we are." He halted the horses and held out one leather-gloved hand, palm up, fingers pointing toward the beauty spread out before them. "Incredible, huh?"

Paradise. It surrounded her in a blanket of deep purple and green, wild violets carpeting a draw carved into the prairie and spreading as far as she could see. The freedom of it filled her soul. "It's like something in a fairy tale."

"Thought you might like it."

"And it smells like paradise." She inhaled the scent of thousands of violets, delicate petals ruffling lightly in the ever-present wind.

It was too beautiful to look at. She had to feel it.

Sarah grabbed hold of the wagon frame and dropped to the ground. "I hadn't realized the ride would be worth the penny."

"I aim to please, ma'am." He circled around the horses, suddenly close.

Too close. A strange tightening sensation rippled low in her belly. Strange, because she *refused* to be attracted to him.

"You look flushed, Sarah. Guess that means it was right to bring you here."

"It's just what I needed."

"Thought so. You have a tough life at the Owenses'." He held up one hand. "I know you don't complain, but it's easy enough to see."

She squinted up at him, standing tall against the

endless blue sky. "Have you been listening to those rumors about me?"

"Kind of hard not to. I can't tell you how many people have mentioned to me how glad they are I've taken an interest in that poor young widow." He winked. "I guess folks need entertainment."

"Glad I can oblige." Although it did rankle deep inside. "Is that how you see me? As poor and unfortunate?"

"I see the good in you." He stared into the distance, fidgeting a bit, and said nothing more.

"I see the good in you, too, Gage." It was so simple, really, his integrity, his strength, his kindness.

What was she doing? Gage wasn't for her, but the beauty of this meadow was. Wonder surrounded her in a pool of delicate flowers, impossibly small, easily crushed.

The blistering summers and the brutal winters came and went, and still these flowers grew in the sweet shade of springtime.

Amazing. She ran her fingers through the leaves and petals, softer than silk to touch, and breathed deep. "This is what hope smells like."

"You could be right." He knelt, too, and the outside length of his thigh lingered against hers.

All her senses focused there, where they touched. The meadow, the flowers, the fragrance and the sky faded into the background. Gage stared at her, his gloved hand settling at the small of her back, his other reaching toward her face.

There was no panic or outrage or shock as the soft texture of fine leather cupped her chin, holding her captive as he eased close. So close their breaths mingled and their lips met in a soft luscious caress.

Her eyes fluttered shut, and she surrendered. Curling her hands into the fabric of his shirt, tilting her mouth for a better fit. Dying a little bit as he caught her bottom lip between his and sucked just right. The sensation was the single best thing she'd ever felt. *Ever.*

Heaven help her, she couldn't move away. She ran both hands up the rock-hard line of his chest. The wet heat of his tongue laved the seams of her lips. Like a flower to sun, she opened up to him.

He was hot satin against her teeth, her tongue. As heady as whiskey, he overwhelmed her. Made her more light-headed with every bold sweep against her tongue. She clutched his shoulders, hanging on for dear life, enjoying his kisses greedily. She couldn't help it. Couldn't let him stop. The magic of desire skidded in her pulse, beat thick in her veins and tugged low in her abdomen.

The rough ragged moan he made low in his throat told her he felt the same. Impossibly tender, he pulled her against his chest, never lifting his mouth from hers. His fingers tugged at her sunbonnet strings until they came free.

She hardly noticed because she couldn't think. There was no room for thought, only the singular pleasure of his kiss. Of the way he laved her top lip, tugging it between his teeth, sucking her swollen flesh.

Then his hands were loose in her hair, untangling her braids, and he was pulling her down into the violets. The scent, the softness, the rasp of his day's growth against her skin, the weight of him as he half covered her were all too luxurious to name.

Tenderly he brushed stray curls from her face. He broke the kiss, breathing as fast and shallow as she, gazing into her eyes as if he were trying to see inside her, to know her secrets and her deepest feelings.

A slow grin curved his mouth, and he kissed her with his smile.

"Are you young folks finished yet, 'cuz you're keepin' an old man waiting."

Sarah recognized that voice. Gage tore away from her, bounded to his feet and rescued his fallen hat from the ground.

"Mr. Luckens. Didn't expect to find you here."

"Guess not, young fella. Next time don't leave your wagon visible from the road. A man like you ought to know that without bein' told." Mr. Lukens winked. "Howdy, Sarah."

"Hello." Mortified, she brushed bits of leaves from her skirt.

Land sakes, she was disheveled, and the reason for it was plain enough. Her hair tangled around her face as she pushed it out of her eyes. Where was her sunbonnet?

Gage settled his Stetson square on his head and faced Lukens. "I was showing Mrs. Redding the violets."

"My eyesight ain't so good, but that ain't the way it appeared to me." The old man cackled. "Got a bunch of folks on their way to your place. Figured you'd need a spot of help with that house of yours."

"What?" Gage stood so Lukens couldn't see Sarah as struggled with her sunbonnet strings. Heck, there were bits of leaves in her hair.

"—comin' by in a few hours, those who can spare the time." Lukens gestured toward the road where a team and wagon were passing by. "Gonna be hard to raise that second story and a roof all by yourself. That's what neighbors are for.''

"I don't know what to say." Mostly because it was damn hard to think with the sweet zing of desire thick in his blood.

The scent of violets clung to his face and whiskers and he could still taste Sarah's kiss on his lips. He had a hell of a time trying to think of anything else. "Folks are coming over? You mean, today?"

"Heck, young man, you've got it bad. Now get that pretty gal of yours in the wagon and head for home. And wipe that dazed look off your face or folks'll talk." With the snap of his cane, he was off, limping away. His mule waited patiently in the narrow clearing near the road.

Hell. Gage rubbed the back of his neck, trying to figure out how to fix this. It wasn't Lukens he was worried about. It was Sarah. Her presence felt as brilliant as the sun. The soft pad of her footsteps in the new grass moved through him like thunder.

He couldn't look at her. Vowed never, ever, to think of the kiss they shared. That incredible, mind-altering kiss. The one that had made him toss away hard-learned lessons about love and women just for the pleasure of tasting her. Of tangling his fingers in her hair. Of feeling her body beneath his.

Nope, he'd never think of her kiss again. Not ever.

"You'd best take me home." She hesitated at his side. Her cheeks were flushed and her lips swollen from his kiss. "You weren't here for the Montgomery's barn raising, but, oh, the fun we had. And all the food. I need to get started cooking."

Woodenly, he steeled his feelings. Forced himself

to look at Sarah and see only Lucy's best friend's mother, to whom he'd offered a ride.

Gage held out his hand, as any gentleman would. When Sarah placed her fingertips against his palm, it all came back—the fire and beauty he'd found in her arms.

Chapter Eight

Sarah knelt before the blazing fire pit, refusing to remember Gage's sizzling kiss. And the iron-warm feel of his sculpted shoulders beneath her hands. And how he'd gazed at her with desire hazing his winter-gray eyes.

There she was. Doing it again. A person would think she'd never been kissed before this. The wrapped potato she'd been reaching for tumbled into the hot ashes. She snatched it and dropped into the bucket, vowing to banish Gage from her thoughts.

Except he was in her view, standing on the framed house, holding a heavy rafter flush for Carl Montgomery to bracket into place. Gage looked as bold and as captivating as he had when he'd kissed her.

Oh, my, the man could kiss.

She eased the heavy bucket onto the edge of the food table and nudged it into place beside a huge bowl of steaming gravy.

What was wrong with her? She had to forget their kiss ever happened. She had to erase it from her mind and blot out the memory of how his commanding lips had possessed hers. His kiss had been both insistent and gentle, the sensual glide of his tongue—

See? If she wasn't careful, Gage's kiss was all she would think about for the rest of her days.

A hand lighted on Sarah's shoulder as Inga Lukens sidled close. "If you'd rather, I can tend to the green beans. Why don't you break apart the batch of rolls Mary just brought? You can do that at the table where you'll be able to keep watch on him."

"Him?"

"The comely stranger that bought the Buchanan place." Inga winked, a robust woman who'd raised six boys and lived to tell about it. She tossed Sarah a knowing look as she cut the string around the turkey.

"If I weren't a few decades too old, I would have my eye on that man." Mary Flannery paused to wave to everyone as she slid a sliced chocolate cake onto the far end of the food table. "I guess you're the lucky one, Sarah."

"Me?"

"Sure. You're looking for a husband. He's got that little girl and no wife." Mary's gaze strayed to where the men shouted to one another as they worked. "Looks like a perfect solution to me."

"What perfect solution?" Sarah lined a basket with fresh dish towels. Here was her chance to set things right and stop those outrageous rumors. "Maybe Mr. Gatlin is much too handsome for my tastes."

"How can a man be too handsome?"

"Take a look for yourself." It was easy to see Gage Gatlin straddling the thick-cut timber high above the ground like a man born to it. What woman wouldn't want to gaze at him for hours?

Inga frowned. "Yeah, I see what you mean. You'd have competition with a man like that."

"Give me a homely man any day." Sarah broke apart the loaf of rolls, tumbling them into the awaiting basket. "I'll leave the handsome ones for the likes of Susan Lockwood."

"Ach, the banker's daughter." Inga waved one hand as if to dismiss the young woman who sat in the shade beneath a parasol, chatting with her mother. "Shameless, here to bat her eyes at our fine Mr. Gatlin."

"She'll probably win his affections." Mary frowned at the injustice. "I'm sure she figures Mr. Gatlin's a wealthy man and most likely to want a banker's daughter for a wife. But she doesn't know what I know."

Mary was wrong. Sarah reached for another loaf, intent on her work. Gage said he wouldn't marry anyone. Yet he'd kissed her.

"To think someone practically famous would live here in our midst." Mary gestured toward the roof of the house where Gage worked.

"It's an honor, it is." Inga spoke up as she set about carving the turkey.

"Who's practically famous?" Sarah followed the women's gazes to the lone man on the timbers above, powerful legs wrapped around the beam as he guided another rafter into place.

"Haven't you heard?" Mary appeared shocked. "It's been all over town, as soon as word got around concerning what Milt did, that is. The sheriff recognized him. Our distinguished Mr. Gatlin is a former Range Rider."

"That can't be." Sarah opened the butter crock. "Gage told me he was a horseman."

"Before that, he was a Rider." Inga thrust a heaped platter of turkey meat at Sarah. "Take this to the table for me, please. Look at him. Yeah, you can see the steel in his spine. Absolute quality, that man."

A lawman? There he was, high above the ground, lashing the timber into place. Not just any lawman, but the best of the best. One of the toughest Montana Territory had to offer.

She shouldn't be surprised. She knew firsthand just how fine he could be.

"Supper!" Inga shouted to the men. "You come down and eat. That is why we have been slaving all afternoon."

"And we haven't?" her father-in-law, old Mr. Lukens, complained with a grin. He patted Sarah's hand as he headed up the food line. "Couldn't happen to a nicer girl. He's a fine one, eh?"

"Almost as fine as you, Mr. Lukens."

"It would be hard to be better." Gage approached, reaching for a plate from the stack at the end of the table. "You're looking fine, too, Sarah. Care to join me?" He held out a plate for her to take.

She stared at it and then at him. "If I did sit with you, then those rumors about us will never stop."

"True, but I prefer the company of the most beautiful woman here."

What a flatterer he was—and a liar. It was hard to hold that against him as he cupped her elbow and began pulling her close.

"Excuse me." Louisa Montgomery cut between them. "Sarah, you're holding up the line. Why, hello, Mr. Gatlin."

Sara blushed. She *was* holding up the line. She might as well shout her feelings for Gage at the top of her lungs in the center of town. That would be more subtle than standing here mooning at him, when it was clear he was out of her reach. He'd been one of the best lawmen in the territory.

Sarah took a step back. Louisa began dishing up her plate, and Gage was distracted by Mr. Montgomery dropping the serving fork. She felt out of place here. And with his kiss still tingling on her lips, she felt out of luck.

Sarah saw her chance and darted away before she made an even greater fool of herself. Now, where had Ella gone off to? It was time for her to eat.

"Howdy, Sarah!" Lucy hopped out of line and grabbed Sarah by the wrist. "Come eat with us."

"Yeah, Ma." Ella flashed an elfin smile. Happiness radiated from her like light from the sun.

As her little girl told her all about the tadpoles they'd found in the creek and a jackrabbit that ran so fast Scout couldn't catch him, Sarah dished up their plates.

"Sarah." Suddenly Gage was at her elbow and stole her plate. "I saved a place for you and Ella at our table. Right this way."

He held her so she couldn't escape. As most of their neighbors watched with interest, Gage led her to the makeshift trestle table where the sheriff and the Lukens family made room on the bench seats.

"That crafty banker and his awful daughter tried to sit here," Mr. Lukens leaned to whisper in her ear. "But Gage wouldn't let 'em. Told 'em he was waiting for you."

"He didn't want to sit next to Susan, that's all."

Sarah wasn't going to be foolish and read something into that.

But she wanted to. Her chest felt tight with aching as Gage eased beside her onto the bench. His wide shoulders and hard thighs pressed against hers and left her dizzy and weak.

Then Gage's fingers curled into her hair. The raspy feel of his calloused fingertips at her nape made her sigh.

"You had a violet stuck there," he whispered, his breath hot on the shell of her ear, and it reminded her of his kiss.

His wonderful kiss.

"I'm glad you let me bully you into sitting with me." He spoke low, so only she could hear. "I like being with you, Sarah."

How was she going to resist him now?

"I am so happy about you and Gage." Inga hefted the last food basket into the back of her husband's wagon. "You with your girl and he with his. Why, it is as plain as day you two belong together."

"We do not. *That* ought to be obvious to anyone who looks at Gage and then at me." Sarah handed Inga the empty butter crock. "Tell that husband of yours to drive safely."

She waited until the Lukens were safely down the road and rounding the bend before she went searching for Ella. It took some doing as twilight fell, lengthening the shadows, darkening the prairie. Finally she tried the stable.

"Look, Ma." Ella peered over the hayloft. "We found kittens!"

"Really tiny ones. Just baby ones," Lucy added,

her excitement shimmering in the rafters above as Sarah headed for the ladder. "Pa, how old do you think they are?"

Gage was up there? Sarah froze in midclimb. She'd done her best to avoid him since supper. Since he'd treated her with kindness and respect and humor, as any friend would, while she'd been unable to forget their kiss.

Why had he kissed her, anyway? Whatever the reason—impulse, loneliness, overwhelming male needs—she wasn't ready to face him without a crowd of people around.

"I noticed the cat was missing this morning when I came in to milk," Gage was saying, the rough rumble of his words pulling Sarah closer. "I figure these kittens had to be born sometime last night."

"They're so little," Lucy cooed.

"And so cute." The adoration in Ella's words was hard to miss.

I'll have to add "kitten" to the wish list. It had been a long time since she'd seen Ella's eyes sparkle quite like that.

A lantern's soft glow lit the way through the hay-strewn boards. Tucked in the corner was a nest of kittens, blind and hairless, sleeping safe against their mother's belly. The calico cat purred contentedly, watching proudly as Sarah knelt.

"She lets us pet them. See?" Lucy traced her forefinger ever so gently over a white kitten's flattened ears. "I like this one the best."

"I like the striped one." Ella touched the sleeping kitten. "Did ya see the gray one, Ma?"

"I see." Sarah could feel Gage watching her.

"Friends," he'd said. They were friends—who happened to have shared a very amazing kiss.

"Don't she look like your kitty?" Ella leaned her head against Sarah's shoulder. "I know you miss Cuddles a lot."

"You had a cat?" Lucy asked.

"Yes, but I had to give her to my next-door neighbor when we moved in with the Owenses."

Lucy's hand crept into Sarah's. "Did it make you real sad?"

"Absolutely. I miss her very much, but I know my old neighbor is taking good care of her. And maybe I'll have another cat one day. You never know."

"Sounds like you had to give up a lot. I didn't realize." Gage stood, moving closer, towering over her. "I hope good times are around the corner for you."

He offered her his hand, palm up, and like magic her hand fit into his. They were skin to skin, and the small contact felt huge. Desire flickered, deep and low, and she couldn't stop it. He attracted her like a moth to flame.

"A good friend" he'd called her, but there, in his intense gaze, was the possibility for more.

"I'll see you home." His fingers threaded through hers, holding tight.

So much was changing between them. Did he feel it, too? Was that why he'd wanted her at his side tonight? Why he was holding on to her so tightly now?

She waited while he extinguished the lantern and let him help her onto the ladder. Ella climbed down next, rosy from the excitement of seeing the kittens, then Lucy, hitting the ground at a run. Gage eased down the ladder with a predatory strength that made it easy to believe he'd once been a lawman. She could picture him in the standard black shirt and trousers, the badge glinting on his chest.

He didn't take her hand again, but he did fall into stride beside her. A companionable silence fell between them as Gage snatched her heavy basket and they followed the girls across the shadowed meadow.

"The first star." Old habit kept her pointing at the faint twinkle at the eastern horizon.

"Let me guess. You're the sort of woman who makes wishes."

"On occasion." Sarah stopped, searching her heart for a wish—she didn't need to dig very far. In the growing dark ahead, Ella and Lucy were trying to talk a shy filly into letting them pet her.

Her first wish was for her daughter. For Ella's health and happiness...

"The second star of the night." The twilight thickened, almost hiding him in its shadows.

The second star would be for her. For her very own wish, just this once. The point of light sparkled jewel-like and true, but when Sarah closed her eyes to wish, it was Gage she saw. His kiss she felt. His love she wanted.

Please, let him find it in his heart to love again. To love me. She opened her eyes at the touch of his knuckles to her chin. Let his finger trace the curve of her bottom lip. The memory of their kiss beat between them, and deep inside she quickened with hope.

Then his hand fell away and he started walking slowly, keeping pace with her shorter steps. "It was pretty nice of folks to show up and help like that."

"I think it was old Mr. Lukens's doing. He's taken a liking to you."

"Then I owe him. My second story is framed, my

roof trusses are up. I can do the rest in no time." He paused to watch the girls dash past. "I appreciate your helping out. Will it make trouble between you and Milt?"

"We'll have to see. He may not even find out about it, since Pearl and the children went to stay with her mother for the day. I don't see a light on in the shanty, so they are probably still visiting."

She didn't want to spoil this perfect evening by thinking of her problems. "Now that I've got you alone, tell me. Are the rumors true? Were you a Range Rider?"

"You know how rumors are. Exaggeration. Invention. Fiction."

"I've known some rumors to be true. Is this one of them?"

"A long time ago."

It made sense. He'd mentioned a job that had required a lot of travel. He'd quit for Lucy. "Do you miss it?"

"Parts of it. Knowing I was doing good with my life. Upholding the law. Stopping cold-blooded killers from harming innocent people. But it was a hard life and came with a price. Lucy's better off having a horseman for a father. I sleep better at night."

"I'm glad you're here."

"Me, too." His knuckles grazed the side of her face. "Your hair smells like violets."

"I can't imagine why." She shrugged, feigning innocence when her pulse thundered through her veins and she would give anything to feel his kiss again.

"I'm glad we're friends, Sarah. Real glad."

There was that word again. Friends. Was he telling

her that he meant what he said, that he would never love again?

He held her hand, helping her through the fence. The sky had darkened so a thousand stars flickered overhead, casting a faint shadow on the silent prairie. The night felt enchanted as Gage laid his hand on her shoulder.

At the back step Gage handed her the basket. "Thanks again, Sarah. Guess I'll be seein' you around?"

"We're bound to run into one another now and then."

"That's what I figured." He brushed a kiss along her cheek.

She breathed in the fresh wood and night scent of him. Nice, so very nice. She turned her face just a bit, hoping he would claim her lips with his…

"Good night." He tipped his hat and disappeared into the shadows.

Boy, that was fast. She couldn't see him anywhere. She'd scared him off. She'd misread his intentions.

Friends. That's why he kissed her cheek. To make it clear how he felt for her.

Embarrassment left her face burning. She'd been foolish tonight, misinterpreting his friendship and letting her hopes for love carry her away.

How was she ever going to face him again?

"'Bye, Lucy!" Ella shouted somewhere in the shadows, her feet pounding as she ran into sight. "Ma, can I go play with Lucy tomorrow?"

"I don't see why not."

"Goody!"

Sarah held the door wide and waited for Ella to hop up the steps and skip inside. It had been ages since

Ella had been this full of life. And she hadn't coughed once today.

The ache in her chest faded away as she shut the door. Her first wish was well on its way to coming true. That was more than enough. What did her own heart matter in comparison?

"He ain't gonna marry you."

"Milt!" Sarah turned up the lamp. There he was tucked in the back corner of the kitchen, boots crossed on the edge of the table, and a half-empty whiskey bottle clasped in one hand.

Sarah shut the door carefully. "Ella, hurry to your room. Now."

Wide-eyed, the girl scurried off through the dark house. The click of the doorknob told Sarah her daughter was safely inside. She hefted the basket into the pantry and tried to ignore the drunk man watching her every move. Her hands shook as she took out a bread loaf.

"If you want a roof over your brat's head, you'll stay clear of Gatlin. No more baking pies. No more favors." Milt's boots struck the floor. "You hear me?"

"Yes." Sarah slipped the loaf into the bread box. Her hands shook harder, and she had to steady them.

"A man like that ain't gonna want you anyway. They say he was decorated five times. Coldest sonof-abitch in the territory. He's got a heart of stone nothin' can break. He's trying to use you. A man has his needs."

Milt paused to take a long pull from his bottle. "You'd best straighten up and do your work here. Understand?"

Sarah closed the pantry door and headed for the

front room. Her shoes knelled in the silence. She tugged the bedding from the chest beneath the window, swearing when the edge of a blanket caught on a nail head. She tried to work it free.

"There's no way that bastard is gonna fall in love with you." Milt wobbled into the parlor.

Sarah gave up, tore the blanket and slammed the bedroom door shut behind her.

"Ma?" Ella sat quietly in the corner. A small lamp on the table kept the darkness at bay. "I don't like it when he drinks."

"Neither do I." Milt had never been this bad, and it troubled her. She pulled a chair over and tucked it beneath the knob. "Don't you worry. We'll have our own place before you know it."

"And my very own bed." Ella covered her mouth to cough.

There was no water in the pitcher. Sarah didn't want to go into the kitchen again.

"How long will it be, Ma?"

"I'm not sure. Before summer, probably."

"That's a long time." Ella rubbed her eyes and coughed harder. "It's all my fault that we're here. I got sick."

"Oh, baby." Sarah sat on the bed and pulled her daughter into her arms. "Getting sick was not your fault. I was sick, too, remember?"

"But I was sicker."

"It's still not your fault. I promise it isn't." She kissed her daughter's brow, wishing she could make everything right again. "You never know when things are going to change. I interviewed at the boarding house in town, and I haven't heard back from them yet. I answered all those advertisements in the county newspaper. Something will work out, I promise. I will make our life better, my baby.''

"I won't get sick again. That's gonna be my promise." Ella rubbed her fists against her eyes. "I'm gonna help out, too."

"You can help by getting ready for bed." Sarah gave Ella one last hug.

"Tell me about my pa."

"Your pa was a good man." She shook the folds from Ella's nightdress. "He would lift you high into the air and turn around in a circle until you giggled. He said you were his twinkling star."

"He'd sing to me." Ella shrugged out of her dress.

"He did." Sarah dropped the nightrail over Ella's head. "Every night he would take his fiddle from the box and sing one song after another until you fell fast asleep."

"And then he'd say, 'Sweet dreams, baby Ella,' and kiss me right here." Ella touched her brow. "I miss him."

"I know." Ella had been too young to remember much, but Sarah knew just what she meant.

How different their lives would have been, if he'd lived.

She tucked her daughter beneath the covers, listened to her prayers and kissed her good-night. Tired from a day spent playing hard with Lucy and the other rancher's children, Ella's eyes drifted shut. Her breathing sounded rough, but not congested, thank goodness.

Sarah pulled the novel from beneath the bed, dusted it off, and settled against the headboard. She'd managed to keep a few books of hers and David's. She had needed them during the long nights spent with Ella, passing the hours between doses of medicine.

The page was still marked with a ribbon scrap. She tried to concentrate on Thomas Hardy's tale of a poor working girl who fell in love with a wealthy man. But couldn't. The story was going to end badly and reminded her of her own life. Of the wealthy, five-times-decorated lawman who'd kissed her in a field of violets.

Who'd told her she was his friend.

And it hurt. She pressed her hand to her breastbone, but it didn't dull the pain lodged deep within.

A confusing tangle of emotions tightened deep inside, and she didn't know how to stop it.

She hadn't imagined her life like this. This wasn't the way it was supposed to be. Troubled, she ran her fingers through her braids to loosen the plaits. Her hair smelled of violets, and tiny purple petals fell into her lap. Evidence of the passion she and Gage had shared.

Friends, he'd said, because he didn't want her.

Sarah heard footsteps behind her and stopped scrubbing. Fiery hot-pains shot through her back as she straightened away from the washtub. She wiped her soapy hands on her apron. "Hi, Lucy."

"Howdy, Sarah. Pa let me ride Scout to school and back all by myself." Pride lifted her up as she skidded to a halt near the rinse water. "Can Ella come play?"

"She's inside—"

Lucy took off before Sarah could finish. Before Lucy made it to the door, the screen door flew open and Ella called out in greeting.

A week had passed since Gage's roof raising, and the days had fallen into a predictable pattern. Every day after school, Lucy came over. The girls would spend all afternoon exploring the meadows and riding Scout.

Sarah had picked up an extra shift at the hotel, and at Ella's scheduled doctor's appointment, he'd pronounced her significantly improved over her last visit. If her lungs remained clear for one more week, he would deem Ella strong enough to return to school. With Lucy as her best friend, Ella was *almost* enthusiastic.

Sarah dipped the long handle into the rinse kettle and lifted a sheet from the hot water. It landed in the basket with a splat.

A footstep padded behind her. "I see Pearl moved back in with the children."

Gage. She had tried her best to avoid him all week long. Sometimes when she'd been taking water at the well or milking the cow, she would catch sight of him across the field. Working on the house, shirtless beneath the pleasant spring sun. Or sitting tall in his saddle, tending his herds. She'd been glad he was busy, and kept her mind on her work.

He had to be uncomfortable, too, because he tugged his Stetson low to hide his eyes and he was doing his best not to look directly at her. If he stood any farther away, they'd have to resort to yelling so they could hear each other.

"Here. Sorry we didn't return it sooner." He thrust the empty pie plate at her. "Lucy kept forgetting to bring it with her."

As soon as she had the plate in her grip, Gage stepped back, keeping a safe distance between them. She tried not to let it bother her.

"I noticed you planted the garden while I was in

town yesterday.'' He rubbed the back of his neck, unable to stand still. ''Appreciate that. Lucy said you told her how much to water and how often.''

Sarah nodded, hugging the pie plate to her chest as if it were a shield protecting her heart. It hurt to see him.

Maybe it was best to put them both out of their misery. ''As you can see, I'm busy here. I have to get this all done so I won't be late to work tonight. Thanks for returning the plate.''

''Sure thing.'' Relieved, he tipped his hat, his mouth a straight, hard line, and he strode away.

Well, that was that. Seeing him now and then would get easier as time passed.

At least, that's what she told herself.

Chapter Nine

"Heard you're taking that job at the boarding house." Beatrice Wagner counted back change on the other side of the postal counter. "It'll be good for you to get out of that house, I wager. This must mean that sweet girl of yours is doin' better."

"She is." Sarah tugged Ella a little closer. "This means she'll start school on Monday."

"Wonderful." Beatrice nudged the candy dish toward Ella and gave her an encouraging smile. "Take two," she whispered.

"Thank you kindly, ma'am," Ella said politely, reaching up on tiptoe to take two peppermints.

"And a couple of letters for you, Sarah." Beatrice shoved the white envelopes across the counter, too. "Hope it's good news this time."

Three answers to her job inquiries stared back at her as she thanked Beatrice, dropped her change into her reticule and maneuvered Ella toward the door.

"Ma, can we stop by the mercantile?"

"We can't afford to get anything, sweetie."

"I just want to look. And I can do that all by myself. Please?"

It was hard to argue with that. "Stay inside the mercantile until I come get you."

"Thank you, Ma!" Ella dashed away, nearly skipping down the boardwalk.

Sarah watched until her daughter had made it safely to the store and disappeared inside before she remembered the letters. Did she open them now? Or wait. They were probably telling her the position had been filled anyway. She'd learned quickly not to get her hopes up—

"You're not going to open them?"

Oh, no. It was Gage, the man she'd done her best to avoid for the past few weeks. She'd gotten so good at it, she'd forgotten to stay vigilant and now here he was, looking finer than ever and more uncomfortable than she felt.

She jammed the letters into her reticule. "Mr. Gatlin. Ella tells me most of your mares have foaled. I couldn't help noticing the fine colts and fillies in the fields."

"Lucy tells me you plan to move to town."

"Today is our final night at my aunt's. We leave for good tomorrow morning." She thought she saw him breathe a sigh of relief. Maybe he'd been trying to keep from running into her, as well. "The position at the boarding house isn't full-time, but it will pay room and board."

"Will you still work at the hotel?"

"That's my intention, until something else comes along. A better job, not marriage," she clarified, just in case that was what he was thinking.

Red crept up his neck and flushed his face. "Bet you're glad to be getting out of that house."

Especially since Milt's behavior had worsened after

his brush with the law—and Gage Gatlin. "I really must go—"

"The garden is growing. Lucy's as thrilled as can be."

"I'm glad. I've got to go—"

"Sarah, wait." She seemed to be in such a hurry to get away from him. Truth be told, he'd nearly dodged into the gunsmith shop just to avoid seeing her.

One thing he'd never been was a coward, and now was no time to start. Besides, he *did* like her. He cared about her. It wasn't her fault every time she spoke her incredibly sweet, rosebud-shaped mouth enticed him beyond all reason.

The fault rested squarely on his shoulders.

"What is it? I have more errands to do." Her face was pale beneath her sunbonnet's gray brim. Dark smudges bruised the delicate skin beneath her beautiful eyes. "I'm afraid I made circumstances worse for you, when I turned in Milt. I'm sorry for that."

"You couldn't let him steal from you." She pulled a list out of her pocket and studied it. Making it clear she was through speaking with him.

"Sarah—"

She broke away, leaving him alone on the boardwalk. He couldn't look at her without remembering how quickly he'd lost control that day on the prairie, when he'd shown her the violets. When he'd kissed her senseless and laid her down in the violets, ready to do more than kiss her.

Much more. His trousers felt a little tighter as he thought about it. Up ahead, she crossed the street and darted into the corner shop.

He ought to feel respect for her. Admire how hard she worked and how deeply she cared for her daughter. Sarah Redding was a damn fine woman. She didn't deserve the thoughts he was having about her.

Thoughts that had him rewriting history and kissing her beneath a star-strewn sky. Except they were alone this time—him and her—and he would pull her down into the soft wild grasses…

Danger. He'd been a lawman a good many years and could scent trouble like a hunting dog on a trail. So he knew where these thoughts were bound to take him.

"Why, good afternoon, Mr. Gatlin." Louisa Montgomery sidled up to him like a panther stalking prey. "What a coincidence. I was just telling Mother—"

"Excuse me, ma'am." He tipped his hat, eager to be off. He wanted to explain away this intense attraction to Sarah Redding as the simple need of a man for a woman.

Then why wasn't it any woman? Why did it have to be Sarah? Only Sarah?

Panic skidded through him. He'd rather face an armed gang of escaped felons than feel this intense need for a woman, for anyone.

Still, his thoughts returned to Sarah.

Frustrated, he jammed the bag of nails into his shirt pocket and unwrapped his reins from the hitching post.

She shouldn't have run off like that and left Gage standing on the sidewalk. He'd been polite, that was all. *She* had been the problem. She looked at him and hoped. She knew better, knew they didn't want the same things from life, and *still* she couldn't help it.

So, she'd been rude, and she regretted it. How could she mend things now? It was too late, anyway. He was busy with his horses and she was moving to town.

They'd likely never have to do more than nod politely as they passed on the street.

The mercantile wasn't busy, and so the bell above the door jangled cheerfully as Sarah stepped inside. The scent of cinnamon and sugar blended with the brine of the pickle barrel, and she wove through the canned goods, looking for Ella.

There she was. Standing at the yard goods counter, her hands clasped behind her back as she gazed into a glass case. Love for her daughter burned deep inside. Forget Gage Gatlin. Sarah had what truly mattered.

"Hey, sweetie." Sarah fished a nickel out of her pocket. "I saved this for you. Thought you might want something special to wear for your first day of school."

"Five whole cents! For me?" Ella's eyes lit like Christmas morning. "I can buy some hair ribbons with that. What should I get? The red is pretty, but I like the pink best."

"The pink would look awful pretty on my girl."

Ella beamed. "Then I want two pink ones, please."

As the ribbons were cut and wrapped, Sarah noticed how Ella lingered at the cotton fabrics. There was a pretty pink calico that would match the ribbon perfectly. Ella didn't say one word as they turned to leave, but Sarah wished more than anything she could afford that cloth.

All things worked out in time. Two weeks ago she feared they would never be able to leave Milt's shanty. Now they had a cozy room at the boarding house.

Who knows? Maybe in two more weeks she wouldn't want to run at the sight of Gage approaching her on the boardwalk. Maybe she'd be able to put aside the memory of their kiss and the thrill of being in his arms.

Surely this affection she felt for him would change like the seasons. With any luck, she'd get a full-time job and move on with her life.

Maybe one of the three letters in her reticule held the answer.

"You're too slow," Pearl snapped as she yanked the platter of eggs from Sarah's grip. Morning light turned the shabby kitchen golden and illuminated the disdain on her aunt's face. "Think you don't owe me nothin' on your last day here?"

Sarah bit her lip. This would be the last morning she would have to hold her tongue while she worked as fast as she could. She flipped the bubbling pancakes and, while they sizzled, forked the salt pork from the skillet.

"She'll be back," Milt pronounced from the head of the table as he chewed with a mouth full of eggs. "This world's too tough for a woman alone. You found that out the hard way, Pearl—"

Sarah handed the full platter to Junior and rescued the last batch of pancakes from the griddle.

Done. She'd let Pearl talk her into cooking this last time, but now she was free. Free!

Baby Davie started crying. Two of the boys began arguing. Sarah untied her apron, tucked it over her arm, and took two full plates with her.

"I'm not very hungry." Ella sat on the back step, staring down at her shoes. They were worn, but a good coat of polish had covered up the scuffs.

"Eat what you can, because it's a big morning."

Sarah settled down beside her daughter. "Lucy ought to be coming along any minute now."

"She's gonna let me ride Scout with her. At least that's the good part."

"The good part will be having your best friend at school with you. You won't be alone."

Ella did her best and took a bite of pancake. "I hope I can sit next to Lucy. Wait, she's coming now."

"That can't be Lucy." Sarah squinted into the sun, trying to make out the driver of the buggy. Lucy was too young to drive a team, wasn't she?

She was holding the reins, but she wasn't alone. Gage towered on the seat next to her.

"'Mornin', Sarah."

What had she promised herself? That this affection she felt for him would eventually fade? That wasn't how it felt when he smiled at her. "Are you driving the girls to school?"

"No, figure they'll be happy enough riding together to town." He whipped off his hat and tossed it into the buggy. "I got to thinking. How are you going to move today with no horse and buggy?"

"I have two good feet. I'll make quite a few trips, but it can be easily done—" That wasn't entirely true, but it was none of Gage's concern. "Ella, don't forget your lunch pail and schoolbooks."

Lucy untied Scout from the back of the buggy and Ella raced to gather her things.

Gage raked his fingers through his tousled hair. "I got to admit it makes me uncomfortable, Sarah. I don't know what happened, but it seems we're not friends anymore."

"Maybe that is my fault, and I should apologize." She lifted her chin. If he could face the truth, then so could she. "I didn't mean to be so bold. I can only claim loneliness as a reason I tried to…well, I tried to kiss you that night."

"I had the same problem." He flashed her a shy grin. "Guess women have the same needs, and as you well know, it's hard being alone."

She blushed, too. "Fine. I guess we've come to an understanding? That you took advantage of me?"

"Is that the way it was? I seem to remember you being to blame—" He chuckled. "Maybe things can get back to normal between us. I'd like that."

"Me, too. I'm glad we can be friends again." She wanted to say the word before he did. *Friends.* "Is that why you're here? To volunteer your horse and buggy?"

"You know I am." He knelt at Scout's side to give Lucy a hand up. "Come on over here, Ella. You're next."

Ella's eyes widened. Always shy, she laid a tentative hand on Gage's broad shoulder and placed her shoe in his hand. He hefted her up and she slid onto the blanket behind the saddle.

He dusted off his hands. "You girls be good. Lucy, keep Scout to a walk."

"I know." Lucy rolled her eyes and touched her heels to the mare's sides.

"'Bye, Ma!" Ella's excitement and trepidation was contagious as she held on tight.

"Hard watching her go?"

"Not at all. As long as my eyes stop blurring."

"She'll be all right. Lucy will watch out for her." Gage rescued his hat from the seat. "You need help loading?"

"I'm not sure how Milt will take that." She gestured to the man on the front porch, mouth clamped tight, face ruddy. "I can manage."

"Fine. Then I'll head home. Better take the road, though. Doesn't look like Milt wants me on his land." Something that seemed like sympathy flickered in his eyes.

She tried not to hold it against him. "I'll return the team as soon as I can."

"I'm not worried. Hey—" he began walking backward down the road "—how did those letters work out? Did you get good news?"

"Good enough. I have an interview at the end of the week." Excitement shivered through her.

"That's great news. I'm glad for you, Sarah."

"I'm not counting my chickens yet."

He lifted his hand, too far away to reply.

She couldn't deny a certain tenderness rising within her as she watched him round a bend and disappear from her sight.

He'd lent her a team and buggy. He'd apologized. He wanted to be friends again.

Was it possible? Would she be able to forget the intense heat of his kiss and the tenderness she'd felt in his arms?

No. Not a chance. Not as long as she lived.

"Ma! Ma!" Ella burst into the room, braids flying as she skidded to a stop on the polished wood floor. "I had the best day ever."

"Baby, I'm so glad." Sarah knelt and felt as warm as toast when Ella's arms wrapped around her neck. "I guess this means you liked your teacher."

"She let me share a desk with Lucy! And guess what? There's this other girl who got sick last year, too, and I'm not as far behind as her. I can't *wait* till tomorrow.''

"Neither can I.'' Happiness filled her up like a big fluffy cloud. "Go take off your hair ribbons and change into your play dress.''

"Lucy's pa said I could come home with them. There's a new filly that was just born and I gotta see her. Please?''

Sarah fetched Ella's yellow calico from the hook in the closet. "Sure. It will keep you busy while I finish unpacking. What do you think of our room?''

"It's the best room ever.'' Ella shimmied out of her good dress. "'Cuz it's ours.''

"That's what I think, too.'' Sarah plopped the calico over Ella's head.

While Ella jammed her arms into the sleeves and buttoned up, Sarah removed the brand-new hair ribbons and stowed them on the bureau that came with the room.

Sunshine streamed through lace curtains, ones Sarah had made long ago. Other treasures dotted the furnished room—her wedding ring quilt, doilies her mother had crocheted and the quilted throw she'd made from scraps of Ella's baby clothes. Tears ached in Sarah's throat as she ran her fingertip across her jewel box.

It wasn't a house, as she'd wanted, but this did feel like home.

A quick rap on the door broke into her thoughts. She wasn't surprised to spy Gage in the mirror's reflection as he smiled down at Ella, who'd pulled open the door.

"Are you girls ready to go? Scout is down there

chomping at the bit.'' He caught Sarah's gaze in the mirror and winked. "Go on, I'll catch up to you two.''

"You can't catch us, Pa! Scout's too fast." Lucy appeared at his side and grabbed Ella by the hand.

The two girls raced off, the strikes of their shoes in the hallway growing more faint until there was only silence.

"Nice place you got." Gage held his hat in his hands, scanning the room. "You and Ella ought to be real happy here.''

"It's a whole new start for us.''

"I hope it goes real well for you, Sarah. Is there anything more I can do? A trunk you need hauled up those stairs? You name it, I'll do it.''

His eyes grew dark. His gaze slid to her mouth. She noticed how fast his chest rose and fell, and a lightning-quick jolt of desire skimmed through her.

As wrong as it was. She was dreaming if she thought Gage desired her. One-sided, that's what this was, and she had to remember that. There was no double meaning behind his offer to do anything she wished.

"As you can see, I'm all settled in. I can't tell you how handy it was having the use of your buggy. I thought moving would take the entire day, but it didn't. I have spare time, and I hardly know what to do with myself.''

"Tell you what. Since your girl will be out at my place anyhow, why don't you come, too?''

There was no flicker of want in his eyes, no invitation in the crook of his smile. Just one friend asking another over to visit. It was as simple as that. "I suppose I could be talked into it.''

"Fine. Then I'll put some steaks on to grill—''

"You cook?"

"Sure. Some folks say I'm pretty good." Dimples dug into his cheeks as he grinned. "Care to find out?"

"I'm not sure I should risk it."

"Worried, huh? Go ahead, doubt my abilities. I'll prove you wrong."

"You sound awfully sure of yourself."

"I'm good and I know it."

The trouble was, that he did. "I wouldn't say good, exactly. More like pompous. Arrogant. Misguided."

"Sure, that's what you think now. Wait until you taste my grill sauce."

"Sauce? You mean, gravy."

"You heard me." He headed for the hallway. "You're in trouble now because I'm going to prove to you I'm a great cook."

"There you go again. Overconfident. Too sure of yourself."

"It's a gift, what can I say?" His wink made her laugh. "See you soon."

She was still laughing as his boots rang in the stairwell. The warmth in her chest remained as she parted the curtains to watch him on the street below.

She couldn't help wanting him. What a sight he was, in denim and blue muslin, untethering his mare. The hardware store owner called out to him and they exchanged friendly words. No wonder everyone thought so well of Gage. He stood tall, unwavering, a man easy to look up to. And as friendly as could be.

Wasn't *that* the problem? Every time she was with him, he made her care for him more. What was she going to do?

She frowned at her reflection in the bureau's beveled mirror. She could see the years on her face. Her dress was plain, the fraying at the cuffs and collar stayed by a careful use of needle and thread, but it was there.

It shouldn't matter how she looked. What mattered was providing a good life for Ella. The trunk tucked beneath the window held her few good dresses, saved over the past year so when she started back to work, she wouldn't need to spend precious dollars on clothes.

She wouldn't lie to herself. It was her pride again, always getting her into trouble, but she wanted to wear something with a little color in it. Something that made her feel like a woman and not the poor relation the Owenses had taken in.

The snap of the buckles echoed in the quiet room and she lifted the trunk's heavy lid. The scent of dried roses tickled her nose as she reached in to lift back the sheets she'd used to wrap her most valued possessions.

There, on top, was her yellow gingham. Trimmed in lace she'd tatted and real satin ribbon. The dress she'd sewn to wear to her best friend's wedding two years ago, during much better times. The best dress she'd ever owned.

Where had the matching bonnet gone? She carefully lifted the hat partition from inside the trunk lid and spotted a yellow strip of matching ribbon.

"Sarah?" Mrs. Flannery, who owned the boarding house, poked her head into the room. "Was that Mr. Gatlin I saw leaving my establishment?"

"One and the same." Sarah stood and shook the wrinkles from her gingham dress. "He was only here for a few minutes. If that's a problem—"

"Goodness me, no. Practically a legend, you know.

Several years back, he used to be in all the newspapers. Then again, you probably knew that.''

"I was in Idaho Territory then.''

"You didn't hear about the prison break, out Deer Lodge way?'' Mary bustled inside the room, holding hard to her broom. "Ten men, some of the most barbarous murderers the West had ever known escaped the night before they were to be put to death.''

"Gage was one of the Rangers sent to find them?''

Nodding, Mary settled into the wing-backed chair by the unlit fireplace. "An entire fortnight the Riders hunted the convicted men, following a path of murder and ruination from Butte all the way to the Badlands.''

"And you know all this from reading the newspaper?''

"Who doesn't? Sarah, you ought to know this. Gage didn't tell you?''

"No. He doesn't talk about being a lawman.''

"Then you listen up. This is the man who's courting you.''

"He's not courting me.''

Mary waved her comments away. "Winter had set in with a vengeance that time of year, but the Riders refused to let up. Every day innocent people—entire families—were murdered in their beds for the little bit of money and food the outlaws stole from them. The toughest lawmen in the territory were on their trail, and killed one by one until only a single Range Rider remained.''

"Gage?''

"He was the only one who stopped them, but not before more innocent lives were lost. And nearly his own.''

"He was wounded?''

"Gravely. It was in all the papers, week after week, the reports saying they didn't know if he would live. He pulled through, but I never read his name again. He gave it all up, and to think he's come here to raise up his girl and marry you."

"Please, Mary, don't start *that* rumor. Gage and I are not courting."

"You were."

"We're friends and nothing more. That's the truth."

"If that's what you want to believe, dear. Now, here's an extra key for your little girl, just in case. I'll just put it right here on the mantel. See you bright and early tomorrow morning."

Mary's story lingered, and as Sarah changed and replaited her hair, the tale troubled her. The image of Gage as a lone lawman tracking ten cold-blooded killers filled her mind.

"A legend," Mary had called him.

"Pa!" Lucy shouted through the kitchen window. "Sarah's here. Quick. You gotta brush your hair or something."

"I like looking disheveled." He snatched the boiler pan off the stove. "The women like it."

"Sarah doesn't like it." Lucy scowled at him in that charming way she had that said she thought he was a lost cause. Then she bolted from the room.

He drained the potatoes, watching through the rising steam as Lucy, leading his mare, and Ella, on Scout, met Sarah on the road.

It was tough to see her beneath the shade of the buggy top. He couldn't see her face, and he still had to fight his attraction to her.

This wasn't going to be easy.

He set the fry pan off the heat and headed for the door. He ought to greet her, after all. They were friends. It was the friendly thing to do.

"Ma, look! I'm riding Scout all by myself." Ella sat awkwardly in the saddle, a little unsure as the left rein slipped from her white-knuckled grip.

Lucy nosed the mare close and caught the rein. Pride filled his chest. No doubt about it, he had a good girl. She'd done a good thing, letting Ella ride Scout, who was as tame as could be.

The girls dashed away, showing off their riding skills to Sarah. The mares took advantage, frolicking a little in the knee-high grasses, fragrant with the first buds of wildflowers. The girls' delighted giggles lifted in the pleasant breezes.

"I brought dessert." Sarah swept from the buggy seat with a basket in hand.

It wasn't the basket he noticed. It was the woman.

She was radiant in a dress the color of buttercups that skimmed her fine breasts and slim waist to perfection and whispered over her hips and thighs. Need knocked through him hard and fast.

He couldn't control it, couldn't extinguish it. It pounded through his blood as she swept gold curls from her eyes and presented him with the basket.

"If supper doesn't turn out as tasty as you claim, then at least we'll have cake."

"So, you don't trust me."

"Not a chance." The twinkle in her eyes said otherwise. "You finished the house. It's beautiful."

"The way Lucy wanted it. I've still got to put on the porch and paint it. Come inside and I'll show you the sights."

"I'd love to."

It was the pleasure of showing his workmanship to an appreciative friend, Gage argued. That's why he felt so...happy. Yep, that was the word. Happy. Not because Sarah was at his side, smelling like roses and sunshine. Nope, he was simply enjoying showing her his hard work. If a little voice in his head called him a liar, then that voice had to be wrong.

"A brick fireplace." She ran her fingers over the real brick. "Folks around here use river rock, it's free for the taking."

"Figure I'll carve a mantel when I get the time."

"And look, a window seat. I've always wanted one." She swept across the room to the white-paned window. "Let me guess. This was Lucy's idea."

"She insisted." And now he knew why. Window seats must be what women like, because Sarah lit up like summer as she ran her fingertips across the polished wood seat.

"You need a cushion so Lucy can sit here and read when it's too cold to go outside. And pillows with ruffles and lace. And you'll need curtains. Millie from the dress shop does custom sewing."

"I'll keep that in mind. 'Course, I'll worry about that after I get some furniture."

Sarah's heels echoed in the empty room. "You're too busy with your horses right now, is that it?"

"I confess, I have a weakness for them. Got the new colts to gentle and an order to fill for two dozen Arabians."

"That ought to keep you busy and out of trouble."

Trouble? He was in it up to his chin. He couldn't help noticing the sway to Sarah's walk as she moved ahead of him to view the empty dining room.

It was perfectly natural for a man to notice a

woman. Nothing to be concerned about. He had will-power.

Until he watched sunlight burn golden in her hair. Until he noticed the full curves of her breasts that pretty dress of hers seemed to accentuate.

"Oh, Gage. The kitchen. Everything smells so delicious. I take back every word I said about you being a bad cook."

"I suppose I can forgive you." Maybe if he did something that occupied his hands and his mind, he'd stop wondering what her breasts looked like beneath that cheerful checkered fabric.

Out of desperation, he grabbed the fry pan and dropped it to the stove with a clatter. "It hurts deep, Sarah, that you doubted me."

She hid a smile as she opened the pantry door. "I may have to whip the potatoes to make it up to you."

"Whip them? You look gentle as can be on the outside, but I know the truth. You're a brutal woman."

"Well, I could beat them if you'd rather."

"Beating vegetables." He pretended to shudder. "No wonder all the town gossips are trying to pair us up. I'm the new man in town and innocent to your ways."

"Did anyone ever tell you that you have a horrible sense of humor?" She uncapped the butter crock.

"Never. What are you going to do now? Butter me up?"

"You're impossible. Where do you keep your bowls?"

"My one bowl is in the lower cupboard near your left foot."

"You have one bowl?" She knelt, found the bowl and refused to let her heart fall any further.

"One fry pan." He ladled his secret oil mixture into the pan. "First it was foaling season, and then I had to get the cattle to the stockyard. No time to shop."

"Did you get a good price for them? I remember folks complaining this year."

"I did all right." He uncovered the meat and forked the steaks into the pan. "The whip's out in the barn if you need it."

"Funny." She tugged open a drawer, saw it was empty and reached for another. "I'll just use the whisk on you if you don't stop it."

"Just proves my point."

What was she going to do with a man who made her laugh? Sarah jabbed the whisk into the steaming potatoes and broke them apart. "Where did you learn to cook, anyway?"

"Here and there." He pinched the last of the seasoning over the sizzling meat.

Sarah shivered as Gage set the salt and pepper on the counter beside her. So close she could feel the heat from his skin, smell the wood smoke on his shirt.

"I'll take over now." His hand closed over hers, taking possession. "You're the guest of honor, Sarah. I don't expect you to work for your meal."

"I don't mind—"

"I do."

He pressed against her, the hard length of his body unyielding against hers. His arms were around her as he slipped the whisk from her fingers. She closed her eyes, savoring the feeling.

It had to be her imagination that his breath grazed the curve between her collar and her ear. It was impossible that he was holding her, moving his hand to her waist and pulling her against him.

That couldn't be his arousal rock-hard against her hip or his fingers curling around the back of her neck to turn her mouth to his...

Like midnight dreams, his lips claimed hers with a raw need she understood. A need she felt in the dark of night, alone in bed, aching for a man's touch.

Gage was more than dreams. He was a flesh-and-blood man whose arms folded her against his wide chest. Desire pulsed through her, gaining strength with every beat of her heart. She wrapped her arms around his neck, taking what she could now, while they were both caught up in the moment. Before reason and common sense could prevail.

His mouth was hungry and demanding, and she opened to him, drinking in his kiss, not caring what he thought or how it seemed. She matched the sweep of her tongue to his and sighed when his hands brushed down her back.

It felt so wonderful. She moaned when his fingers curved around her hips and pulled her harder against his arousal, unmistakable against her stomach. He held her there, groaning, too, breaking their kiss to nibble his way down her throat.

"The steaks," she gasped between fast, shallow breaths.

"You were waiting for me to burn them." His kiss at the hollow of her throat was part chuckle, and it vibrated through her entire body, making her toes curl.

"I think I can reach it." He lifted one hand from the small of her back and he strained to catch hold of the pan's long handle. "Supper is saved."

"I'm impressed."

"Notice how I still have you right where I want

you?'' He leaned his forehead against hers so they were eye-to-eye, lip-to-lip.

"I noticed." He was still hard against her stomach, and desire kept jolting through her like a spring lightning storm. "I thought we agreed to just be friends."

"We are friends."

"Yes, but don't you blame this on me like you did last time." She swirled away from him and reached for the pitcher of milk. "You were shameless."

"I blamed you because you were at fault." He winked as he forked the steaks from the pan to a platter. "You wanted me to kiss you. Admit it."

"Me? You trapped me against the counter. I was innocently making the potatoes." She poured milk into the bowl and reached for the salt and pepper shakers. "You forced your kisses on me."

"I don't know what came over me. Suppose I need to apologize?"

"Absolutely."

He gazed at her through lidded eyes as he stirred flour into the pan. "That was a pretty great kiss."

"It was." She grabbed the whisk. "Watch out, I'm heavily armed. Try it again and take your chances."

"I'll be good." He winked. "Or even better."

Chapter Ten

I'll be good. Or even better. Gage's warning haunted her all through supper. They ate outside at a trestle table with the girls both talking a mile a minute.

Their heated embrace filled her thoughts as she cut Ella's steak into bite-size pieces and dished up more potatoes for Lucy.

That was a pretty great kiss. He wasn't the least bit sorry, either. He could sit there and laugh at Lucy's jokes and try to fish for compliments on his cooking as if nothing earth-shaking had happened.

A great kiss? No, it had been better than that. Spectacular. Extraordinary. She would never want another man's kiss ever. Only his.

While he rode off to check on his hired hands at the beginning of the second shift, Sarah bustled the girls into the kitchen.

Fast as could be, she washed dishes while the girls dried. As soon the last pan was washed, Sarah dried the rest and watched the girls race off to check on the kittens.

Contentment filled her as the setting sun cast a soft glow through the window. It was hard not to wish as she put away the dishes and covered the half-eaten cake. Gage had kissed her right here at this counter, hard with need.

With desire. For her.

Could a man like Gage fall in love with her?

"You cleaned my kitchen."

She hung the dish towel up to dry. "It seemed the least I could do, since you did prove me wrong. Supper was one of the best I've ever had."

"Me, too. In my case, it was the company." He tucked her hand in the bend of his arm and escorted her outside. "C'mon."

"Where are you taking me?"

"Don't look so worried. You doubted my cooking abilities and now I plan to punish you."

"By hauling me outside?"

"Yep. I might even force you to watch the sunset."

"You're a cruel man."

"I try."

The world seemed perfect with Gage at her side. The bright orange disk of the sun set the whole sky aflame, suspended above the distant mountains. The plains were alive as birds searched for bugs in the last light of the day. Does with new fawns grazed in the tall grasses. An owl glided low, her low who-who a harmony to the melody of the birds and wind and rustling grasses.

There was a peace to the prairie she couldn't explain. "I'm going to miss this when I leave."

"Why not stay right here? You don't have to go to the next county to find work."

"I've been looking for work here, but no luck. I suppose the prairie will be about the same in Price."

"Is that where your interview is?"

"Yes. A rancher and his wife need a housekeeper and cook."

"Will that be a good situation for you and your daughter?" Gage's chest tightened as Sarah nodded. Her hands were red from hard work, and that wasn't about to change anytime soon. It troubled him. "Maybe something will work out right here. For the girls' sake. I'd hate to separate them."

It couldn't be for his sake. Gage knew from hard experience that he didn't have what it took to love a woman. Not through the years, or for better or worse.

Yet, this woman could tempt him. "It's good of you not to mention my lack of manners in the kitchen."

"Lack of manners?"

"Fine. My bad behavior."

"That's more like it." Her hand on his arm was as light as air, and yet her touch was all he could think about.

He pictured her tender hands on his shoulders, on his chest and then trailing down his abdomen. He swallowed. "You could lecture me the way I did you, about the two of us being no more than friends."

"I could."

"The simple truth is that I liked kissing you. A lot."

"I noticed." A blush stole over her, turning her cheeks an attractive pink.

Damn, she was gorgeous. He fought the urge to kiss her there, where her skin flushed with modesty. Maybe desire, and that was going to get him into trouble. He leaned on the fence, propping his elbows on the top rail.

She joined him, washed with pink light from the setting sun. Her skirts swept his leg. Her arm curled through his arm.

"What are we going to do about this kissing thing?" he asked.

"We've tried ignoring it, but it hasn't gone away."

"I guess we have to face the truth. You're a good kisser and you wear down my willpower until I can't stop myself."

"I notice this keeps being my fault."

He chuckled. "It sure as hell isn't mine."

"No. You were not at all aroused in the kitchen when I was shamelessly kissing you."

"Glad you noticed." He kissed her hair, loving the silky feel against his skin. Gossamer strands caught on his day's growth, and that was nice, too, as she leaned against him.

That sweet body of hers was going to be his undoing.

"Trouble is," he confessed, "I'm aroused again."

The pink flushing her nose and cheeks deepened two shades. "*That* is a comfort of marriage. Keep that in mind, you scoundrel."

"Hey, I never said it wasn't. Just that there was a rising predicament."

"Stop with the puns. This is not proper conversation." She was laughing, though, all sparkle and life.

He couldn't help pulling her into his arms, holding her sweet body to his.

"Just want to be honest with you," he murmured in her ear. "I can't offer you what you want from a man. But you make me want to."

His eyes had turned as bleak as a winter storm. His confession held so much sadness it made her sad, too, as she splayed her hand over his chest. His heart beat strong beneath her palm. So very strong.

"It's different for you, Sarah. Sounds like you had

a good marriage. They're rare, that's for sure. You don't understand how it was.''

"Maybe I do.''

His brow furrowed into deep lines. "What do you mean? You had a bad marriage?''

"I had a tough one. I was young, I thought I was in love. I didn't know what it meant to commit to another person.''

Her lower lip trembled and he laid her cheek against his chest, cradling her head in the palm of his hand. "Sorry, I just assumed. I didn't mean to bring up any pain. You don't have to tell me.''

"I do. You think something that isn't true, and I want you to know. That first year of our marriage was hard. David came with wounds from his family, and I had mine. Loving someone is harder than it looks.''

"I know.'' His throat ached, because he did know. "Failing someone you love is worse.''

The crown of her head nodded against his chin. "Then Ella came along, and it was harder.''

"I know.'' More responsibilities. Another person depending on him. A small child he didn't want to fail.

"David was at wit's end. So was I. Maybe we were finally wise enough to understand those vows we'd made in the little mountainside chapel where we married. I don't know. But we made it better.''

"Better?'' His marriage had only gone from unhappy to worse.

"The six months before David died were the most wonderful of my life. I think of all that time we wasted, and I regret every minute we were unhappy.''

He knew about regrets.

"If I'd only opened my heart sooner.'' She released

a shaky breath. "I won't be happy until I can find that intimacy again."

"I can't."

"I'm not asking you to. I learned the truth about love. It's a gift that's best freely given, without condition and without end. Anything less than that only brings heartache."

"I'm telling you. I don't have that in me. I wish I did." There had been times his marriage had been good, but they had been short-lived. Sarah was an optimist, and maybe she hadn't been married long enough to see the way things were. That the honeymoon phase came to an end every time, followed by more resentment.

But he liked her vision of things.

He pressed a tender kiss into her hair. "Turn around and look at the sunset."

She twisted in his arms and leaned against him.

"It's beautiful," she breathed. "So much brilliance and color."

"Yes." She was like that sun to him, lighting up the entire sky, and he held on tight.

"The sunset is better watching it with you, Gage."

He didn't dare answer. An overwhelming tenderness clawed painfully right behind his breastbone, and he couldn't tell her about it.

So he held her in silence for as long as he could. They watched the sun set the sky aflame at the horizon to slowly fall behind the endless line of rugged mountains.

He breathed in the rose scent of her hair, savored the rise and fall of her ribs beneath his hand and loved the soft-firm feel of her against him. Warm and comforting and thrilling all at once.

Until the last curve of the sun had disappeared, and darkness came. Then he released her, changed because he'd held her.

He desired her, and it wasn't because he was lonely. When she smiled, he lost his heart.

Gage halted his team outside the boarding house, windows gleaming with lamplight. "Here we are."

"Home." The word had never sounded so good. "You didn't need to drive me into town."

"I wanted to." He didn't touch her, but his words were intimate, emotion clear in his voice.

The closeness of the evening lingered between them, unspoken but felt.

"We might have to do that again." Gage climbed down. "I make a mean pan of chicken and dumplings."

"Ah, but are they better than mine?" Sarah slid her palm over his and let him help her down. Not because she needed help, but because she wanted his touch.

"I'll have you know I never back down from a challenge." His words tingled against the back of her neck as he held her for a moment longer than necessary, one hand at her waist, the other on her elbow. "Duel or cooking contest, I'm man enough to win."

"Just because you're a legendary lawman doesn't mean you can't be defeated. I may be the woman who beats you."

"Just don't hurt me." He winked.

"What am I going to do with you? No, don't say it. If you bring up whipping one more time—" She had to adore a man who made her laugh, even if it was with puns.

"I'll behave," he promised with a saucy grin. He

rescued her empty basket from the floorboard. "I know you work tonight. If you need someone to keep an eye on Ella, she could bunk with Lucy."

"Really?" Lucy squealed from the back seat of the buggy. "Can she, Pa? Please? Please?"

He rolled his eyes. "I made the mistake of saying that louder than I meant to."

Sarah took one look at Ella and wished she could say yes. "Maybe another time. I have everything arranged with Mrs. Flannery. She's going to keep watch on Ella while I'm at the hotel."

"Just let me know if you need help. I'll ride to the rescue. It can't be easy juggling two jobs."

"It's an improvement, believe me." The air was starting to turn chilly, and Sarah pulled Ella into her skirts. "We best get you inside, sweetie."

The girls said goodbye, as Sarah tugged Ella toward the front door. Although Gage said nothing as he leaned against the side of his buggy, she wanted to believe it was longing she felt in his silence.

Later, as she scrubbed down the hotel kitchen, she couldn't help going over the evening's events in her mind. Treasuring each memory. Of his kiss. His embrace. The hard feel of him—of all of him—when he held her tight.

"My, aren't you in a chipper mood tonight." Ms. McCullough bustled in with her slate. "I wager it has something to do with that wonderful Mr. Gatlin driving you to the boarding house this evening. After dark."

"Lucy had Ella over to play."

"Hmm. That's awfully cozy." Mrs. McCullough opened the pantry closet. "Guess what I heard is true, after all."

"I'm afraid to ask." Sarah wrung soapy water from her cloth. "When are the rumors about Gage and me going to stop? Surely there's someone more exciting to talk about?"

"Who could be more exciting than Mr. Gatlin?"

Remembering the blazing heat of his kiss, Sarah could not argue with that. She'd never experienced anything so amazing.

"We need more brown sugar. Better write that down." The stylus scratched on the slate. "And flour, too, and how was supper?"

"Gage is a great cook." Sarah stopped scrubbing. She looked up in shock at the woman grinning ear to ear on the other side of the kitchen. "You tricked that out of me."

"Years of experience, missy." Mrs. McCullough looked proud of her accomplishments. "Did I hear you right? He *cooked* for you?"

"Oh, no." Sarah went back to washing the counters. "I'm not giving you any new gossip."

"He *cooked* for you? Honey, let me give you a good piece of advice. You listen up and stop scouring that counter for a minute." Mrs. McCullough took a deep breath, setting down her slate so she could gesture with both hands. "In the thirty-five years I was married, not once did my Herbert cook for me. Not so much as boiled water for a cup of tea or a poached egg. In thirty-five years."

Sarah exchanged her cloth for a brush and dunked it into the wash water. "Gage is a widower. He had to learn so he could feed his daughter."

"He didn't have to feed you." Mrs. McCullough placed both hands to her throat. "He *cooks*. Why, that man would be a blessing to any woman smart enough to marry him. You'd best snatch him up right now, before word of this gets 'round town. Women will be falling at his feet.''

''I'll take your advice under consideration.''

''See that you do.'' She closed the pantry doors, rescued her slate and tapped across the floor to the swinging doors. ''A man like that comes around once in a lifetime.''

That may well be true. Sarah tightened her grip on the brush and scrubbed hard enough to bring up the grease stains around the stove.

Gage was a once-in-a-lifetime man. Handsome, wealthy and kind. A retired lawman and still a hero. A wonderful father and a gifted horseman.

Trouble was, he wasn't *her* once-in-a-lifetime.

The house felt lonesome after midnight, the silence so loud he couldn't clear the nightmares from his head. He rolled out of bed, pulled on his denims and padded into the hallway.

Starlight glowed silver beneath Lucy's door. He eased it open to get a look at her. She was sprawled out, the blankets to her chin, still and peaceful, her dark hair tangled across the pillow. Tenderness washed through him, love for his little girl.

She'd talked nonstop during the return trip from town until he'd tucked her in and kissed her tonight. She'd worn herself out, she'd been so happy.

''Know what, Pa?'' He could still hear her, clear as a bell in his memory. ''Sarah had a rope swing when she was little, too. Know what, Pa?'' Sarah this and Sarah that, her eyes glittering with dreams. ''Know what, Pa? One day, if you do get a hankering to get married, it would be like today, when Sarah came.''

Ah, hell. The truth hit him like a falling brick and he sat in the middle of the staircase before his knees gave out.

Marriage was nothing like what had gone on tonight. Marriage was serious business. It was responsibility and meeting expectations and making sure everyone had what they needed.

His chest knotted up, remembering how hard it had been. How hard he'd tried. How often he'd failed.

After all this time he could still see the anger on May's face. Feel her disappointment in him... He cut off his thoughts.

He could put a bullet through a target at any distance, as long as he was in range. He could track the most clever criminals who'd ever passed through Montana Territory and find them.

He'd survived twisters and blizzards and flash floods when he wore a badge. He'd done all that, but he hadn't been able to fix the wound in his marriage.

He'd always figured he was the problem.

It wasn't fair to Lucy to be saddled with a father like that. He couldn't blame her for wanting a mother. Most men with children remarried, after all.

He couldn't do it, not even for Lucy.

He made his way through the house. The emptiness echoed around him in the dining room without a table and the parlor without a sofa.

He'd only meant to be practical with more work than he could do alone. Men to hire and train. Fences to mend, animals to gentle. The new bunkhouse to shingle and side.

Hell, there was always some excuse. He figured he must like things this way, never permanent, so nothing would look or feel like home. As a Rider, he'd spent his life on the road. As a wrangler, he'd moved from ranch to ranch, wintering over in whatever town they ended up in, always moving on when the Chinook blew.

That didn't matter so much when Lucy was smaller. Now she was a schoolgirl, wanting what other little girls had. A comfortable home, stability, friends… permanence.

You can do this, Gatlin. He dragged in a deep breath, letting the night air fill him up.

He wasn't a kid anymore, a little boy terrified of his stepfather, afraid for his beaten mother. Wishing he was big enough to take his mother away. To take care of her and his baby brother so no one would hit them again.

He'd spent the next eight years of his life trapped, his stepfather's cruelty wearing him down.

When he couldn't take it anymore he'd pulled on his patched boots and walked away. Never looked back.

But those years were still affecting him. His failed marriage only taught him what he'd already known. He was better off not needing anyone.

Except Lucy. She needed him. She needed him to fill this parlor with permanence—sofas and chairs, pillows and cushions and those doodads females liked.

She needed a home, so when she grew up she'd know how to be happy. How to stay. How to love the family she would have one day.

He could do this. He *had* to. She was the one person he never intended to fail.

That meant he had to be careful. Gage splayed his palm across the counter where he'd trapped Sarah and kissed her hard and long.

Right here they'd laughed together and she'd scolded him and she'd filled his arms as if she belonged there. Fitting beneath his chin, against his chest, as if she were made for him. The heat of her breasts, the curve of her hip against his hardness.

He wanted her. Wanted to know the heat of her thighs. Needed to hear the sigh she would make when he entered her in one slow thrust…

Gage yanked open the door and let the cool wind breeze over him. It didn't help. He was still hard. Still wanted her.

After rummaging through the pantry, he found the whiskey bottle. Tossed back a few shots, let the liquor burn like fire in his guts. Made his way in the dark to his empty bed and stretched out on the wide mattress.

Hours passed without sleep because he wanted her.

That bad, and that much.

Gage squinted through the glare of the dining room front window in the boarding house where Sarah worked. Oh, hell. Just his luck the place was as packed as cattle in a stampede.

Maybe he ought to wait. Finish his errands and head back to the ranch. Make sure the hands were moving the breeding mares to the right pasture. Check on the new fences being built.

Anything would be easier than facing Sarah. Could he pretend that he didn't desire her?

Buck up, Gatlin. Just do it. He'd done harder things in his life.

But it didn't seem that way as he shouldered into the boarding house dining room.

Mrs. Flannery gave him a wide smile and the best table, tucked in the corner by the window, where he didn't feel so walled-in. Thinking too hard about his feelings could do that to a man.

He ordered, then asked Mary about Sarah.

"Just finishing up her shift." Mary appeared so pleased he'd asked. "Should I send her out?"

"Please."

He took a sip of lemonade to calm his nerves. He'd no sooner set down the glass than she appeared through the swinging doors. Golden hair twisted into a knot on top of her head, accentuating the delicate cut of her high cheekbones and the curve of her chin.

He'd kissed that chin. Found himself wanting to kiss her there again...and anywhere else she would let him.

She carried two plates and set one on the table in front of him. "Mary said you wanted to sample my chicken and dumplings."

Vaguely he remembered their teasing remarks from the other night, but he was too busy watching her mouth move to remember what had been said.

Stop thinking about kissing her. He gathered his stray thoughts while he stood and pulled out the chair for her.

"You're a gentleman when you want to be." She tossed a shy smile at him.

Damn, she was remembering, too. How on earth was he going to get this done?

She settled into the chair with a rustle of petticoats, and he nudged the chair forward until she was comfortable. Breathing in the intoxicating rose scent that clung to her hair made him weak.

You can do this. He took his seat across from her and grabbed his fork. "Guess this is the moment of truth."

She watched expectantly as he took his first bite.

The creamy gravy and fluffy dumpling melted on his tongue. A grin tugged at the corners of her generous mouth, reminding him of her kisses, passionate and tempting and better than anything he'd ever tasted in his life.

"You like it."

"Damn good." He wasn't sure if he was talking about the food or her. It didn't matter. "You win hands down."

"That was too easy. We'll have to set up an unbiased judge. Maybe Lucy. I'll save some for her and Ella for an after-school snack."

"That's right. She's spending the afternoon here." He hadn't forgotten. He just couldn't seem to concentrate and be in Sarah's presence at the same time.

"What are you doing in town?" She spread her napkin across her lap. "You seem to have enough to do on your land."

"I'm meeting the afternoon stage. I hired a man and his son. Used to work with him on one of the horse farms I was at last summer. Good workers, and they were willing to come here for a job."

"Sounds like you'll have that bunkhouse filled up before you know it." Sarah's slender fingers curled around the fork's steel handle.

Such pretty hands, he couldn't think. Couldn't hear what she was saying. He remembered how it felt when she clutched his shirt in her fists, then ran her hands over his shoulders when he was kissing her.

What would her touch feel like on his bare skin?

Oh, hell. Wasn't he going to try to behave himself? He grabbed his glass, the ice jangling in protest, and downed a long swallow of cold liquid.

"Are you all right? Is there something you're not

telling me about the food? Let me guess. You actually hate my chicken and dumplings and don't want to hurt my feelings.''

''That's not it. I just—'' What was he going to say? The truth? He fumbled a little, then remembered why he'd come in the first place. ''I know you've got that interview tomorrow. Didn't know how you were going to get there.''

''I plan to rent a horse and buggy from the livery.'' Sarah seemed unconcerned as she cut a bite of chicken with the edge of her fork.

Unconcerned? ''That just doesn't make good sense.''

''*What?*''

''It's nonsense to pay when I have a perfectly good buggy I'm not using.''

''I see.'' Her mouth thinned into a straight line. ''I thought we had an agreement. You were going to stop treating me like a poor widow in need of charity. Remember?''

What in blazes did that have to do with her job interview? Gage shook his head. ''I was only saying I'd feel better if you took a rig of mine. If you're going to go, that is. Jerry over at the livery doesn't maintain his vehicles like I do, and you might have a breakdown, is all.''

Poor widow? Did she have any notion that when he looked at her he saw an attractive woman that made him rock-hard?

The little gray buttons on the front of her bodice strained over her extremely fine-looking bosom as she inhaled deeply, eyeing him like a U.S. Marshal ready to make an arrest.

''Are you telling me the truth?''

"Absolutely. I wouldn't drive one of Jerry's rigs farther than across town. You're headed into the next county."

"I hadn't considered that."

"Tell you what. Maybe you ought to look closer to home."

"I am looking. I'm not finding anything. That's the problem."

"Maybe you just haven't looked hard enough. You've got a nice room, and you're working for room and board. Maybe you ought to stay here, instead of uprooting your daughter and moving to another county."

"I haven't been hired yet." She gave him a scolding look. "Not that it's any of your concern."

"You've be surprised how nosy I can be. What you need is a job around here that pays well."

"While you're dreaming, why don't you add in a new horse for Ella, and a husband for me, oh, and a thousand dollars in shiny gold coins. I could really use that."

She stole his water glass, which he hadn't touched, and took a sip. "Enough about me. These men you're meeting at the stage. They'll be your first live-on hired hands."

"That's the plan."

"Does that mean your new bunkhouse is finished?"

"Yep." A plan was forming in his head, and she kept trying to divert him. "Tell me about this job over in Price. What would you be doing?"

"Cooking for two dozen cowboys." She shrugged. "The pay is good and we would get our own cabin. I'll know if it's something I would like when I get there tomorrow."

"Cooking for cowboys, huh?" *You could do that for me.* He bit his tongue to trap the words. Sarah work for him? What was he thinking?

He was losing his mind, that's what. Gone plumb loco. Remember how it had been in the kitchen? He hadn't been able to keep his hands off her. His iron will melted like soft butter when he was near her.

He wanted more than kisses. He wasn't going to lie about that.

So what was he really wanting? He stirred the green beans on his plate as he tried to figure out what to say.

"Don't like beans?" she asked. "I'm not surprised. I think men have an aversion to green vegetables. I sprinkled a little bacon crumbs over them, to give them more flavor."

"Do you know what I'm thinking?"

"I'm afraid to ask."

"Maybe you ought to work for me instead."

"You?" She shook her head. "Oh, no. I..." She opened her mouth, stopped, then shook her head. "I don't think that would work. Besides, you'll only have two hired men. That's not enough to need a full-time cook."

"There's the house." Now where had that come from? He hadn't even been thinking about that, had he? And yet it felt right to keep Sarah here. It would be better for the girls. Better for Sarah.

Better for him.

In all truth, the thought of her packing up and leaving, of never seeing her again, made him hurt. Right in the middle of his chest. It hurt to breathe. It hurt to move.

"It would take an hour to dust and mop the entire place. You don't need a housekeeper."

"School will be out soon enough, and Lucy will need someone to take care of her. Plus, I've got a few dozen horses to deliver and that's going to take me out of town. I'll need someone to stay with Lucy then. Why not hire you now?"

"For an hour's worth of housework a week and cooking for two men?"

"You're making this difficult, Sarah. I'm in a real bind here. You can help me out."

"Sure, a real bind." She didn't look as though she believed him one bit. "I can't work for you. You know why."

"The kissing, right?" The solution seemed clear. "I won't kiss you anymore. My word of honor."

"Well, I wasn't complaining about the kisses." She blushed a little.

His chest swelled. She liked his kisses, huh? He'd already figured that out. "No kissing during working hours. I figure you can fix up the place the way Lucy wants it. Find pillows and curtains and whatnot. That ought to keep you busy for a while."

"You act as if I've already accepted."

"You ought to. For the girls' sake," he clarified because it was easier than the truth. "If you worked for me, you wouldn't have to uproot Ella. You could stay right here in town, like you're doing. For someone who cooks the way you do, I'd pay well."

"Is that so?"

"Sure. So, are you going to accept my brilliant offer or not?"

"Brilliant?"

"Yep. I know you're one of the smartest women I've met, so I expect you'll accept."

Oh, he could charm the skin off a snake. Sarah ran

her finger through the beads of condensation on the glass in front of her. Work for Gage? She didn't want to be his employee. She wanted more of what she'd felt last night.

As if he remembered, he covered her hand with his. All trace of humor was gone. "I want you to stay, Sarah."

She envisioned how it would be working in his home, the easy laughter, the warm companionship.

"Think about it?" he asked, more a command than a question. But there was a plea in his eyes. A need for her.

It changed everything.

He needed her. Not a housekeeper. Not a cook. Her, Sarah Redding.

"Maybe I'd like the job in Price better." She watched him carefully. "But I suppose I'd rather stick close to home. I like our room upstairs, and Ella is settled here."

"See? I knew you were a smart woman." He took the water glass she'd drank from and took a long pull from it, gazing at her over the rim.

His silence said what he did not.

Chapter Eleven

Her first afternoon in Gage's kitchen. Sarah wiped up the last of the egg she'd dropped, glad that at least Gage was out in the corral. He would have taken one look at the floor and changed his mind about hiring her. She couldn't seem to keep her hands steady, wondering when he was about to walk in the door—

The screen door banged open. Gage? She whirled around, the washcloth in hand. When she spotted Lucy bounding into the kitchen with Ella close on her heels, Sarah released the breath she didn't realize she'd been holding.

"Do you know what, Sarah? The kittens are even bigger than they were yesterday."

"They're bigger, Ma," Ella confirmed.

"Know what, Sarah?" Lucy jumped across the room. "I like that you're here."

"Really?" Sarah dropped the washcloth in the wash pile. "You've only told me so five times since you've been home from school."

"I just like you here." Lucy bounded up on tiptoe. "Whatcha makin'?"

Ella grabbed hold of the counter, too. "I know. It's meat loaf."

"That's right." Sarah pulled Ella into her skirts and gave her a hug. "What are you girls up to now?"

"We're gonna make mud pies." Ella's face was pink from running, and she looked a little healthier, as if she were finally starting to put meat on her rail-thin bones.

It was good they were staying here in town, Sarah decided. She owed it all to Gage.

"This ought to help the mud pie bakers." She rescued a battered muffin tin from the lower cupboards. "Let's see. You're going to need a spoon."

"And a bowl." Lucy eagerly took the bent spoon Sarah handed her and dove into the cupboard.

"The mixing bowl is mine. Here, take this kettle. It should work."

"Okay. C'mon, Lucy!" Ella dashed off, leading the way for once, the muffin tin clutched in both hands.

Lucy followed eagerly, letting the screen door slam shut with an ear-splitting *thwack.*

"Who were those wild girls?"

"Gage." She hadn't heard him come in, but there he was, leaning against the door frame with the smile she couldn't resist. The one he seemed to smile only for her.

"I'm not sure, but they looked a lot like your Lucy and my Ella."

"They look like they're having fun." Gage strolled into the kitchen, his hat bent and his shirt torn. A dusty hoof print adorned the upper right side of his shirt.

"What happened to you?"

"The usual. That colt and I had a disagreement

about who was going to wear a bridle and who wasn't. Believe it or not, I won.''

''Doesn't look like it.'' She wiped her hands on her apron hem and dug in her pocket for a clean handkerchief. ''You're bleeding.''

''I do that a lot.''

''And it's dripping all over the floor.''

''Next you're going to say you just cleaned that floor.''

''Not exactly, but I'm going to have to.'' She pressed the cloth to the corner of his brow. ''What did you do? Land in a bramble bush?''

''I'm not that clumsy.'' But his sheepish grin told the truth.

''You did. A respected lawman, indeed, falling into the sticker patch. If the women in town knew, your sterling reputation would be tarnished a bit.'' She grabbed him by the shirtsleeve and pulled. ''Come over here into the light where I can get a good look. Yes, I'm going to have to dig out those thorns.''

''That's where you're wrong. If I bleed enough, they'll come out on their own.''

''That's one method. Here's another.'' She rummaged through the cupboards. ''No, you stay right where you are. I'm not about to let my boss expire because of an untreated festering wound.''

''You care about your paycheck more than me?''

''I'm ruthless that way.''

''I'm crushed.'' Gage glanced toward the door as if he were planning an escape. ''I came in for a clean shirt, not to be fussed over. I'll just head on upstairs—''

''Why are you in a hurry?'' She uncapped the little brown bottle. ''You're hurt.''

"Why am I in a hurry? Well, I've got two dozen horses that need to be ready to go by early next week and not enough days to do it. But I want the contract, so there you have it. I don't have time for doctoring. Besides, I've been hurt worse."

"Not enough time, huh?" She reached into her apron pocket, glad to see she had the upper hand. "Fortunately for you, I know exactly what to do. You don't have to go to the trouble of heading to town. Wait one minute."

"What are you up to, Mrs. Redding? And say, what's for supper. My hired men are going to be hungry—"

"Is that fear I hear in your voice? A big strong man like you?" She withdrew a pair of small scissors and watched his eyes widen. "You *are* afraid."

"I'm not partial to doctors or doctoring."

"Those wounds could fester and then where will you be?" She tsked, shaking her head slowly, as if to scold him, but her eyes were laughing. Her mouth, soft and generously cut, a mouth made for kissing, curved into a gentle grin.

He'd kissed that mouth and he wanted to again. Right now. This very minute. And he had to fight the urge. It was like a blind, raging impulse rolling over him with the force of a spring twister. Destroying every drop of willpower and control. Leaving only a tenuous thread of resolve. He would not kiss her.

At least not until suppertime, when she was no longer his housekeeper for the day.

The cool cloth touched his brow. Pain clawed through the cut on his forehead.

"Ow. That hurts. Worse than the sticker bush." He tried to pull away, but Sarah pushed him into a chair and wrapped her hand around his head. She held him there, eye level with her breasts.

He might not be a gentleman to notice, but it was damn hard to look anywhere else since she had held him captive, rubbing that hellish medicine into his cut without mercy.

"Angel, I don't need doctoring."

"Too bad. Just stay still and let me pull out these thorns."

That hurt, too. Still, the view was good. He had to appreciate that. She had nice breasts, soft-looking and full. Just the right size to fill his palms. His fingers itched to hold her, to feel the weight of her.

A man could lose his willpower gazing at those breasts.

"There, now hold this while I cut a bandage." She placed a cloth on his cut and reached for the evil little medicine bottle.

He watched her breasts sway slightly and it made him wonder. Imagine how would her breasts move when he had her astride him naked and...

"There, it wasn't too bad, was it?" She smiled at him. "You ripped your sleeve right here. It's bloody."

"Is it?" He couldn't get the image of her naked and astride him out of his head. He didn't want to.

A little curl had escaped her braid and he brushed it away from the side of her face. Her skin was like heated silk, far more fine than anything he'd ever touched.

"Take off your shirt."

"What?"

"So I can bandage this." She tapped his arm right above the cut.

Pain broke through the haze of his thoughts. He

cleared his throat. Now, see how far this had gone? Good thing he had willpower, because he was going to need it. "Sorry, darlin'. I thought we agreed to no kissing during working hours. I assumed that included nudity."

"You know what I mean." She gave him a no-nonsense look as her nimble fingers plucked at his buttons.

Fabric fell away in a whisper, and his pulse thudded so loud in his chest it was a shock that she couldn't hear it. He was hot and bothered and gritted his teeth as her fingertips grazed his shoulder. The shirt slipped away entirely.

Reason tumbled away as her hand splayed at the base of his neck, taking him to a place where there was no logic, no rational thought.

Overwhelming need hammered through him, leaving him weak. He yearned to pull her onto his lap and to loosen the gray buttons marching down her prim-and-proper bodice. To peel away layers of starched muslin and secret lace and suckle her until she cried out his name...

"Ow."

"There, I got the last thorn. It's over." She stroked her stinging medicine across his upper shoulder. "Lift your arm."

"I'm afraid to. What are you going to do?"

"Trust me, you big baby."

"Hey, I'm tough. Don't you ever doubt it."

"Tough as stone. Sure." She laughed as if she didn't believe him, a warm wonderful sound filling the kitchen like sunlight. "I'm almost done torturing you. Lift your arm."

"Not without some sort of reward."

"Reward? Like a cookie?"

"No. I want something sweeter." He caught her around the waist and pulled her onto his lap.

She tumbled against him with a shriek. "You and I had an agreement, buster."

"Yep. I might have warned you I'm a dishonest sort. Break my word constantly."

"I noticed that about you first off, that you are a disreputable sort of man. You fooled other people, but not me."

He hooked his forefinger over the lacy edge of her collar and tugged. Her laughter became her kiss, and he took what she offered, deep and hard. He found pleasure in her moan.

She liked that, did she? He plowed his fingers through her hair, holding her captive, loving the feel of golden silk against his hand. He smoothed his fingers along the graceful line of her back to her hip.

She dragged her mouth from his, breathing fast and shallow, her eyes glazed with pleasure. "Supper is likely to be late and what will my boss think of that?"

"I'm not your boss." He could feel the beat of her pulse at the base of her throat, and he kissed her there, where her skin was as white as satin and as sweet as spun sugar. "You're not here to work for me. You're here to see how this works out. This. Between us."

He nudged her just right against him, and her eyes went black as she realized how much he wanted her. Beyond reason. Beyond what he believed to be true.

He pulled her close for another kiss, his hand grazing the outside curve of her breast. When she didn't pull away, he whisked his thumb along the peak of her and felt her nipple harden.

"What are you doing to me, sir?" She leaned her forehead against his, breathless.

"I might ask you the same question, ma'am." He caught her bottom lip between his teeth and sucked just enough to make her groan.

Bootsteps thumped on the step outside and a knock rattled the screen door. "Gage? You in there?"

Sarah shot off his lap, and he caught her by the wrist so she wouldn't go far.

"He can't see us. Don't worry." He kissed her brow as he shrugged into his shirt, breathing in the scent of her, of roses and woman. So damn good. "I've got to go."

"A good idea." She blushed a little, touching her kiss-swollen lips, as if to let him know she liked his kiss, his touch.

She was a mature woman. She'd been married. No doubt she missed the pleasures of the marriage bed as much as he did. That gave him hope as he met Juan at the door.

"More trouble with that colt?"

The hired man shook his head. It was something worse. They headed outside, and Gage lowered his voice so Sarah couldn't hear. "Trouble at the creek?"

"Yep. Knocked out the fence posts the boys put in yesterday. Happened sometime in the night. They're replacing them. We'll have to see what happens next."

"We bring in the sheriff, that's what. No violence. There are children around. A stray bullet could do serious harm."

"Right." Juan nodded once in agreement before he headed off, ready to solve the problem.

Milt was a problem, but nothing Gage was going to let ruin his day. The property line dispute was a matter

of law. Milt would have to understand that and leave
the fence posts alone. Or there would be trouble.

Gage figured he'd set up a night watch, just to be
safe. That ought to be a good solution.

Heading toward the corral, Gage tried to turn his
thoughts to the colt he was training, and failed. Sarah's
scent was on his clothes. The lingering memory of her
embrace warmed him from the inside out. Filled up
the lonely places deep within.

"Pa! Look at our mud." Lucy held a mud-caked
spoon in her hand while Ella set the mud-filled tin on
a rock to bake.

"Good job, girls. Looks like great mud to me."

This felt right, somehow. He had work he loved, a
happy daughter and an amazing woman in his house
who made him laugh.

When he looked over his shoulder, Sarah was in the
window. She lifted her hand in a quick wave, and it
struck him then where this relationship was headed.
That he just might want a woman more than his freedom.

Sarah disappeared at the window but never from his
thoughts. Not from his moment forth.

Sarah caught glimpses of Gage the rest of the afternoon through the window while she worked.
Glimpses of his bronzed shoulders and back through
the corral rails, burnished by the warm sun.

As she shredded potatoes, she couldn't help noticing
the way he held the leather lunge line in one hand.
Sometimes, if the wind blew just right, she could hear
the low rumbling timbre of Gage's voice as he spoke
to the colt.

You're here to see how this works out. This. Be-

tween us. Those words he'd said to her. Tender words
that were so hard to believe. But they were true. There
was something unexpected and remarkable between
them. Something that didn't happen every day.

Gage had kissed her the way a man does when he
loves a woman. He touched her and laughed with her
and made her feel more cherished than she'd ever felt.

Was Gage falling in love with her? She hoped so.

Because she loved him.

Gage landed in the bramble bush a second time. He
wanted to blame the colt, but that wouldn't be fair. It
was his own darn fault. He hadn't been concentrating
on his work.

He'd been thinking about Sarah. Knowing she was
in his kitchen right now, not a hundred yards away,
and knowing she was a passionate woman who welcomed his touch, why, it was amazing he could work
at all.

"Got troubles, Gatlin?" Juan planted his hands on
his hips, shaking his head slowly. "Never thought
woman trouble would happen to you."

"Trouble? Don't use that word." Gage climbed to
his feet and inspected his knees. No real damage. He
was lucky this time. "Think that's enough for the colt.
We'll work him first thing in the morning."

"Right. Want me to bring out the dappled mare?"

"She's coming along fine. Why don't you put her
through her paces? Work on her lead-change a little
more." Gage brushed bits of leaves and dirt off his
denims. "Work your magic on her."

"I'll see what I can do. In the meantime, be careful,
Gatlin."

Alone again, Gage dusted off his pride, rescued his

hat and realized what Juan meant. Sarah swept through the green-tipped grasses, coming directly toward him. She paused to snap off a handful of wildflowers, intent on her work.

There was something about her, something that clutched tight in his chest. He liked the graceful line of her neck and the elegant line of her arm as she moved. The way she walked. The way she held a flower to her nose and inhaled deep.

He couldn't explain it. He only knew that he'd never wanted a woman the way he needed Sarah. Like breath. Like water. Like the earth at his feet.

"I have supper ready and keeping warm in the oven." She leaned her slim forearms on the top rail. "Land in the bramble bush again?"

"Heck no. I'm not that clumsy."

"I saw you go sailing over the fence." She looked as if she belonged here, on this land, in this place, with the house behind her and the prairie surrounding her.

It felt so right as she went up on tiptoe to study his bandage. Right to have her here with him.

"You're not bleeding." She peered at him. "You hit pretty hard."

"I'm as rugged as they come."

"You're practiced in being thrown off a horse."

"You wound me, darlin'." He clutched his chest.

"What did you say you were? The best horseman this side of the Rockies. So what are you doing in the brambles?"

"I was trying to impress you that day."

"Well, you didn't succeed. Because look." She pointed to the horizon. "The Rockies."

"They always used to be farther away than that.

Maybe I should have said something else. Like I'm the best horseman this side of the Colorado.''

"Yeah, but that wouldn't make you stay on your horse any better."

"You know what I do really well?" He pulled her close, his arm slipping around her shoulder. He steered her away from the sticker bushes and toward the house. "Kiss."

"Says who?" She leaned against him, savoring the luxury of being in his arms again. "You kissed me and I didn't notice anything great."

"No? I guess I'll just have to try again. See if I can't do better." His lips grazed her jaw in the faintest hint of a kiss.

A light, barely there kiss that made her want more. Much more. "You're awfully bold, Mr. Gatlin."

"I'm bad that way."

"I noticed."

Dust rose as men worked a horse in the corral. Gage called to them, letting them know supper was ready. It felt so perfect with the lark song trilling in the air and the soft bunch grass at their feet.

She had to be dreaming. Sarah leaned her cheek against his chest. The world had never been so beautiful.

"Do you know what, Pa?" Lucy hopped into bed and dove beneath the covers. "Sarah makes the very best meat loaf ever."

"It was pretty good." Actually, he didn't notice the food, only Sarah. Dishing up seconds for the girls, teasing that there wasn't enough food for him, and sending him secret little looks when she didn't know he was watching.

"And she put flowers on the table. I like that." Lucy folded the coverlet into place. "She's always humming. Did you know that?"

"I noticed."

"And she didn't get mad when Ella and me got all muddy." Lucy dropped back into her fluffy feather pillows and folded her hands over her stomach. "She's awful pretty."

"I know where this is going, darlin'." He rescued her book from the night table and handed it to her. "Remember when I told you I'm not getting married?"

"No." All innocence. "I musta forgot."

He wasn't fooled. "Well, if I ever change my mind, you'd best not get your hopes up. There's a whole lot to work out between a man and a woman long before they want to get married."

"Like the wedding dress. A lady always wants a pretty dress. Do you know what, Pa?"

"Read your book." He tapped the binding. "Stop worrying about what may or may not happen. There's no telling how things will work out. Or if they'll go the way you want them to."

"Sarah likes it here." Lucy was like a speeding train on a downhill track. "She'd be awful good to marry. If you wanted to."

"I hear you loud and clear." He kissed her brow. "Don't get your hopes up too high, darlin'. Okay?"

"I guess."

He turned down the lamp, leaving just enough light for her to read by. "I'm coming up in a half hour and this light better be out."

"Pa?"

He halted at the door. "What is it now, Luce?"

"I love you."

How could he argue with that? "I love you, too."

"Pa?"

She could go on like this all night if he let her. "Read your book, darlin'. I'll be right downstairs if you need anything."

"A ma." She hugged the book to her, looking so small and alone, with genuine want in her eyes. "Maybe you could think about it, cuz I like Sarah real well. *Real* well."

This was dangerous ground he was walking on. Walking as if he didn't have a care in the world. Lucy was his entire life. Everything he did, he did for her.

Except this.

He had to be honest. He had to face the truth. There were reasons why he'd asked Sarah to work for him, to take care of Lucy and the house and the light cooking for them and two ranch hands. Reasons that had nothing to do with Lucy needing a mother and him needing a cook.

He'd been attracted to Sarah from the first moment they met. If he closed his eyes, he could see her in the soft light of a new dawn, chicken feathers in her hair and stuck to her skirt. He knew she was different, even then, from all the other women who had baked welcome cakes and pies.

He pushed through the screen door and sat on the front step. Darkness fell like a curtain over the prairie, inching across the sky. A storm was brewing, angry clouds streaking from the west. Good thing he had the roof on the bunkhouse. Glad the feed was stored and covered. Glad Sarah had made it home by now, in the horse and buggy he'd talked her into taking.

He didn't need to close his eyes to bring back the

way she'd climbed into the buggy, so proper, so elegant. He'd shared the longing on her face, in the brush of her hand on his as he'd handed her the reins.

The girls were chattering, reminding him they weren't alone. That was good, because it kept him from acting on impulse. On the thoughts that circled around in his mind. Of what he wanted to do to her when he had her all to himself.

Dangerous ground. He couldn't deny it. It was natural to think ahead, to wonder where this was going. And panic, because no doubt Sarah would want marriage if he took her to his bed.

But jumping ahead wasn't going to tell him anything. So he'd take it one step at a time. Because there was no telling where the journey would lead. Or how it would end.

Ella hid a cough behind her hand as Sarah turned down the covers on the trundle bed. "I'm not getting sick. Honest, Ma."

"Is your throat sore? Does your chest hurt?"

"No."

"Okay. In bed. You had a big day, missy."

"I got to ride Scout all by myself. And on the trail, too. Lucy and me were like real cowgirls and I know what kind of horse I want. A girl horse that's all snowy-white with a long white mane and tail."

"Sounds really pretty." She kissed Ella's cheek— because it's always good to dream—and reached for the hairbrush. "What would you name this horse?"

"Sugar. Just like the one on Lucy's ranch."

"I see." Sarah untied the end of one braid and then the other.

"Her name is Sugar and she's so sweet. She likes me, too."

Sarah loosened the tightly plaited hair with her fingers, liking the sound of happiness in Ella's voice. "You've petted her, have you?"

"Have I! She only wants me to pet her. Not Lucy. Maybe it's because I save all the sugar for her."

"Sugar?"

"From the stable. Lucy's pa keeps it to sweet talk the horses. And peppermints, too, but Lucy and me eat those instead."

"Does Lucy's pa know about this?"

"Yep. He's the one who showed us the peppermints."

Sarah wasn't surprised. Gage had a soft side when it came to his daughter. The man who didn't believe in love. Remembering the welcome weight of his arm on her shoulder and the way he'd complimented her cooking with a low ring of tenderness in his voice made her blood heat from head to toe and everywhere in between.

Oh, she loved that man. She had to believe he was falling in love with her, too.

Love. She'd wanted to be loved again. The hope for it had gotten her through the hard year at the Owenses's. Yet to think dreams could come true, just in a blink of an eye. It was a gift, rare and wondrous, one she intended to hold on to with both hands. She intended to love Gage with all of her heart. The way love should be.

"Lucy says Sugar is gonna go away soon. When Mr. Gatlin takes the horses to sell."

"I wish we could afford to buy her from him. I bet she's expensive."

"I know." Ella's shoulders slouched a little. "Ma? Lucy says I get to stay over then."

"That's right." Sarah forgot about the brush in her hand.

When Gage took his horses to sell, she would be sleeping in his house. In his bed.

"Lucy said her pa bought special treats at the mercantile. For when he's gone."

"Is that right?" Sarah returned to brushing Ella's hair in long, smooth strokes. The fine locks crackled.

"Lucy says he got popcorn. Popcorn!"

"That is a treat." Sarah set the brush aside. "Time for sleep."

Ella curled up on her pillow. She sighed, a content sound, and closed her eyes. She coughed again, harder this time. "I'm fine, Ma."

"All right. Good night, baby." Sarah kissed her brow, smoothing the sheets into place. "Sleep tight."

"I'm gonna dream about my very own horse. With a long snowy mane that ripples in the wind."

Sarah turned the lamp low and curled up in the corner. She threaded her favorite needle by feel, lost in thought.

Lost in dreams.

The sound of a gunshot echoed in Gage's dreams. Bolting awake, he thought it was another nightmare. Another muffled boom told him it wasn't.

In a split second he was in his trousers and digging out the Colt Peacemaker from the back of his closet shelf. Dumping a handful of bullets into his shirt pocket, not bothering to take the time to button the garment, he flew down the stairs.

"Pa. I'm scared. What's the matter?"

"You stay in this house, Lucy. In your bed. Do you hear me?" He meant business, and she knew it. Her eyes grew wide and she nodded solemnly.

He didn't bother with his boots. Buckled on his holster and whistled for his mare. She came at a trot, nickering at the wooden fence. He climbed up the rails and onto her back, sending her into a full gallop.

He headed straight for the creek, thumbing bullets into the Colt's chamber as the mare flew through the field and skidded to a stop at the crumbling fence. Milt's rifle was cocked and slung against his shoulder. The man's stance threatening. His two sons at his side, both with weapons drawn.

"Boss, we've got a disagreement." One of the hired men ambled close, his gun at his hip. "Milt says this land is his. We say it ain't."

"I happen to agree with you, Wally." Gage tucked his Colt into its holster. "According to the deed, this creek is mine."

"This fence has been here for years." Milt patted the butt of his rifle. "I intend to see that it stays that way."

"I'm not looking for trouble, Owens. According to the deed's legal description of this land, the fence ought to be on the other side. If you think the deed is wrong, I'll be happy to take the matter before the county judge. He would tell us for certain who is right."

"Ain't no judge gonna tell me what's mine and what ain't."

Gage caught a strong scent of whiskey. "The sheriff, then."

"You'd like that. Always hidin' behind the law."

Milt slid the battered Henry carbine off his shoulder. "Well, Mr. Lawman, we settle this here and now."

"I'll say it again. We'll handle this according to the law. Put down your guns and walk away." In a split second Gage had his Colt in hand, cocked and pointed, before the other men could blink.

Milt paled. He fumbled with his gun, easing it to the ground. His sons did the same.

"Turn around, boys, and go on home. The sheriff will be out to talk to you in the morning."

Milt swore, muttering what sounded like threats as he retreated through his unkempt fields, his sons following.

"That didn't solve anything," Wally complained. "I followed orders and didn't draw on them, but I don't like it."

"We have the law on our side. Those men will have to abide by it." Gage patted the cowboy's shoulder. "Good job."

He watched Milt in the shadows. Waited until he saw a flash of light as the shanty door opened and then closed. Headed in to check on Lucy, who flew into his arms. She'd been so worried.

He took her to bed, tucked her in safe and snug, and headed back to his room.

But he was too troubled to sleep, so he watched the fields from his window. There were no more signs of trouble.

He hoped it stayed that way.

Chapter Twelve

Gage lifted the bucket straight from the well hook and dumped it over his sweaty head. Cool water cascaded over him, shocking his overheated skin. Didn't do much for his thirst. He sent the bucket back down when he saw his good friend climbing between the corral rails.

"We ought to be ready on schedule, except that colt is still saddle shy. I'll keep working him." Juan wiped his brow with his kerchief. "Heard that the sheriff visited Milt's shanty this morning and stayed over an hour. Haven't seen him or his boys, but his wife left with the rest of their children in the wagon. Guess she wasn't too happy to have a husband in trouble with the law. Maybe that will solve our problem."

"It's never that easy. But I hope so. We'll keep on guard and keep moving the fence. I need that water."

"I figure Owens needs it worse. His crops are going to fail without it. He's got a lot to lose, but the sheriff's visit may have done it. We might not have any more trouble."

"I think you're right. Milt has a family to think of, and I'm counting on that. He'd be better putting his muscle to digging a well to water his crops instead of fighting for land that isn't his. Hope he's smart enough to see that." He handed Juan the dripping, cool bucket. "I'll be right back."

"Not if you're heading to the house and the pretty lady." Juan wasn't fooled and his wink proved it. "You behave now, Gatlin."

"You know me."

"That's the problem."

Gage couldn't argue. He'd been up since dawn in the corral, working to the sweat. But about the time Sarah ought to be driving up in the buggy, he made sure to keep an eye on the road.

Today she wore a light green dress and carried a thick package in her arm as she let herself in the back door. It felt right. He wanted no other woman in his house. No other woman humming in his kitchen while she cooked.

He could hear her through the open window, a song he didn't recognize, but it was pretty with her voice to it. Happy-sounding. He hated to interrupt her, so he stayed on the step a minute or two. Watching her at the counter as she mixing spices with flour into a bowl. Wanting her beyond all reason.

"You startled me." She changed when he walked in the room. Not as relaxed. Tension straightened her up, as if she felt desire, too…and feared it.

"Sorry. Just watching you work." He pulled her into his arms and kissed her, slow and deep and thorough. When he pulled away, he took pleasure from the glazed look in her eyes. Knew this was right as he pulled a hairpin from the crown of her head. "You make me crazy, you know that?"

"Me? No, I think this is your fault. You make my common sense fly right out the window."

"Then you know why I'm here."

"Yes."

He tugged free another pin and her hair tumbled loose over her shoulders and breasts. She'd said yes; it was all he could think about as he cradled her head in his hands and kissed her again. Deep enough to drag a moan from her throat. To elicit a tiny sigh of longing.

He wanted her. More than anything. He caressed her bottom lip with his tongue, suckling and nibbling gently. She arched her neck, encouraging him to press kisses along the delicate curve of her throat. He stopped where he met a tiny row of lace at her collar.

The button was so tiny it slipped in his fingers, but he managed to release it and another just like it. The first glimpse of her pale skin beneath had him groaning. And aching for more.

"We won't go any further than you want to." He swept her into his arms, settling the weight of her against his chest. "I promise, no pressure. I'm prepared to go as slow as you want."

"I think I've forgotten to tell you what a wonderful man you are." She kissed him this time, and he tasted her passion, the need in her.

Gentle kisses, and the caress of her lips to his made him hurry up the stairs. He knocked his shoulder against the wall and stubbed his toe against the door frame, and he didn't feel a thing but Sarah's kiss. She took his lip into her mouth, sucking, and teased his sensitized flesh with her tongue. Hell, his knees about gave out from under him and he dropped her on the bed.

She bounced, surprised, then laughing. "Going slow, are we?"

"Yep." He jumped on the mattress, sending her bouncing and laughing some more and into his arms.

He loved how she welcomed him against her, pulling him half over her. She didn't move away from the hard length of his shaft against her hip, only smiled as he unfastened the buttons marching in a straight line between her breasts. His hands brushed those soft mounds as he went, making her eyes go black.

He wanted her right there. His trousers were tight and he loosened his buckle. Fit his knee between her thighs and peeled back layers of cotton and lace. He groaned at the sight of her creamy-white skin and smooth breasts, half hidden by her corset.

"I can take that off," she offered.

"I can manage it." He laved the upper swell of one breast and caressed the other. This is what he'd dreamed of all night, tortured by images of everything he wanted to do to her.

It had to be a dream now, too. Any minute he was going to wake up and the taste and scent of her was going to fade away into darkness. And be gone forever.

He couldn't believe he was here, in broad daylight and not a dream, touching her, kissing her. And that she would want him to, watching him with dark eyes as he slipped the dress from her shoulders so he could reach around and tug loose the bow at her back.

Her fingers curled around his nape, holding him to her as the cumbersome garment came unlaced, exposing the dark rose peaks of her breasts. He hardly had time to contemplate their beauty as he caught a pebbled nipple and pulled it into his mouth. She held him there as he suckled, laving her with his tongue. He loved that she grew restless beneath him, lost in the pleasure he was giving her.

"Like that, do you?"

"Oh, just a tiny bit."

"A tiny bit, huh? Then maybe I ought to stop, since you aren't enjoying this more."

"Don't you dare."

He chuckled, his breath a warm sensation across her damp, sensitized nipple. Sarah guided him back to her breast and let her head roll back against the thick pillows, grateful when his mouth captured her again, taking her to where there was only feeling.

His hands were caressing her, everywhere. Her stomach, her hips, her thighs. He was like a cyclone, sweeping her away, leaving her breathless and weak and clinging to his shoulders as he smoothed the cotton skirt away from her thighs.

She groaned, anxious and needy, wanting this man she loved. His touch was like no other, bold and possessive and tender all at once. His touch left no doubt she was his woman, his love.

"Oh, Gage." She sighed as he stroked his way up her inner thighs. Teasing, circling, never quite making his way beneath the hem of her drawers. The core of her ached for his touch. Never had she wanted anything so much. Restless, she lifted her hips, desperate for his touch.

"There's no hurry," he whispered, his words a hot caress on her throat.

"I want you." She ought to be embarrassed, admitting such a brazen truth, but she only saw the way Gage raised up on his elbows to meet her gaze. So much was mirrored there in his eyes. Affection and friendship and respect and want. And love.

Yes, she saw that as dark and deep as his desire for her. Felt it in the most tender brush of a kiss to her mouth, the weight of his hand as he molded her breast to fit his palm.

"It's been a long time for me, too," he admitted. "I want this to be right, Sarah. I want you well pleasured, so you'll stay with me."

"I'm not going anywhere." She stroked his chest, curling her fingers into the light mat of dark, downy hair, coarse and soft at the same time. Delighted in the texture of his skin, so different from hers, browned by the sun, and the hard ridges of muscle that rippled beneath her hand.

He was touching her again, easing down her drawers, the heel of his hand brushing low and lower still. Such exquisite pleasure. Hot and sharp and fierce. His fingers crept lower, exploring and teasing and circling that central place that made her cry out in near abandon.

A knock rattled the door downstairs, echoing in the empty rooms. Gage's hand stilled.

"Who in the blazes is that?" He shook his head. "Doesn't matter. I'm sure it's a traveling salesman. He'll go away."

"The door's unlocked."

"He'll go away," Gage insisted as he slid two fingers inside her. His thumb stroked and circled and she was lost. Completely, utterly lost.

The knock thudded louder. A man's booming voice shattered the moment. "Gatlin? Are you in there?"

"It's my foreman." Gage shook his head. "We could ignore him. Pretend we're not here."

"Duty calls, sir. We can always finish this later." She blushed a little. Gage had finally taken his hand out of her drawers and now she felt embarrassed. Realizing she'd done all but surrender completely to him, she smoothed her skirt into place and wondered what happened to her corset. Searching for her garments was far easier than having to look him in the eye.

The door banged shut downstairs. "Gatlin? We need you at the creek."

Gage shot off the bed and refastened his denims. "I'll get rid of him. You stay right here. Please." He kissed her, deep and wet, leaving her tingling.

"It's nearly ten-thirty. Time for me to start work." She blushed again because she'd come early today. And Gage knew why.

He swore, buckling his belt. "Tonight, then. After work."

"But I—"

"Have Ella spend the night with Lucy. It would be all right if you came along, too. I suppose I could make room for you in my bed. If that's what you want."

"My reputation—"

"Don't worry about it, angel. I'm leaving anyhow in a bit to take the horses to the capital, and you'll be staying here." He grabbed a clean shirt from the closet. "We might call this a test. To see if you feel comfortable staying in the house while I'm away."

"You think of everything, don't you?"

"Ma'am, I sure try. Will you stay?"

"My common sense says no. Absolutely not."

"And your body says?"

"Yes."

"Then tonight can't come fast enough." His dimples flashed and he left, his boots thudding down the stairs and echoing through the downstairs. The screen door slammed and he was gone.

Oh, heavens. She sank onto the edge of the bed, rumpled from their lovemaking. She hid her face in her hands, wishing her common sense would come back and save her.

Then again, maybe she didn't want to be saved. Gage loved her. She knew he did. He might not say the words, but this was serious. He knew it. She knew it.

And this, the way he'd pleasured her in his bed, it was just the beginning.

Desire curled deep inside. She was still tingling from his touch, breathing hard from wanting him.

She still wanted him.

It was hard to concentrate as she prepared the noon meal for the four ranch hands and the newly hired wrangler Gage had lured away from a ranch in Wyoming. The men talked over her fried chicken and buttermilk biscuits about the problems with Milt. He'd taken to drinking, sitting in the fields with his loaded rifle. Watching as the men finished the fence.

She couldn't help feeling somehow responsible. Milt was her uncle by marriage, but her offers to speak to him were met with a loud round of nays from the armed men at the table. Wally grabbed an extra piece of chicken, leaving before the meal was done, to ride for the sheriff. Milt wasn't breaking the law yet, but a fence line wasn't worth a man's life if it came to that.

"Don't worry about Milt, angel." Gage followed her into the kitchen after the other men had returned to their duties. "It's a matter of common sense. Any more trouble, and he'll find himself in jail. That will make him back away."

"I know times are tough for them." She'd seen it with her own eyes. A barely producing piece of land Milt had unwisely purchased years ago was only the start of it. "I heard Wally say my aunt Pearl left with the children. Despite his faults, he does love his family. Losing them makes his drinking worse."

"That's a problem they need to solve." He took her into his arms. "The men and I told the sheriff we would help Milt dig a well to replace the water. That may be a solution, if Milt isn't too cantankerous to accept my assistance."

"Like me, you mean?"

"You used to be rather prickly when I tried to help you, but you're became amazingly agreeable." His lips brushed hers once, and again. "If I can get that blasted colt to behave before I leave for Helena, I'm going to leave the white mare here. The one Ella likes. Figure she needs a horse if she wants to keep up with Lucy."

"You mean Sugar? The mare Ella wishes for every night before she goes to sleep?" When he nodded, she couldn't help loving him a little bit more. "Thank you. That's the best gift you could have given me."

"I know." He kissed her again. "It's one o'clock. The day is going so slow, so at this rate it'll be damn eternity before tonight comes."

"The reward may be worth it." She blushed. Had she really said that?

Throughout the afternoon, it was all she could think about. The hunger in Gage's kiss. The anticipation shimmering in her blood, making her tingle. The day felt extraordinary as she passed the time doing ordinary things. Hemming gingham curtains for the house, or snatching time to daydream about Gage.

Instead of fantasizing about making love to Gage, she ought to be trying to locate the common sense she'd obviously misplaced.

But what did common sense matter when compared to how alive Gage made her feel? The caress of his hands, the tug of his mouth at her breast, the way he'd touched her so intimately…

Tonight *did* feel like centuries away.

She heard a clatter in the yard and set down her sewing. Scout was wandering up the drive, with Lucy and Ella on her back. In the distance rang the shouts of children on the main road to town, walking home from school. Lucy and Ella waved at someone out of Sarah's sight and Scout broke into a gallop, taking the girls flying past the door.

"Hi, Ma!" Ella yelled with glee.

Then Sarah remembered. The cookies! She'd do better to keep at least half of her mind on her work. Grabbing the mitt, she rescued the cookies from the oven, relieved they were a golden brown and not crisped at all. Perfect. Warm cookies for the girls to enjoy with a glass of milk.

"Ma!" Ella tumbled through the door, Lucy traipsing in behind her. "I won the spelling bee."

"She did. I came in second 'cuz I couldn't spell 'impertinent.' "

"Impertinent is a pretty big word." Sarah scooped the last cookie onto the wire rack to cool. "I'm proud of you both. And first place, baby. You're doing so well."

"I know!" Ella threw her arms around Sarah's waist.

Lucy did, too. "You baked ginger cookies. My very, very favorite."

"I heard that somewhere. Lucky for us, it's Ella's favorite, too." Sarah gave each girl a kiss on the brow. "Now go upstairs and change out of your school clothes. Hurry."

"We're awful hungry right now, Sarah." Lucy's fingers reached toward the counter.

"Awful hungry," Ella agreed breathlessly. "We're about to starve."

Was that a wheeze? No, Ella was simply excited. Sarah felt her child's brow to be sure. Well, she felt fine. "All right, one cookie each, and that's it for now. Off you go."

The girls thundered up the stairs, talking a mile a minute, their voices ringing in the stairwell. The sounds of happiness had Sarah humming as she set the baking dishes near the pump.

Was this joy real? Or was she dreaming? Happiness made her feet light as she retrieved the bowl of bread dough from the windowsill. Contentment made the task of handling the sticky dough agreeable.

If this was a dream, she never wanted it to end. This, right here, was everything she'd ever wanted. She caught sight of Gage through the open doorway, in the saddle, trotting a buckskin around the corral. His head bent to his task, his back straight and strong, he looked like the hero he was, an invincible man of might and tenderness who loved her.

She could not ask for more.

It was there between them through supper and into the evening, unspoken but humming beneath the surface. Sarah couldn't ignore the flicker of want inside her that happened every time she looked at Gage.

The evening seemed to last forever. After supper Sarah ironed the curtains she'd finished hemming and Gage hung them in the dining room, according to the girls's instructions. Later, after bedtime stories and a lot of orders to quiet down, the girls seemed to be asleep, each tucked into their own bunk bed.

"Finally." Gage commented as he stole into the parlor. "It's only eleven."

"Are they actually asleep? And not faking?"

"I say we give them a few more minutes and we'll know for sure." He joined her on the front step and pulled her into the curve of his side. His arms held her tight as he nuzzled her ear. "I've been waiting for this all day. Couldn't think of much else."

"At least you didn't land in the sticker patch again."

"That's because I took a machete to it this morning. It's gone." His hands caressed the curve of her shoulders. "I didn't know if I could take another session of being doctored by you. I may have lost all control."

"What about now?"

"Close." He laved an extremely tender spot behind her ear.

Pleasure shivered through her and she leaned back against him. "That's nice."

"Nice? I don't want nice." He kissed lower, where her neck curved into her shoulder, while his hands circled around her waist. "I intend to ravish you, my sweet lady."

"I might like that." She arched her back as he

cupped her breasts, kneading and stroking until she bit her lip to keep from crying out.

"Seems to me you definitely like that." He plucked at her buttons again and slipped inside her dress. "Left your corset off, did you?"

"Hmm." It was all the speech she could manage. Pure bliss. She felt every muscle in her body relax. So good. So very good. She moaned when he withdrew his touch, leaving her breasts heavy and aching.

"I think we're officially alone." He helped her up, keeping her close at his side. "Let's find someplace more private."

"Not your bedroom. The thought of the girls right across the hall—"

"One day you're going to have to get used to that." His fingers curved around her nape, then trailed down her back in slow, sizzling strokes. "For now, I understand. We'll find a place to be alone, together."

"I'd love that."

"Good." His fingers stole into her gaping dress and caressed her. "I want you tonight, Sarah. I've never wanted anyone the way I want you."

His words knocked away the last of her disbelief. The doubt she'd been holding inside. The part of her that thought this was too good to be true, too incredible to be real. That Gage, heroic and strong and kind, would want her, Sarah Redding.

Because he did want her. His touch, his words, the tender brush of his lips against her temple. She wanted him, needed him, more than the earth at her feet.

As if he understood, he pulled her into the grasses. There was no need for words as he pulled the clothes from her until she was naked in the moonlight, sheltered by the roll and draw of the prairie, but exposed to the night. To him.

"You are worth the wait. Do you know how much I want you?" He untied the ribbon from her braid and loosened the tight plait. "You're mine, Sarah. All mine."

She plucked at his buttons and slid the soft wash-worn fabric away to expose the hard gleam of his torso and the heat of his skin against her palms. Moonlight caressed him the way she wanted to. Over every ridge and ripple of muscle. Over every curve of arm and rib.

"I'm more crazy now," he whispered in her ear as he laid her onto their clothes, spread out beneath her. "Do you feel how much?"

Did she ever. The hard length of him jutted against the curve of her stomach. She could feel him plainly through his thin cotton drawers. Then he moved away and there was no barrier between them. Just his blunt stiffness hard against her, and the answering curve of her own desire.

A desire that coursed through her with the fury of a spring river, crashing and speeding and knocking away everything in its path. She wasn't aware of the sky above or the grass below or the call of a coyote in the fields.

Only the weight of Gage as he eased over her completely, one knee between her thighs, capturing her mouth with his, kissing her deep and fast until she was breathless and her hips were arching up to meet him. His hardness pulsed between them, and her body answered.

She wanted him. Needed him inside her. Was about to snap into a thousand pieces if he wouldn't hurry—

"Please, Gage." She heard her own desperation.

He smoothed the tangles from her face, breathing hard. "You want me, do you, angel?"

"No. Not at all. Please, I—" *Need you.* The words caught in her throat and became a tortured groan as he pressed her thighs apart with his knees. His shaft nudged against her inner thigh. "Gage, please—"

"As you wish, my lady." His words were a kiss as he entered her in one long, slow thrust that tore a moan from her throat. He settled deep and held there, thrumming inside her. "Is this satisfactory?"

"Oh, yes." She wrapped her arms around his shoulders and held tight. There was so much of him, hard and thick inside her, and he felt so good. No, that wasn't the word. Magnificent, amazing, stupendous.

Sharp thrills of pleasure ripped through her, spiraling through every nerve ending. Gage set a rhythm that sent her over the edge in a sudden, fierce climax. Wave after wave of tight, rippling sensation left her helpless and clinging to him.

"Hmm, you're a pretty easy woman. Just what I like."

"You think you're funny."

"I am. Like I told you, I'm the best rider in all of Montana." He rocked against her, determined to prove it.

"Enough with the puns. You have a bad sense of humor."

"Yeah, but maybe you like me a little bad, eh?"

"Maybe."

He lifted her hips, bringing her knees high enough so that she could wrap her legs around him. She'd never been this vulnerable and open to a man. Locked together, they moved as one, his breath was her breath, his kiss hers. The orgasm that rocked them both began with him and ended with her.

Drained, wrung out, overwhelmed with a fierce love that had no end, she clung to him. Couldn't let go. Gage remained inside her, kissing her and stroking her without another word until he was hard again, until she was ready.

They made love as the stars wheeled around in the sky and the moon set quietly in the west, leaving them alone with in the night.

The morning looked damn good from where Gage was sitting, astride his mare. Probably because there was Sarah at the kitchen door, carrying a platter of eggs and sausages to the trestle table.

She looked different today. Just as lovely and every bit as tantalizing as she moved the basket of biscuits to keep the red tablecloth from flying away in the wind. *He* was the one who'd changed. Last night had been the best lovemaking he'd ever had. That could give a man a whole new perspective.

"'Mornin', Pa!" Lucy slammed open the screen door and leaped down the board steps, her school dress flying around her as she raced across the lawn. "Sarah made blueberry muffins. Hurry!"

Ella skipped up to Lucy, looking like a miniature version of Sarah, sweet and pretty and as good as gold. "Yes, please, Gage. Ma makes the best muffins ever."

"How can a man argue with that?" He dismounted and handed the reins to the girls. "Suppose you two are skilled enough horsemen to tie her up for me?"

Two "Yesses!" rang in unison and the girls importantly led the mare to the iron ring on the post in the yard.

Sarah set the milk pitcher on the table, looking more beautiful today than he'd ever seen her. Desire lingered in his blood, and the memory of last night had him pulling her into his arms.

"I suppose you'll want an encore for tonight." He nuzzled her neck where she was ticklish.

"It's a sure bet." She giggled against him and felt like heaven. "Last night was amazing."

"Yes, you were." He would have kissed her more, but the girls interrupted, each carrying a kitten. The kittens had wandered out of the barn, they said, and the mother cat had moved them from the loft a few days before.

The table was merry as the girls chattered on about this and that. Sarah tossed him secret glances that said it all. He'd pleasured her well and she couldn't wait for more.

It was a once-in-a-lifetime occurrence, this connection they had. He was grateful for it. And being a smart man, knew what he was going to do about it.

Sarah belonged in his life. He was going to make sure she stayed right here, so every morning could be this happy and every night could be a passionate one.

When the meal was through, he told Ella there was something waiting for her in the barn. Something that might help her get to school that morning.

Lucy squealed. "I know!" The girls bolted from the bench seat, running all the way.

"I don't know how to thank you." Sarah's hand lighted on his shoulder as she began stacking the plates. "You don't know what this means."

"Maybe I do." He could look in her eyes and see it. "Don't you know that I want to make your life better? And your daughter's? You're here for a reason, Sarah.''

"I know.'' Her kiss was tender, her touch magic.

His whole life was changed. Sarah had done that. She made everything new and wonderful.

"Mr. Gatlin!'' Ella's squeal was a half cry as she rode into view, with Lucy on Scout at her side. "Do you mean I get to ride her? Really? To school?''

"Sure I do. She's yours forever, Ella. You take good care of her, now.''

"I will.'' So serious. "Thank you so much, sir. I'll take the best care of her. I swear.''

Sarah's hand slipped into his. "You girls are going to be late. You'd better get going.'' Her words gentle as she waved goodbye. "Have a good day, baby.''

"It's the best day. I got a horse!'' Ella brimmed with joy because it wasn't every day a wish came true. "Come on, Sugar. Let's go.''

"'Bye, Pa!'' Lucy hollered as she led the way down the road. "'Bye, Sarah!''

Sarah's hand fell to her chest as she watched her daughter ride away. "Did I mention how wonderful I think you are?''

"Sure, but not nearly enough.'' He kissed her thoroughly, because they were alone. "I'd haul you inside the house right now and demonstrate to you what I'm thinking about, but the sheriff ought to be here any minute.''

"More trouble with the creek?''

"No, and don't worry. It's being handled.''

"I know.'' She breezed away with a stack of dishes and disappeared into the kitchen.

The problem with Milt was being handled. Gage would make certain of that. Already he felt fiercely protective of Sarah. He had that trip to make, and the thought of having to leave made him crazy. With the sheriff's help, at least he knew Sarah would be safe.

If Gage looked just right, he could see her through the window. His life was changing and he didn't even know it.

"Is that everything?" Clancy asked from behind the mercantile's front counter. "I have candy on special today."

"You're tempting me to spend more money in your establishment."

"Yes. Is it working?"

Sarah dug in her reticule for the nickel she knew was in there. "How much peppermint will this buy me?"

"Enough to make two little girls very happy." Clancy reached for a paper bag and filled it. "No, keep your money. This goes on Mr. Gatlin's account."

"The fabric and the candy are separate, and don't you dare try to say otherwise." She found the nickel and added it to the pile of greenbacks on the counter that would pay for her yard goods. "Gage Gatlin is not paying my bills."

"Hear he leaves tomorrow with a bunch of horses he's selling to the governor's cousin. Impressive. The banker plans to buy a new driving team from him. Quite a reputation he's getting. Don't suppose Gage will be gone long to Helena, when he's got you waiting for him."

She blushed. "He plans to be gone only a few days."

"You tell him I'm interested in a good horse for my daughter." Clancy placed the bag of candy on top of the wrapped package of fabric. "Oh, and I'll be seeing the rest of the groceries are delivered today."

"Thank you kindly." Sarah slipped the wrapped peppermints into her reticule and tucked the heavy package of fabric into the crook of her arm.

It felt wonderful to have a little extra to spend. Ella was going to love the pink calico fabric, enough to make a new dress and a matching sunbonnet. Both girls were going to love what she planned to do with the yarn and bleached muslin she'd bought—matching rag dolls for them to play with. She could not wait to get home and get started.

Had the sun always been this cheerful? She didn't think so as she headed down the boardwalk. Town was busy this time in the afternoon, right before school let out. After a quick check at her timepiece, she had just enough time to stop by the furniture store.

"'Afternoon, Sarah." Sam, old Mr. Lukens's son, greeted her from the back. "Hear you're keeping house for that beau of yours. Has he asked you to marry him yet? My wife is already crocheting a wedding present. Judging by that smile on your face, I say she's right."

"I have no comment to make, but thank you for asking. You wouldn't be willing to sell me a table and chairs on credit, would you? It's for Gage."

"Sure it is." Sam didn't look as though he believed a word of it.

Since there were no other shoppers in the store, Sarah was able to walk the aisles of beautiful furniture and wish a little. She couldn't help picturing her future with Gage. With that oval cherry table in the dining room and that green brocaded sofa in the parlor.

"I could drop the price on that sofa, if you're interested."

"Just the table and chairs for today, please." She was tempted. She'd rather wait for Lucy's and Ella's advice about the rest of the furnishings, but she wasn't willing to wait any longer for a real table. A house wasn't a home without one.

After making the arrangements for delivery, Sarah left the shop and checked her list. She still needed to have the tear in her shoe repaired at the shoemaker's, but that could wait.

The school bell clanged merrily, announcing classes were done for the day. She had just enough time to fetch the buggy—

"Livin' pretty fancy, aren't you, from what I hear."

Sarah whirled around, surprised by the venom of those words. More shocked by the haggard lines on her aunt's face. "Pearl. I've been wondering how you are getting along. I've been meaning to stop by."

"You wouldn't be welcome."

"Are you still at your mother's?"

"Don't see what concern it is of yours, seeing as you're in bed with that man." Pearl's mouth pursed disdainfully as she looked Sarah up and down. "Never saw you wear that when you were livin' with us. Did he pay for that dress?"

Sarah knew Pearl's life was hard. Very hard. She tried to forgive her those harsh words. "I know there are tensions between Gage and Milt. I was hoping—"

"Tensions? I would call it trouble. That Gatlin has done nothing but rile Milt into a rage. My husband ain't the same after what that man done to him. Those animals were his. From helping that worthless old man that lived there. And now the creek. That ought to be ours. We claimed it.''

"That's not right, Pearl, and you know it. Gage has offered to help build a well. Maybe you could ask Milt if that wouldn't be a good solution. He would be gaining a well, and that's valuable. It would help with his crops.''

"You just stay out of this, missy. The last thing I need is more meddling from the likes of you. Folks say that Gatlin fellow is just toying with you while he takes time to find himself a real good wife.''

Sarah bit her lip. Her relationship with Gage wasn't her aunt's concern. "Maybe you could consider what I said about the well.''

Pearl sniffed, as if she smelled something unpleasant. "A man that rich ain't gonna love you. When he leaves you pregnant without a penny to call your own, don't you come knockin' on my door. You just remember that.''

"Aunt Pearl, I—''

"You're no relation to me. Now get out of my way." Pearl shouldered past her, walking fast, anger ringing in her step.

"Don't you let her worry you none, missy." Old Mr. Lukens tapped his cane near her shoe. "That Gatlin is a good man. Came across me havin' trouble, and nailed on a new shoe for my donkey. You can't get better than him.''

Old Mr. Lukens had caught her and Gage kissing that day in the violet patch. "You ought to come over and have supper with us one evening.''

"Ma'am, I would enjoy that very much. You let me know." He tipped his hat and ambled off, cane in hand, leaving her feeling relieved.

He was right, but she wished Pearl's situation could be better. Pearl had been the only relative who'd taken her in. That had to count for something, even now. There, at the far end of the street, Pearl's school-age children gathered at the family wagon.

It reminded Sarah of how lucky she was. To have the love of a good man. A job where she could take care of Ella at the same time. A life filled with love and tenderness. A future that promised more.

"Sarah!" Lucy halted her little mare in surprise.

"Hi, Ma." Ella waved from Sugar's back. Her hand dropped as several coughs shook her hard. "Were you lookin' for us? Can we go look in the mercantile?"

"Too late, I already finished shopping." Sarah tugged the candy from her reticule, wondering if she ought to take Ella home and get her resting.

"Goody! Enough for both of us. Oh, thank you, Ma!" Ella unfolded the paper and offered Lucy first choice.

"Thanks, Sarah!" Lucy crunched on the end of her peppermint stick.

"Wait and I'll drive home with you. Besides getting you a nap, Ella, we have a lot to do this afternoon."

"Are we gonna make new curtains?" Lucy guessed.

"Are we gonna make cherry pie?" Ella asked.

"You'll have to wait and see." Sarah clutched her package tight. "The buggy's up the street. I'll meet you there."

Ella coughed again, and Sarah made up her mind. She'd stop by the doctor's clinic and have him take a look at Ella, then they'd head home. There would be plenty enough time for sewing and baking.

Up ahead, the girls chattered as they rode side by

side along the busy street. Two sets of braids, one dark and one light, swayed with the horses's gaits.

Determined not to worry about Ella, Sarah hurried after them.

"How am I gonna leave you?" Gage murmured in her ear, snuggling against her in the warm afterglow of another night spent making love. "You are the best thing that has ever happened to me, and I have to leave you for two whole nights."

"I'm not sure I can survive it." She curled into him, contentment making her warm and sleepy. Except she didn't want to sleep. She kissed the center of his chest. "I suppose you have to go and sell your horses. Too bad."

"Hmm, isn't it?" He found her breasts and caressed her lazily. "I would spend the rest of my life right here without one complaint."

"Except who would cook for us?" She moaned when his hand swept lower. "Then again, who needs food? I just need you right now."

"I thought so." Gage rolled her onto her back and settled his weight over her. She was wet and ready and he filled her slow and deep. "Two whole nights without you."

"I will miss you every moment."

"Every second." He couldn't get enough of her. Hated that dawn would soon be coming. He couldn't hold back the night, so he held on to her and loved her until the night began to fade to shadows.

"Ready to go, Gatlin?" Juan called from atop his gelding. "Wally has the horses ready, and I'm anxious to get you out of my hair."

"Hold your horses. I'll be gone soon enough." Gage checked the cinch, let the stirrup fall into place and mounted. He was ready to go. Didn't want to.

"Pa!" The screen door slammed and Lucy raced across the lawn. "I forgot to tell you. You can't forget my present."

"Wouldn't dream of it, darlin'." He hauled her onto his lap for a final hug goodbye. "I'm gonna miss my little girl."

"I'll miss you lots and lots, but Sarah is gonna stay here." Lucy's eyes sparkled with delight. "Just like a real mother."

"I'm glad you like her."

"I don't like her. I *love* her." She kissed him with a smack on the cheek and slid down the horse's shoulder. "Get me somethin' good."

He held his feelings still as he gave the mare a nudge with his heels. "You be good while I'm gone. Mind Sarah."

"'Kay. 'Bye!"

Gage lifted his gloved hand to wave, but there was Sarah in the road behind Lucy, in her pretty yellow dress, her hair unbound and shimmering in the morning light. Sarah who gazed at him with longing in her eyes.

A longing he felt, hard and deep.

She missed him all the day long and now lying alone in his big bed in the room where his clothes hung, it was impossible to put him out of her mind. To close her eyes and forget how much she missed him.

Was he sleeping now? She tried to picture him in a hotel room, his hair tousled and his big body sprawled across a snowy sheet, dreaming of her. Desire licked through her veins and she tossed and turned in the empty bed, restless and wanting him.

What was the use? She threw back the covers and reached for her robe. She might as well get up, because she wasn't going to get to sleep anytime soon.

Her feet padded on the stairs, so new there wasn't a squeak to wake the girls. She opened the door to listen to Ella's breathing. It sounded a little congested. Maybe the mint balm she'd rubbed on Ella's chest would clear her up by morning. It often did.

She closed the door tight and felt her way by memory and paused for a moment in the dining room. Emptiness no longer echoed around her as she gazed at the moon, shadowed by moonlight, where a cheerful tablecloth draped the new table, and chairs were neat in their places. A bouquet of wildflowers sat in a chipped mug in the center, flowers the girls had picked for her.

She knelt for her sewing basket, tucked away in the corner, when she heard a cough through the ceiling boards. Ella's cough.

There was no cause for alarm. Ella couldn't be sick. She'd been perfectly fine when Sarah had tucked her into bed. She was thirsty, that was all. A glass of water should do the trick.

Ella coughed again when Sarah opened the bedroom door. She could make out the shadowed outline of the little girl sitting up in bed, her hand to her mouth, her shoulders hunched.

"Here's some water, baby." Sarah eased down onto the mattress, careful not to wake Lucy fast asleep on the other side of the bed. "Drink up. It's nice and cold."

Ella coughed again, spilling the water as she took the cup. Sarah held it steady for her as she drink, one sip and then another. There was no more coughing.

"Better?"

Ella nodded. "I don't want to get sick again. Not for anything."

"I know." Sarah pulled her girl into her arms. She loved her so very much. "You go back to sleep. I'll leave the cup right here in case you get thirsty again."

Ella leaned back in her pillows, already half asleep. She didn't feel hot, and her breathing sounded clearer. The chest balm was working.

See? Everything was just fine.

"'Morning, Sarah!" Lucy burst into the kitchen, her hair tumbling down her back and her stockings crooked. "Are we gonna have pancakes?"

"Already made and in the oven. Sit down and let me braid your hair." Sarah took a ribbon from her apron pocket and turned Lucy around so she could finger part her hair into sections. "Ella, is that you?"

"Yes, Ma. I had to find my speller. Today's the spelling bee, and I'm the best in my class."

"I know, smart girl. Why don't you fetch the maple syrup from the pantry for me? I'll finish Lucy's hair, then I'll do yours."

Ella trotted off, looking perfectly healthy with her rosy cheeks and quick grin.

"Do you know what, Sarah?"

She plaited the very end of one braid, then tied it tight. "What?"

"You could stay here forever. I'd like that."

"I'd like that, too." Remembering Lucy's dreams

for a mother, Sarah's heart melted a little more. "Hold still while I finish."

"Do you know what, Sarah? I sure miss Pa."

"Me, too." Sarah quickly worked her way down the braid, tucking and turning.

"My turn, Ma." Ella sidled close, and coughed hard into her fist.

This time, something wasn't right. Sarah felt Ella's forehead. No, she felt fine. "Sweetie, doesn't your throat hurt?"

"No."

Ella's color was a little high, but she was also excited about the upcoming spelling bee.

Sarah decided that she couldn't risk it. "We'll pay another visit to the doctor this morning."

"Aw, Ma. No." Ella stomped her foot in protest.

Proof enough that her daughter wasn't feeling as well as she claimed. "Just a quick stop. If you're fine, we'll take you straight to school so you hardly miss a thing."

"I don't wanna go." Ella's eyes filled.

"I know, baby. But we want to be careful." Sarah held her child close. "Come on, let's get breakfast or you girls are going to be late."

She kept her voice light as she rescued the pancakes and sausages from the warmer. Everything was going to be fine. She had to believe it.

Chapter Thirteen

Home. Gage had never been so glad to be anywhere. While the house was dark, a single lamp burned in an upstairs window. Sarah was waiting for him.

He'd thought of nothing else but her the entire trip. Even had a few surprises in his saddlebag for her. One that he'd chosen from a jeweler's case. One his entire future hinged on.

He didn't bother to light the lantern, and put up his horse in the dark, going by feel. Scout nickered a welcome, begging for sugar. He gave her some, rubbed her nose, and poured grain into her feed tray when he filled the bucket for his mare.

He followed the light to the back door, where his key fit the lock. The instant he stepped into the house, he knew his life was different. Better. Because of the woman upstairs.

A flicker of light tumbled into the kitchen, showing the tidy counters and new curtains at the window. A wicker basket of colorful napkins perched on the counter next to an enamel cookie jar in the shape of a beehive. He breathed in the lingering scent of roses.

Sarah. He warmed to the marrow of his bones,

thinking of her in his bed. Waiting. His trousers grew snug as he climbed the stairs, not bothering to kick off his boots as he went.

The light glowed beneath the door, and he felt for the ring in his shirt pocket. It was there, a reassuring presence as he turned the knob.

Would she be naked beneath those sheets? Or wearing a soft white gown he could take off, button by button?

Anxious to find out, he opened the door.

She was on the bed all right, her long hair spilling over her shoulders like liquid gold. She sat propped against the headboard in a pretty white nightgown, little Ella asleep, her head pillowed on Sarah's thighs.

The desire ebbed away.

"She's sick. Just the croup, and a light case of it. We're lucky. But her lungs are weak, and..." She caught her bottom lip between her teeth and said no more. She stroked Ella's hair.

"I'm sorry." He didn't know what to say. Wasn't prepared for this. His mind had to make an abrupt turn and he faltered a little, making his way to the bed. "You had the doctor come out?"

"We went in to see him. He's coming to check on her in the morning."

"Good." He cupped Sarah's neck and stole a kiss. "You look exhausted. Did you get any sleep last night?"

"Barely."

She'd spent the night watching over her daughter. Gage knew that. She didn't have to tell him. He hated how tired she looked. How dark those smudges were beneath her eyes. How pale her skin.

"It's almost time to change the mustard compress." Sarah gently lifted Ella onto the bed.

"I'll get the fire started." He stopped her with a touch. "You stay here with your girl."

"Oh." She caught his hand and pressed a kiss to his knuckles. "You're a good man, Gage Gatlin."

"That's not what you told me the other night." He nuzzled her cheek, then headed for the door.

Sarah loved Gage a little bit more for that. Her love for him grew and grew. When he returned with a steaming mustard plaster for Ella, made just right. When he carried away the cold plaster-caked cloths so she could stay with Ella. Then he returned with a cup of mint tea, so she could relax while Ella slept.

When Ella's croup broke before dawn and the worst was over, Gage promised to watch Ella for a few hours and tucked Sarah into bed beside her child.

Her last image before she closed her eyes was of Gage sitting tall and vigilant in the chair beside the bed, beyond the small pool of lamplight. He was cloaked in darkness and shadow, invisible in the night.

She had never seen him more clearly.

The early morning sun hurt her tired eyes, but the few hours of sleep had made a difference. Sarah slipped into a fresh dress as quietly as she could, for Ella was asleep, curled on her side beneath the blankets.

"Sarah?" Gage kept his voice low and his step light as he carried a tray into the bedroom. "Figured you could use some breakfast."

Her stomach growled at the scents of coffee, crisp bacon, cheese-topped scrambled eggs and sliced potatoes in thick buttery wedges. "You did this? Of course you did. I just— It's unexpected."

"See how useful I am?" He bussed her cheek with a hint of a kiss and set the tray on the window seat. "Ella needs her sleep, and her mother needs sustenance. You clean your plate or there'll be hell to pay."

"Hell, huh?" She leaned into his embrace, drinking in the bliss of his strength and his touch. "I would call this heaven."

"Me, too." Her hair snagged on his whiskered chin as he held her safe. "Everything is going to be fine. The doctor ought to be here soon. I'll get Lucy her breakfast, and we'll watch for him."

"I can't believe you're doing all this."

"This is just the beginning, angel." He released her. "I'll be downstairs if you need me."

She nodded, too overcome to speak. See how much Gage loved her? She'd never been so cherished. Never felt such devotion.

Ella stirred in her sleep, breathing evenly, and her color was good. Sarah resisted the urge to brush blond locks from her daughter's dear face, because she didn't want to disturb her. Ella needed her sleep to recover. And she *was* going to recover.

How lucky they were.

Sarah curled up on the window seat with the plate of food Gage had made for her. As she ate and watched the sun rise over the peaceful prairie, she counted her blessings. Every single one.

The doctor placed his stethoscope into his medical bag with slow precision, and Sarah didn't need to hear the words as he nodded toward the hallway outside the sunny bedroom.

Her knees wobbled as she forced her feet to carry her over the threshold. Her hands were ice as she pulled the door closed behind her. "I watched her so carefully. The croup broke around four this morning. She's breathing fine."

"I know, but I heard something with the stethoscope that concerns me."

"Not pneumonia. No. Ella can't go through that again. I almost lost her last time and she's only starting to be as strong as she ought to be—"

"Sarah." A hand settled on her shoulder, gripping tight. It wasn't the doctor's touch, but Gage's. "What do we need to do, Doc?"

"Sarah's been through this before. I'll be back to check on Ella around noon. If we can keep her from worsening, she'll be just fine."

This couldn't be happening. Not to Ella. Not again. Numb with fear, she couldn't think of any questions to ask. She opened the door slightly and peered through the opening to see her daughter, so little and fragile. She didn't deserve to be ill.

"Ma? Do I have to take more yicky medicine?"

"Probably, sweetie." Sarah stumbled into the room, tamping down her fear.

"I'm not sick anymore. Honest." Ella shoved off the covers. "I can sit up and everything."

"I see." She could also see the fine trembles that shook Ella's body. Sarah helped her back onto the pillows. Heavens, she was as weak as a kitten. "You close your eyes for me, baby. You need your rest."

"No-oo." Tears filled Ella's eyes. "I don't wanna be sick."

"You're just a little ill. There's nothing to be afraid

of. Some medicine, a few poultices, and in a few days you'll be playing in the sunshine with Lucy.''

''I'm so sorry, Mama.'' Ella sobbed into her pillow.

''There's nothing to be sorry about. Don't be sad. Think of only good things, baby. Like Sugar waiting in the pasture for you to ride her.''

Ella didn't answer, and Sarah rubbed her back in small comforting circles. Wished she could take away her child's pain.

Muffled clangs and thuds sounded from the kitchen downstairs. Sarah knew she ought to go down and help the doctor. He was probably heating water for the powdered medicine he would bring for Ella. But she hated to leave. Lucy tiptoed into the room and climbed onto the far side of the bed.

''It's gonna be okay, Ella.'' Lucy traced the stitching on the comforter with her forefinger. ''My pa doesn't let little girls stay sick. He always makes sure I get better.''

Ella sighed, as if too sad to say one more word.

The day passed in a blur and became night before Sarah had a chance to sit down. The doctor had stayed most of the afternoon as Ella's condition worsened, fearing pneumonia could set in.

It was after midnight as Sarah wrung cool well water from a cloth, folded it in thirds and draped it over Ella's brow.

The door hinges creaked. There was Gage, his brow furrowed, holding two blue enamel cups. ''Thought you might join me for some tea. With fresh honey from Mr. Lukens's hive.''

''Was that his donkey I heard braying outside this afternoon?''

"Yep. He had me look over the shoe repair I did on his animal." Gage kept his voice low as he crossed the room and settled next to her on the window seat. "Heard about Ella and came to offer his personal remedy."

"I'm afraid to ask."

"Two shots of whiskey, followed by honey and tea." Gage handed her the steaming cup. "He said it was a surefire cure."

"Yes, but for what?" Sarah breathed in the steam. The earthy, sweet scent was pure comfort. "I have a favor to ask you."

"Name it."

"I knew you were going to say that," she joked because this wasn't going to be easy. "You need to find someone else to take care of Lucy and cook for you. Ella needs me. I can't work as long as she's ill."

"I don't expect you to."

"The cooking needs to be done."

"I'll manage." He held her so tight. "Don't you see? You are welcome here. You and your daughter can stay right here forever. I'd like that just fine."

Her throat knotted, and she couldn't speak.

"You're not alone, Sarah. Not as long as you have me."

"What luck." She kissed him, savored the velvet heat of his lips and the caress of his tongue to hers. Desire rose as fast as a flash flood, snapping through her nerves, sweeping away all thought.

In the quiet between them, she felt his love in a hundred different ways, from the brush of his kiss on the crown of her head to the weight of his hand on the curve of her hip. With every breath he took. With every beat of his heart against her ear.

Gage stayed with her as the hours ticked by. He brought cool water to bath Ella's face. Mixed the putrid-smelling poultice the doctor had sworn would help her lungs, and steeped a new pot of tea. They worked side by side, in perfect synchrony, until the first light of dawn.

Gage could see how hard it was for Sarah. See with his own eyes the nights she went without more than snatches of sleep. There were bed linens to wash daily so there would be fresh sheets for little Ella to lie on, broths to make and poultices to prepare. By the end of the week, Sarah looked as thin and pale as her child.

He was lucky to hire a girl from town—one of Mr. Lukens's granddaughters—to cook twice a day for the men and to help Sarah where she could.

There was Sarah's room rent due, and the doctor's bill to be paid. He handled it quietly, paying ahead on the room. When he heard the amount she owed the doc, he had to see the written accounts to believe it. The doctor was a fair fellow, but Gage hadn't realized how hard things had been for Sarah.

He'd brought the ring out twice before from behind the loose brick in the fireplace. Twice he'd considered this band of gold and twice he'd returned it to the hiding place behind the corner brick. He held it, studied it. Debated what to do.

Marriage was serious business, but it was a decision he'd made when he had made love to Sarah. From that moment she'd become his responsibility and now was the time she needed more from him than a job or a lover's touch.

Ella was out of danger, and he'd waited long enough.

He heard her bare feet whisper on the stairs and the hush of her skirts around her ankles. The hair on the back of his neck stood on end as she came close, his body sensing her presence. That was all it took. He was rock-hard and ready and wanting her.

Yep, he was definitely going to have to propose.

"What are you doing alone in an empty room?" She hunkered down beside him on the hearth bricks. "Before Ella came down sick, I was going to ask Lucy to pick out the sofa."

"Do you think that's wise? Her favorite color is purple and she has a fondness for fringe."

"I happen to like purple. And fringe. That would certainly liven up this room."

That's what Sarah had done—bring life to his world. He thought of the ring he held in his fist. "How's Ella?"

"She ate the broth on her own, and she's sleeping peacefully."

"The doctor was pleased when he left today. Said she'd turned a corner."

"Thankfully." Sarah rubbed her face with her hands.

"Then that means we can be together."

"You want me, huh?" She nestled against him, finding just the right place beneath his chin. "I suppose you came home from your trip thinking to climb right into bed with me."

"I have to confess it's true. I'm a man longed denied his needs. Not that I'm complaining. Your girl comes first. But I've been a mighty patient man, considering what you so freely offered."

"Hmm. That makes me sound like a certain kind of woman."

"And me a fortunate man." He wanted her. He squeezed his eyes shut, holding her tight, fighting control. What a good wife she would make. Loyal and hardworking and sensible. She was a devoted mother, a good friend and a passionate lover.

"Ella *is* better." Sarah glanced at the front door, open to let in the warm night air, considering. "Maybe I could—"

Something flashed in Gage's hand, a brilliant sparkle of pure light. A ring lay in his palm, a row of diamonds nestled in a gold band. An expensive ring.

A wedding ring.

She blinked, not trusting her eyes. No, it was still there, shimmering like stars in the night.

"I bought this in Helena when I was delivering the horses. I'd already made my decision then. Do you like the ring?"

She nodded, daring to touch the diamonds that winked and twinkled against his skin. Warm from his touch.

He took her left hand in his. "I wanted to do this right. Figured maybe I ought to ask you in the moonlight and figure out the pretty words you want to hear. But the plain truth is that I want to marry you. Please, be my wife."

Smooth gold slid onto her ring finger, over her knuckle and into place.

A perfect fit.

"There are five diamonds. One for each of us and

our two girls, and one to represent the promise of more.''

"Oh, Gage. I can't believe—'' But it *was* true, the diamonds and promises still glittered in the ordinary lamplight. ''I want to be your wife. More than anything.''

He kissed her tenderly. Slow and deep. It was more than a kiss. More than a promise. They were going to be married.

"Does Lucy know?''

"Figured I'd wait until you said the magic word. And since you have.'' His eyes glittered with meaning.

Desire flickered low in her stomach. ''You have a celebration in mind, do you?''

"Sure. Figure a kiss is too small. We ought to make a grand gesture. Something climactic.''

She buried her face in the crook of his shoulder, refusing to laugh. She really shouldn't reinforce such behavior. ''You're a bad man.''

"Sure, but I don't hear you complaining.'' His chuckle rumbled through her like her own. ''Lucy's tucked in her bed, and Ella's fast asleep. She might not need you for a little while.''

"I want to be close, just in case.''

He kissed her again, taking his time, a promise of the passion to come. ''Go check on her first.''

She loved his kisses, but she loved his thoughtfulness more. Lifting her skirts, she took the steps two at a time, bare feet padding against the warm boards. Sure enough, Ella was asleep, her forehead cool and her breathing relaxed and clear. Not a cough or rattle to be heard.

The ring on her hand felt strange and new, and Sarah studied it and considered all Gage was pledging to be. The love he felt for her.

He caught her the moment she stepped through the door. Made sure the door clicked shut before he guided her into one of the empty bedrooms in the long hallway. Where he'd been sleeping through Ella's illness.

"You'll be close by if she needs you later," he whispered as he shut them in with a low lamp burning and the top sheet turned down on the straw tick he'd been using. "Right now, I want you naked and moaning beneath me."

"Moaning, huh? That's going to take some work on your part."

"Yes, and I'm up to the task."

"I'm not even going to comment on that—" His kiss cut off her words and drank in her laughter as he guided her to the mattress in the corner.

Where he entered her in one slow thrust and loved her until the stars faded from the sky, until dawn peeked into the room, and still he loved her.

Sarah dropped a freshly laundered nightgown over Ella's head. It was hard to concentrate when she was brimming with joy. The morning was lovely. The room was already warm, filled with bright sunshine.

"Ma, I'm tired of staying in bed." Ella coughed into her hand, her shoulders shaking hard.

"Here, baby." Sarah handed her the cooling cup of lovage tea and held it steady while she sipped. Ella's thin shoulders stopped shaking and her coughing faded.

"It hurt, Ma."

"I know. Finish the cup. The tea will help."

"It tastes bad." An ill-tempered frown creased her brow.

Being cranky was a good sign. "I'll see if I can't round up a piece of peppermint to take the bad taste away. Finish the cup, and I'll let you sit on the window seat for a while."

Ella perked up. "And you'll read to me?"

"Absolutely." Sarah reached for the hairbrush and the sun caught the diamonds on her left hand.

"Ma!" Ella grabbed the ring. Her eyes grew round. "Married ladies have those. Like the rich ladies in town."

"I know." She couldn't help it. She liked the ring, but more than that, the man who had given it to her. "I'm going to marry Gage. What do you think about that?"

"I'd get to live here forever and ever in Lucy's room? And ride horses and have a kitten?"

The hinges on the door whispered open. "Sarah!" Lucy screamed, streaking through the room and jumping onto the bed. "Pa didn't tell me. He didn't tell me! Do you know what?"

"What?" Sarah braced herself as Lucy launched into midair and wrapped her arms around Sarah's neck.

"I knew it! I knew Pa ought to love you. Because when we first came here, and all them ladies brought him cakes and fawned all over him, he liked your cherry pie the best. The very, very best.''

''What's all this noise? Don't you know I'm trying to cook downstairs?'' Gage eased into the room, a spatula in hand. ''Sounds like there's a party in here.''

''Pa! I knew it! I did, I did, I did!'' Lucy raced into his arms, hugging him fiercely.

''I'm glad you approve, darlin'.'' He swung Lucy up into the air and back down. ''I've got breakfast almost done. Ella, do you want me to carry you down to the table?''

''Yes, please. I can sit up real good now.''

''You sure can.'' Gage shot Sarah a hot, meaningful gaze. He hadn't forgotten about last night. Nor had she.

She felt thoroughly loved and deliciously sated as he wrapped her into his arms for a noisy smooch that had the girls giggling.

This was how it was going to be, a house full of sunlight and laughter and love. Especially love.

''Now that Ella's recovering, I can't stay here night after night.'' Content and deliciously sated, Sarah snuggled against Gage's side.

''I don't see why not. I'm glad you're here.'' His thumb grazed one swollen nipple, sending delicious shivers of pleasure through her. ''*Real* glad.''

''I noticed.'' His tongue replaced his thumb, dampening her flesh. She arched her back, and he took her into his mouth. ''You're forgetting something important.''

''I'll get there, angel.'' He winked.

"I'm talking about a wedding." She sighed when he blew on her damp nipple. "We're not married yet."

"We can remedy that situation easy enough. We ask the minister to marry us. Tomorrow, maybe."

"Tomorrow?"

"The next day, then."

She raked her fingernails gently down the center of his chest. "What's your hurry, cowboy?"

"I think you already know." He was hard against the curve of her stomach, proof that he was ready for her again. "I want you, Sarah. *Now.*"

His hands on her hips guided her over him, and she sheathed his thick shaft with one slow slide. "You're a demanding man, Gage. I'm not sure I should give in to your desires."

"Too late."

Such exquisite sensation. Sarah closed her eyes, savoring the heavy thrum of him inside her. This was something she could never get enough of, holding him so intimately, feeling the love for him well up from deep in her heart. She cried out at the tight, sharp pleasure coiling within her, where their bodies joined.

She wanted it slow, but he surged upward, driving into her, setting a fast rhythm that tore away her control. The tension gathering inside her unraveled. Wave after wave of searing pleasure, hot and deep and sharp, rolled through her. Leaving her so weak she sank onto his chest and surrendered.

She held him as he came, shuddering hard and thrusting deep, holding himself to the hilt as he pulsed within her. She kissed him as he sighed, as his arms enfolded her. His lips claimed hers in a slow, gentle caress.

This man was hers. Emotion overwhelmed her as he rolled her onto her side, kissing her with more tenderness than she'd ever known.

He was her life, her future and every dream come true. "I love you, Gage," she whispered.

His arms stiffened. His kiss ended. "I care for you, too, Sarah." His lips grazed her cheekbone and he snuggled against her, tucking her against his hips.

His lips nibbled and kissed the nape of her neck. His hands stroked her breasts and stomach and thighs. But he said nothing more.

No words of love. No whispered declarations of great affection. Not even a good-night as he drifted off.

She counted the hours, too troubled to sleep.

Chapter Fourteen

Sarah opened her eyes and knew she was alone in Gage's bed. Dawn was changing the dark to shadows, so she didn't bother with a lamp as she found her clothes by feel. She wanted to catch him alone before he headed out to the stables.

Just her luck. He was already gone. The fire snapped in the cookstove, the oven door propped open to feed the new flames licking at the dry kindling. That could only mean—

The back door swung open. The hired girl rushed into the kitchen carrying two pails full of milk. "Beautiful morning, isn't it, Mrs. Redding? Let me feed the fire before I start the salt pork."

Maybe she could catch Gage alone in the stable. It was worth a try. Sarah shouldered through the door and out into the yard. Morning came in a hush of peaches and golds as she made her way through the tall, seed-heavy grasses and the wild roses twined on the rail fencing.

There was Gage, not in the stable at all, but out in the pasture with one of the hired men, inspecting a sorrel mare's rear hoof. She wouldn't likely be able to get him alone now, not between his work and the girls. Troubled, Sarah watched him a minute, before she turned around and hurried back to the house.

Last night she'd told him that she loved him. And he hadn't been able to say the same.

He did love her. This much she knew. So why were the words so important?

She helped Ella wash and dress and plaited her blond hair into two braids. Lucy bounded in, wanting her hair braided, too. While she worked, Sarah listened to Lucy's ideas for the wedding. Ella chipped in a few of her own.

All the morning through, she couldn't set aside the doubt she felt. *I care for you,* he'd said. Care.

Not love.

There was an enormous difference between the two. She'd made the mistake of marrying a man she'd cared for, thinking that was love. And it had been a hard road to haul to make a good marriage from that. She wouldn't do it again.

"Can I go out and play, Ma? *Please?*"

"Not today. You're still coughing, baby."

"But it's hot out, Sarah." Lucy turned on the charm. "What if she don't run? Or, I know, what if she stays out of the creek? Or we could sit quietly on our horses and keep 'em to a walk. That wouldn't hurt none."

"Tomorrow, if today goes well." Sarah spoke above the chorus of disappointed "Aws" and searched through Gage's top bureau drawer for her buttonhook. "Lucy's right. Today is already hot. I don't see why we can't sit outside in the shade and do something quiet."

A round of "Yippees" rang in the happy room.

Sarah dug Ella's shoes out of the closet, joy filling her up until there was no room to breathe. The girls were giggling on the bed, Ella was pale but stronger, and the ring on her finger sparkled.

Sarah stopped at the window and leaned her forehead against the glass. There he was, astride a gray Arabian, lasso in hand, Stetson shading his face as he rode flank, moving a herd of horses to another pasture. Half a dozen cowboys rode with him, following his lead. He sat tall and straight, always patient when a spirited colt broke free.

She melted, watching him. She thought of all he'd done for her. He was steadfast and unfailing, tender and true. Love was not only a feeling, but an action, too. With everything he did, Gage showed her beyond words what his feelings were.

So she ought to stop borrowing trouble. Gage loved her. He might not say the words, but he felt them, right?

Still her doubts remained.

After a long day in the hot summer sun, seeing Sarah was more refreshing than if he'd jumped in the well. Gage ambled to a stop midfield and let the sight wash over him.

She was sitting on a quilt in the shade of the house, in that yellow dress he liked so well. Her hair was pulled back in a loose braid at her nape, and escaped curls framed her face and tumbled over her shoulder to touch her breasts. The girls sat on either side of her, heads bent over needle and thread.

As if she could sense him, she looked up from her sewing. The smile that lit her up tugged at the hard closed places inside him.

"Pa!" Lucy hopped up, waving a blue piece of fabric for him to see. "Look. Sarah's teaching me to make a dress. A real dress."

"That's nice, darlin'." He loved seeing his girl so happy. Right there, that told him everything he needed to know. Marrying Sarah was the best decision. "That's an awfully small dress. How is it going to fit you?"

That made her laugh, as he knew it would. "It's for my *doll*. Sarah's making her right now!"

"I'm making a dress, too." Ella added quietly. "Ma's making us matching dolls so they can be like sisters."

"That sounds like a great idea." Gage hunkered down on the front step and knuckled back his hat. "Hate to interrupt such beautiful girls while they're sewing, but I just got back from town. After stopping by the saddle shop, I looked up the minister. Seems he's got time to perform a wedding tomorrow afternoon."

Over the girl's excited squeals, Sarah tucked her needle into the seam she was working on and set her work aside. "It seems sudden."

His pride took a small hit seeing that she was acting uncertain. "If you want to wait, we will. It's just sensible, that's all. We've got the girls to consider, and with you living in the house and all."

She blushed, knowing exactly what he meant. He couldn't tell her in front of the girls that having her in his bed, so warm and willing and incredible, was what he wanted. And he didn't want to feel guilty about it. Didn't want to worry that folks might start to talk about Sarah in a bad light.

He wanted to marry her. He knew he'd be happy

with her. Look at them right now. The girls content, the afternoon pleasant, and even when it came to a disagreement, he and Sarah were talking rationally. There was no arguing, no fury, no heartache, no accusations as had been the case in his first marriage.

It wasn't going to be like that with Sarah. She would never know how grateful he was, to find a woman who fit into his life, like a piece missing suddenly found and it made him whole.

She tucked her lip between her teeth, the curls framing her face ruffling in the wind. He itched to touch her, so he did, cupping her jaw in the breadth of his palm. She came against him like poetry. Made him feel a beauty he didn't believe in.

"No, you're right." She sounded shaky, and there were shadows in her eyes that hadn't been there before. "There's no sense to waiting. I love you. You love me. And we have the girls to consider. Look how happy they are."

"We want cake for the wedding," Lucy informed them, swirling around in circles, catching Ella by the hand and tugging her 'round and 'round, too. "A big chocolate cake with flowers on the frosting. Like at the hotel."

Gage tried to figure out what Lucy was saying. Her mouth was moving, but suddenly the world was spinning. The ground moving.

Sarah snuggled against him, smiling at the girls.

She thought he loved her. She thought…

Wait. He knew exactly what she thought. She believed she'd found her happily-ever-after.

The problem was that life wasn't a fairy tale. Sarah ought to know that, too.

His guts knotted, always the sign of trouble. Had he made a terrible mistake?

Sarah's ring sparkled as she splayed her hand on his chest, stealing a kiss from him. "I have supper almost ready. Did you get a chance to buy more popcorn?"

"Sure, but will I share?"

"Popcorn!" Lucy and Ella shouted in unison and stopped twirling. "We want it, Pa! Yeah, we want it."

"One place it isn't, is in the wagon."

The girls were off, running at full steam to be the first to find the special treat. Lucy was happy. He was happy.

"I bet I can make you share some of your popcorn with me." Sarah winked at him, blushing a little, before she disappeared into the kitchen, leaving the screen door to bang shut behind her.

This is what it could be like forever. With Sarah's smile to renew him at the end of a hard day. With Sarah's supper waiting on the pretty cloth-covered table. With Sarah to pull close and hold through the night.

This is what he wanted. This happiness he'd never thought was possible. A marriage between them was going to work. He could feel it deep in his bones.

And if it troubled him what Sarah said, he decided to ignore it. Love was a word for something that didn't exist. If she wanted to use it for this incredible feeling of happiness, then that was fine by him.

By this time tomorrow, she would be his wife. His wife to make love to, to hold and to cherish. As for the wedding night. His blood kicked at the thought of what he intended to do to Sarah once he got her alone in his bed.

Yep, he was going to like being married just fine.

* * *

It happened again. It was all Sarah could think about as she felt Gage relax in the bed beside her. She'd told him she loved him and this time he hadn't said anything at all. Except, "Good night."

He'd been a thoughtful lover. Every touch tender and passionate. He'd told her that she was the one he wanted. And his ardent lovemaking had left her in no doubt of that. He'd possessed her completely.

Good night, he'd said.

His hand was heavy on her bare hip and she carefully lifted his wrist so she could scoot out of bed. He didn't stir, breathing heavy and deep, the sheet twisted around his knees. The moonlight spilled through the window, worshiping every inch of him, leaving no doubt. He was a desirable man, and love rose in her heart like an ocean's tide, so powerful nothing could stop it.

She grabbed his cast-off shirt and shrugged into it, breathing in his pleasant man and wind scent. Desire twisted low in her stomach as she curled on the window seat and gazed out at the night. Calm and peaceful, with the moon only a thin sickle hanging low in the sky.

"Hey. Thinking of me?" The bed ropes groaned as he shifted. "You ought to be deep in a satisfied sleep. Since you're not, that can only mean my work isn't done."

"I guess not." A satisfied sound escaped her throat as he settled behind her on the seat and pulled her against him. His arms enfolded her until she was snug.

"I hope you admire how hard I'm willing to work to satisfy you." He nibbled her earlobe. "And how big my work ethic is."

"Stop it." She swatted him playfully on the shoulder. "You are not going to get any more pleasure if you keep that up."

"That's not a problem." As if to prove it, he placed her hand on his aroused shaft.

"That's it. I'm not going to marry you."

"We'll see about that. Come back to bed with me and I'll change your mind." He moaned as her fingers tightened around him. "Forget the bed."

He guided her over him. The swollen head of his shaft nudged against her, stretching her, and every worry tumbled away, leaving only desire. Only the feel of him pushing inside her, inch by slow inch. She took all of him, loving the feel of his thickness, his length, nestled deep. Pleasure twisted like a fire-hot blade as she rocked against him. Intense as it was, it paled against the emotion building in her heart.

He suckled one breast and the other as she set a slow pace. This feeling, it swelled each time they came together. A feeling so raw and aching and vulnerable she fought it. Tried to keep from surrendering her entire heart to this man who couldn't say that he loved her.

He came first, thrusting hard, muscles rippling, tendons straining. She could feel the pulse of him, like a life force that moved through her, too, pulling her into a slow, powerful release that left her spent and crying against his chest.

"Angel." He stroked her hair, kissing her face, his touch so cherished. "This window seat is nice, but let's get you back in bed."

That wasn't what she wanted him to say. Was she the only one feeling this way? "I have to ask you something."

"Anything you want." He growled against her throat. "As long as I'm on top this time."

"No, Gage." She sat up, moving off him, moving away. "You think we should get married tomorrow, but—"

"Tomorrow, two o'clock." He brushed tangles from her face, not understanding, still thinking she wanted to talk about the wedding before he hauled her back to bed and made love to her.

She closed her eyes, afraid of saying what was on her mind. Afraid of saying nothing at all.

"I told Mrs. Flannery I'd be by tomorrow or the next day to pick up your things. She was pleased I was making an honest woman of you." He kissed her wholly, with lips and teeth and tongue, a hungry possession that told her he wanted her all over again.

"Mrs. Flannery knows we're getting married?"

"Sure. Probably the whole town by now."

She closed her eyes. Everything was spinning away from her and she felt as if she couldn't stop it. Couldn't make it right.

"Tomorrow night you'll be mine." His hand wound through her hair, the weight of his palm cupping her nape as he nudged her toward his jutting shaft. He bumped his knee against hers, pressing apart her thighs. "I want you, Sarah. For the rest of my life, I want to have only you."

Have, not love. Pain clawed through her and she pushed away, standing on her own two feet. "Do you love me?"

"If that's what you want to call this between us, that's all right with me." He wrapped his arms around her waist from behind, his whiskered chin rough on the curve of her shoulder. "You are the best thing that has ever happened to me, Sarah. Come back to bed. Please.''

His plea shivered across the shell of her ear, sending arrows of desire down her spine and through every inch of her body. ''What do you mean? If this isn't love, what would *you* call it?''

He tugged her backward toward the mattress. ''Come on, angel, I'll show you want I mean.''

''I want you to say it.'' Her heart was breaking and he didn't notice. ''I need you to tell me how you feel about me. I need to know if you love me.''

''Oh, Sarah.'' He sat heavily on the edge of the bed. Planted his hands on his knees. Bowed his head.

A horrible chill lanced through her. The silence between them grew until it was so enormous she couldn't speak. The few feet separating them felt as wide as the plains. She eased onto the window seat and crossed her arms over her breasts.

''I won't lie to you. I'm not going to have that kind of marriage. Where I say one thing to keep you from getting angry with me, but it's a lie. Over time a little lie here and there gets to be a habit, and it's not right. I want honesty between us.''

''Me, too.'' Her own voice sounded so far away. She brushed her thumb over the ring on her hand. ''Do you love me at all?''

''I don't believe in love. You knew that from the start.''

''But I thought—'' *That I was special.* She couldn't say the words.

''Oh.'' He seemed to hear them, anyway. There was a rustle of sheets as he moved off the bed and knelt in front of her. Took her hands in his. ''Isn't what we have enough?''

She couldn't nod. Couldn't agree.

"We get along so well, you and me. Isn't that right?" He waited. "Damn it, I thought you were more practical than this."

He hated being frustrated. He hated that she was looking as lost as he felt. "Sarah, I'll say the words if you want me to."

"I want you to mean it." She withdrew her hands from his. "I need you to love me, Gage. Or what's the point?"

A blade through the chest wouldn't hurt this bad. Why was she doing this to him? "There is no point, Sarah. There's just you and me and what we can have together."

"But what is that? I have to know."

"I don't know what it is. Compatibility, maybe."

"Compatibility?" She didn't look any more pleased with that.

Hell, he was doing this all wrong. "Sarah, I care for you. We have a good relationship, don't we?"

She nodded, her hair tumbling forward to hide her face.

"We get along. We don't hurt one another, don't argue, don't blame, right?" He waited for her to nod again. "There's no unhappiness, no heartache, no disappointments. It's just you and me, getting along, raising our girls and making a life together. Right?"

She nodded again. Perfectly reasonable, after all.

"What I have with you is real. It's not a fairy tale of impossible love that doesn't last anyway. You've got to know there are no shining knights, no rescued damsels or no happily-ever-afters. Life is what you make it, nothing more, nothing less. And, Sarah, I want to live my life with you. It's not a fairy tale, but it *is* real. I'm a man you can count on forever.''

She hooked a shank of thick locks behind her ear, exposing her face. Not smiling, not sad, not anything. He didn't know if she'd heard him or not. Heard what he was offering her—everything he was, everything he had, everything he would be.

She came into his arms like dawn to the mountains, gentle and quiet and perfect. Relief slipped through him like a morning breeze. Losing Sarah was the one thing he didn't think he could handle.

He kissed her tenderly, so she would feel how important she was to him. Gently, the way he intended to kiss her for the rest of his days.

Sarah watched her wedding day dawn in a slow procession of black to silver-gray before a gentle rosy-peach light glowed on the windowpanes. Gage stirred, stretched, and cuddled up behind her.

"Good morning, beautiful."

He looked so handsome with his sleep-tousled hair and day's growth raspy on his jaw. She wanted to hold him forever. To forget last night's conversation. To do anything to have the right to call this man her husband.

But would it be enough?

Ella's cough shattered the stillness and gave her reason to pull back the covers, snatch her nightgown from the bedpost, shiver into it and hurry across the hall.

"'Morning, Sarah," Lucy whispered from the top bunk. "Do you know what? You're gonna be my ma today."

"Oh, Lucy." She didn't know what to say as she reached for the pitcher on the bed table and eased onto the bottom mattress.

Ella was sitting up, drinking as much water as fast as she could. "I'm all right—" Her shoulders shook with the effort not to cough. "I'm not sick anymore. Not at all. Honest."

"I see that." Sarah refilled the glass and held it steady while Ella drank it down. "Sounds like I should make you some tea. Lucy, you make sure Ella stays here."

"But, Ma, I'm not sick. Really. See?" The coughing stopped, and Ella didn't feel too warm to the touch. "Are we really going to live here for keeps?"

There's just you and me and what we can have together. That's what Gage had told her with true sincerity. *I want to live my life with you.*

He'd stood to offer her his faithfulness, his companionship, his future and his prosperity. There would be passion in his bed whenever she wanted it, a good life without want for her daughter, and the promise of more children. Her babies, hers and Gage's.

He was offering her so much. Everything that would make her life comfortable and happy.

Everything but his heart.

"You two get dressed. And, Ella, come straight downstairs to take your medicine." Sarah grabbed the hairbrush and ribbons on the way to the door. "No dallying."

Lucy hopped to the floor with a two-footed thud, and as Sarah closed the door she saw the girls jumping up and down together.

"We get to be sisters today." Ella's joy spilled into the hallways, following Sarah where she stood on the landing. "Real sisters. Not just best friends."

"Forever and ever."

Weak-kneed, Sarah eased onto the top step. The

ring on her hand felt heavy and she stared at it, all the uncertainty rushing up into her throat. She couldn't breathe, couldn't think. Could only see the flash of the diamonds in the peaceful morning light.

She could do this. Gage loved her. She felt it last night in his touch. She experienced it every waking moment of every day. The thousand things he did for her, to make her life better, big and small, said the words he could not.

That was love, wasn't it? A love that would strengthen and deepen through time? A love that would bring happiness to them all?

Sarah's feet touched the boardwalk, noticing how Gage held her several moments longer than necessary to help her from the buggy.

"I'll see you at the church in an hour." His lips brushed her cheek in a secret kiss, hidden by the brim of his Stetson and her bonnet. "I can't wait to make you my wife, Sarah."

Anyone could see how much he cared for her. His steady hand guided her to the front door and opened it for her. His respect, his friendship, his affection were unmistakable and yet...

It's enough, she told herself as Ella and Lucy came running, hand in hand, their happiness contagious. Hiding a cough in her free hand, Ella told Lucy good-bye and the girls waved as Gage tugged Lucy back to the buggy.

"I'll see you soon," he promised.

Not, I love you, Sarah.

It troubled her as she led Ella upstairs and unlocked their door. The room was as she'd left it, the bed neatly made and the curtains pulled back to let in cheerful light.

"I wanna wear my new pink dress, please, Ma?" Ella coughed. "And my new shoes."

New dresses, new shoes, everything Ella could ask for. See what a good match this was? "Your new calico would be perfect. And we don't want to forget the new ribbons."

Sarah helped Ella into her dress and found the buttonhook so they could put on the shiny shoes. With matching pink ribbons tied at the end of her braids, Ella looked adorable. No, perfect.

"We need to get you some hot water so I can steep the herbs—"

"Sarah? Are you in there?" Mary Flannery was on the other side of the door, teapot in hand. "I thought that was you coughing, little Ella. I heard you got yourself mighty sick."

"But not for long. We didn't have to move in with Aunt Pearl." Ella swirled. "Look at my new dress."

"Just right for a wedding. Now, here's a pot of tea that will help with that cough of yours. Why, Sarah, look at you. You're not ready yet."

"First things first." She found a cup for the tea. "I have plenty of time."

"Less than an hour, dear, and your dress isn't laid out yet." Mrs. Flannery tsked as she marched into the room and pulled open the wardrobe door. "Goodness, I don't see a thing fitting for a wedding. And to one of the richest men around."

"I didn't have time to make anything."

"There's a dress shop right across the way. Oh, this is a disaster. Simply unacceptable. You can't get married to Gage Gatlin in a calico work dress."

"And why not?" Her yellow calico was nearly new, well, she'd hardly worn it, for it had spent most of its life tucked away in the trunk. "It's perfectly fine."

"Fine? I'm afraid that won't do at all." Mary shook her head, studying Sarah from head to toe. "A calico work dress. Why, I've never heard the like. A man like Gage Gatlin won't be wanting that, I assure you. No, you need a dress to represent this momentous event. This love the two of you have found."

Mary's words were like nails into the most vulnerable places of her heart, and Sarah couldn't find breath enough to protest. To tell the truth.

There was no momentous event. No love to celebrate between her and Gage.

A calico work dress—a *sensible, practical* dress—would do just fine.

"Here, Ella." Sarah pulled out a chair and placed the steaming up on the small corner table. "Come drink this up."

Mary headed for the door. "You wait right here. Goodness, a *work* dress. Wait until I tell Millie."

Sarah felt the glimmerings of embarrassment, but not because she didn't have a nice dress. It was because she hadn't thought of it.

He was getting married. Gage didn't think it would be happening to him twice in his lifetime, but he didn't feel a bit of panic as he shrugged into his black jacket. He knew this was the right decision. For himself, his daughter, and for Sarah.

"Do you know what, Pa?" Lucy burst through the door in her best dress with the lace that Sarah had helped her choose. "It's almost time. We gotta go to the church. Sarah's gonna be my mother!"

"She sure is." Gage checked his tie in the mirror, figured it was good enough, and plucked his hat from the bedpost.

"Hurry, Pa! You're too slow." Lucy leaped in place, lace and ribbon fluttering. "Hurry, hurry, hurry!"

"What's the rush?" he teased, tugging on one of her braids. "Sarah will wait for us if we're late."

"Pa!" Lucy was clearly tortured as she grabbed him by the hand and yanked him into the hall.

This was it. His last half hour of freedom. Gage didn't mind so much as he tugged on his boots in the kitchen.

"Hey, Pa." Lucy ran to the door. "The sheriff's here."

What was it this time? More trouble with the neighbor? "Howdy, Sheriff."

"Gage." The lawman touched his hat brim. "Just been out to the Owens place. Evicted him on behalf of the bank. His land was repossessed."

"Sorry to hear that. I hate to think I had a hand in that."

"You did offer to help, but he refused. Wasn't much more you could do, anyway. His money problems have been going on for a while, the way it looks now. I just got back from riding him to the county line. Told him I wanted him to keep going, but it doesn't mean he will. He could come back here and cause trouble. He's stolen your livestock before. Who's to say he hasn't been doing that for years?"

"Think he's a danger?"

"I think he's a concern, no more. I'd keep my eye out, if I were you. He might not stick around, or he might make good on his threats. I can have one of my deputies out here if you want protection.''

''I have enough hired men, thanks. You think he's a real threat?''

''It's a possibility. I'd keep watch over my herds if I were you.''

''Fine.'' It looked like his biggest problems with Milt were over. He'd inform Juan, keep a lookout at night for thieves, and with any luck, Milt would hit the road and keep on going *without* any of Gage's horses.

The sheriff nosed his horse toward town. ''Good luck with your wedding.''

''Thanks.'' Luck? He didn't need luck. He knew deep down that this marriage would be different. Better. With no romance getting in the way of things. A good marriage wasn't based on love. But on something better. Duty. Respect. Friendship.

''Pa!'' Lucy pulled him across the yard. ''We've got to hurry!''

''We sure do, darlin', because I can't wait, either.''

Yep, it was going to be different this time. He was going to be happy with Sarah as his wife. Without a doubt. He knew it down deep.

Chapter Fifteen

"Are you certain you want to walk to the church alone?" Mary turned around in the hall. "I'd be happy to wait for you. Ella won't mind, would you, dear?"

Ella shook her head, looking like a princess in her pretty new things. So happy, she sparkled.

"I need to fix my hair and I'll be right along." It would be so easy, to tie up her hair, grab the pretty blue pin Mary had lent her and tuck the antique scrap of lace at her throat, borrowed from the seamstress, and walk straight to the church. "You two go on ahead."

"It's a big day, and a bride always needs time to dream a little." As if she understood, Mary took Ella's hand and closed the door.

Leaving Sarah alone. But not to dream.

I can do this. She took a breath and unclasped Mary's beautiful pin. A golden lacework butterfly that matched her dress perfectly. The satin gown that draped her figure like a wish come true.

She hardly recognized herself in the mirror as she reached for the comb. It wasn't the expensive dress, proper for the wife of Gage Gatlin, but the woman who stared back at her. A convenient bride.

A woman who'd vowed to marry only for love.

I can't do this. She couldn't stand in front of witnesses before God and vow to love a man who could not love her. Who'd kept his heart tucked away. As generous as he was, Gage could not give her the one thing she wanted.

How could it be good for Ella? She would never see what a loving marriage should be. Neither would the other children who might come along. How would they feel loved if there was no true love between their parents?

If the vows spoken at the altar were lies.

She could love Gage with all her heart, to try to make up for the words he could not say and the emotions he could not feel. Would it be enough? Would his affections for her strengthen and grow deeper over time?

How could she know? It was too late to change her mind, too late to cancel a wedding half the town knew about by now. No, she had to do this. It was for the best. Even if she did not have Gage's heart, she had him. In her life, in her future, in her bed.

It was enough. It had to be.

Tears burned behind her eyes as she wound her long hair in a loose ponytail and separated a hairpin between her teeth. There, in the beveled bureau mirror she saw a woman with tears streaming down her face. With heartbreak in her eyes.

It was five minutes to two, according to the small clock on the mantel. Five minutes to finish her hair and make her way to the church. Where Gage would be waiting to marry her, a woman in a silk gown, with flowers in her hair.

Sarah brushed the soft pink petals of the wild roses she'd picked for today. Could not pick them up and place them in her hair.

Four minutes to two. Three minutes to two.

Gage would be waiting at the church in his black suit, the one that made his shoulders so wide, his chest so strong. Like a legend of old in his proud Stetson and scuffed riding boots.

He would be waiting for her, ready to take her for his wife. To give her passion and children and one of the finest houses in the county. He would laugh with her and hold her and trust her with his life. But he would never give her his heart. He didn't think he had to. Not now. Not ever.

The clock chimed the hour. Two o'clock.

No man was going to love her, after all. Especially not one as fine as Gage Gatlin. Who would look at her in her beautiful wedding dress and not find enough inspiration to love her.

She crumpled to the floor in her silken gown and felt her heart break into a thousand pieces.

Where was she? Gage rubbed the back of his neck. It was damn hot in this suit in the middle of the afternoon. He felt what had to be fifty pairs of eyes watching him from the pews. Folks who had invited themselves out of curiosity. Their whispers buzzed in the back of the church, speculating on what was delaying the bride.

No wedding dress, someone had murmured, then their words fell away and he couldn't hear what was said.

Hell, he didn't care what she wore. She had a few real pretty dresses. Any one of them would be fine. He only wanted to make her his wife. That was all. She looked beautiful in anything she wore.

"Gage." Mary Flannery tapped him on the shoulder and pulled him away from the front row of curious onlookers. "I spoke to Sarah, Gage."

"She's just late, is all. I understand that. I didn't give her much time, and with Ella's illness…" He shrugged. "I'm not angry she's late. I'd wait forever to marry her."

"Oh, Gage." Sadly, Mary shook her head and spoke with quiet sympathy. "Sarah isn't late. She isn't coming. She doesn't want to marry you."

"That can't be right." What was Mary trying to pull? "I get it. This is a joke, right? Playing a game with the poor nervous groom. All right, fine. Tell Sarah it worked, so she can walk down that aisle and become my wife."

"This is no joke, Gage. Sarah really isn't coming. She's in her room at the boarding house and she refuses to leave. She asked me to keep little Ella for a few hours." Mary patted his arm. "I'm so sorry. You two are made for each other. Anyone with eyes can see it."

Sarah wasn't coming? She ought to be right there, coming down the aisle with his ring on her hand. What was wrong? Why didn't she want to be here?

"I don't understand." He wiped his hands over his face, suddenly angry. Blood rising, he could hear the gossip sweep through the church like a wildfire. *She jilted him. Sarah Redding left Gage Gatlin standing at the altar.*

It wasn't true, damn it! He marched down the aisle

and flung open the door so hard it slammed against the clapboard wall. It was probably eighty or more degrees in the shade as he stalked through town, his boots ringing on the boardwalk so that shoppers and anyone else in his path scattered.

He knew what this was about, embarrassing him like this. Hurting his pride and his feelings and making a mess out of everything that was right in his life. It was those words he couldn't say to her. That's what she'd been so upset about last night, and he thought he'd settled the matter. Fixed the problem.

But no, she decided to do it this way. Instead of listening to reason, she'd decided to hurt him and his daughter in front of half the town. Not that he gave a damn what people thought, but it was the humiliation of it. He'd taken a punch to the guts and it hurt.

His anger grew with every step he took across the street. By the time he yanked open the boarding house's front door, he was livid. Ready to let her have it. She wanted to play tough, that was fine by him. He pounded up the stairs and raised his hand to slam his fist into the door.

And heard her sobbing, muffled through the wood. Raw and painful. The way heartbreak sounds.

The fight drained right out of him. He dropped his fist to his side and took a shaky breath, trying to figure out what in the hell to do.

She was crying on the other side of that door. Crying. All because he couldn't play make-believe.

He hated that she was hurting that much. Over something foolish, something that was impossible to have. What a mistake he'd made, thinking what he had to offer her was enough. Half the women in town would have jumped at what he offered, but no, not Sarah.

The door was unlocked, so there was no resistance as he opened it. The hinges creaked and the floorboards groaned beneath his boots as he dared to ease inside.

There she was, in a puddle of blue silk on the floor, her hair tumbling over her shoulders, her hands to her face, shoulders shaking.

"Go away." She didn't look up.

"Oh, Sarah." What in the blazes did he do? He closed the door and tried to figure it out. If he went down on one knee, she'd know she was right. That she'd won the argument.

But if he didn't, was there a way to repair this?

He decided to stand. It was safer, keeping this the way he meant it to be. Realistic. Pragmatic. Logical. "The reverend said he'd wait. If you want to go now—"

"I c-can't." She raised a tear-streaked face. Her skin was ruddy, her eyes red.

This wasn't fake crying, and he eased onto his knees. Wiped a teardrop from her cheek with the pad of his thumb. "Sure you can. We can get a little wash water and some hairpins. It's not too late to mend this."

"How can we fix this? You don't even know what's wrong."

"I figure it's got something to do with last night. Look how hard you've been crying. You're miserable, Sarah, and I hate it. I hate seeing you hurt like this."

Her lower lip trembled. "It hurts when the man you love doesn't love you in return."

"Oh, angel. There's enough hurt going around right now."

"I'm sorry."

"No, it's all right." He took her hand in his, the diamonds sparkling pure and true, a symbol of everything they could have together, and it heartened him. This could still work. If he could find the right words. "See why I think romantic love is a bad ingredient in a relationship? It gets everything all confused and turned around. It hurts too much."

"And so it's better never to love so you don't have to hurt?" That wasn't right. She wasn't reacting the way he thought she should. More tears brimmed her eyelashes but did not fall. "Love is the only thing that matters. There are a thousand practical reasons why I ought to marry you. It's convenient, we're compatible, it's good for the girls, I never have to work two jobs again. But there's only one reason why I can't marry you."

"Sarah." This was killing him. Couldn't she see it? "What I feel for you is honest and real enough for you to touch and see. It's not a myth, it's not something that will fade. This lasts. This matters. This, right here." He twined his fingers through hers. "This is what lasts. Faithfulness. Duty. Responsibility. Mutual regard. We can get along just like we've been doing. I'm my happiest when I'm with you."

"Stop it." She scrambled to her feet in a froth of blue silk and shimmering ribbon. "I can't do this. Don't you see? You don't love me. You don't love *me*."

All she could hear was the words "duty, responsibility, mutual regard" over and over in her head as she looked at him. This man still willing to marry her.

Still believing the best she could hope for was a dutiful, mutually satisfying, *friendly* marriage.

She wanted to be his one true love. The woman he cherished above all else.

Sarah wrapped her arms around her middle and wished she could hold him instead. That a hug and a kiss and wedding vows would make this all right.

It couldn't.

So she said what needed to be said. Found the courage to end a relationship with the best man she had ever known. The man she'd had the privilege to love.

She pulled the ring from her finger and presented it to him, the diamonds sparkling in mockery of the promises he could not keep.

His eyes clouded. "I gave that to you to wear forever."

"I know." This was so hard, but she had to do it. She blinked fast, keeping the emotion down. It was what she had to do.

"Here." She pressed the ring into his palm as he towered over her, all formidable man. "I hope you can find it in that hard heart of yours to forgive me. I know I'm hurting you."

"Disappointing me." His chin shot up as if nothing could ever wound him. He was tough to the core and looked it. As he bowed his head to stare at the ring, a dark shank of hair tumbled over his forehead.

She itched to touch him one more time, even in the pretense of brushing his hair into place. But she'd returned his ring. She wasn't the woman he loved. It wasn't her right.

"I'll be out to fetch my things." She cleared her throat. "And to say goodbye to Lucy."

"Goodbye?" What for? Was she leaving?

"I won't be seeing her anymore." Sarah looked distant, like a stranger, as she opened the door for him. Gestured for him to go.

Just like that. He would walk out of her life. The best thing that had ever happened to him. Not that he loved her. But it felt as if he'd lost everything.

"Take care of yourself, Gage."

He caught a brief glimpse of anguish on her face as she closed the door on him and locked it. The clink echoed down the hall and in the empty places within his chest. Where his heart was supposed to be.

"Sarah is gonna come. You wait and see." Lucy sat stubbornly on the ranch house front step and refused to budge. She had her sewing in her lap, hemming the doll dress Sarah had helped her make. "I'm gonna get this done, 'cuz, you know what? She's gonna be real surprised I did this all by myself."

"Lucy, I know this is tough, but you've got to accept this. Sarah isn't coming back. She doesn't want to marry me."

"Does, too." Lucy poked the thin needle through the fabric, head bent. "Sarah loves us."

He couldn't deny it. Wouldn't do any good to argue about it. Sarah did love them, that was the trouble. She had to go and turn this compatible connection between them into a romance.

He wasn't going to have anything to do with it. He wasn't going to open himself up to that kind of pain again. He feelings shut down, he felt numb remembering what it had been like. The cold silences. The angry accusations. The aching disappointments. May's tears in the night, tears he couldn't console.

The same way Sarah had been crying. Raw and

hurting, and it was a waste, that's what it was. A plain waste of emotion. What he and Sarah had together was ten times—no, a hundred times—better than any marriage he could think of. Passion and laughter and honesty. His way had worked just fine. The girls had been happy. He and Sarah had been happy. Why did she have to go and ruin that? Look what she was doing to Lucy.

"Do you know what, Pa?" Lucy tugged the thread through the fabric. "Sarah needed a dress. That's why she didn't come. Know what? We could go to the store and buy her one."

"It's not that simple." He settled on to the step next to her. "I wish it was."

"You just gotta buy a dress, Pa. You don't gotta make it." Lucy glared at him. "Hitch up the buggy and we can go. I'm gonna help. I sew now, so I know about dresses."

"No, darlin'."

"But Sarah loves me. Just like a ma." Lucy's voice rose, thin and trembling and full of pain. "She made me a doll and she braids my hair and she's just like a ma. She was gonna marry us. She *promised*."

He tugged Lucy onto his lap, holding her against his chest while she cried. Horrible, wrenching sobs that shook her little body. He couldn't help feeling angry. This was Sarah's doing. Hurting Lucy like this.

He'd been crazy, that's what. Plumb loco to think a relationship with a woman could have worked out. Sarah may be special, but she was a woman. She wanted fancy words and romance and fairy tales, and that kind of thing could ruin a man's life. And his daughter's.

Never again, Gage vowed as he comforted Lucy the

best he could, holding her until there were no more tears, and holding her some more. There was trouble in the fields, but Gage waved Juan away. Let him deal with it the best he could—he was more than capable. Gage wasn't about to leave his child alone like this.

He wasn't ever going to expose her to this kind of pain again.

Next time he saw a beautiful woman with kindness in her heart and a smile that turned him inside out, he was going to keep on riding. Next time he felt this amazing connection, this understanding with a woman, as if being with her was the most natural thing in the world, as if he were made to do it. He'd remember Lucy's tears and walk away.

What have I done? Sarah sat in the dark, the lamp turned low as midnight neared, and listened to Ella's muffled tears.

Had she made the wrong decision? Her finger felt bare without the golden band. It was amazing how quickly she'd gotten used to it, and how much she'd treasured it. Not because of the gold and diamonds, far more fine than any material possession she'd ever owned, but because she thought it represented Gage's love.

When he'd wanted duty. Friendship. Passion in the night. And nothing more. He didn't harbor a deep emotional love for her. Never had. What had he said? That love was a fairy tale. He didn't cherish her love. Didn't believe in it.

Ella had taken the news hard. She'd wanted to be best friends and sisters with Lucy. To ride horses and play in the green fields and make mud pies in the shade of a pretty white house.

She was still crying, silently into her pillow, her hopes shattered, too. What of Lucy? Sarah hated to think of Lucy, who'd wanted a mother so badly, crying, too. And Gage?

No, Gage wouldn't be devastated. He hadn't loved her, so how could he be hurting? He wasn't in love. He hadn't lost his heart's desire.

Sarah felt cold, even though the breeze filtering through the curtains was warm. She was lost without Gage. How was she going to live without him? How was she going to move on, get through each day? See him on the street and wave, as if nothing had ever happened between them?

She couldn't. What she had to do was leave. Make a new start in a new place, where she wouldn't have constant reminders of Gage and how she hadn't been enough for him to love.

Why, she hadn't planned on staying in this town anyway. Ella was well. There were other opportunities in other places. She had to find the right one. Somewhere out there, there could be another man with eyes the color of the wind. A wonderful man with a touch that seared her to the soul.

But it didn't seem likely.

Damn it, he couldn't sleep. Gage tossed back the sheet that smelled faintly of Sarah's rose soap. He should have changed the sheets. The scent was driving him crazy. His feet hit the floor and he grabbed his denims. Maybe a hard ride would help him get Sarah out of his head.

The sound of her crying. The way she'd said, "You don't love *me*," as if it were something personal. As if he couldn't see what a special bond they shared.

And how wounded he was that it wasn't good enough for her.

At the back door, he jammed his feet into his boots. Tried not to remember it was that place at the counter where he'd kissed Sarah for the first time. First tasted her passion that made him hunger for more. The stove where they'd cooked together. The garden patch outside she'd planted for Lucy. Well tended, with lacy carrot greens marching in a neat row, the young peas and beans strung up on poles, and the silky tassels of growing corn.

Reminders of Sarah were everywhere he looked. In the barn where the kittens slept. The buggy she used to drive. Each sight lashed through him with the sting of a bullwhip, and he didn't bother with bridle or saddle. He rode bareback into the night and came across the field where he and Sarah first made love.

It felt as if someone had taken a knife to him and carved out his heart. Left him bleeding and mortally wounded. Nothing had ever hurt like this. Nothing.

A pack of coyotes streaked by, crouched low, nothing more than wraiths moving through the dried grasses. Then he heard it, a faint rapport that disappeared across the vast plains. Growing louder. Birds scattered from the grasses, squawking with alarm. Antelope breaking around him sailed over the split-rail fence.

Gage smelled the smoke, faint, but unmistakable.

"Gatlin!" Juan's warning rang above a distant thundering from somewhere near the creek.

A stampede, coming his way. But that wasn't the trouble the foreman meant. Smoke scented the air as the earth quaked and the night felt thick with the terror of stampeding animals.

A horse whisked past him. Another broke stride and nearly bashed straight into the mare.

His heart kicked as his mount bunched and strained beneath him, ready to bolt. He tightened the reins, riding the bit hard, leaning forward to talk low to her. "Easy, girl. You keep right on going. I'll get you through this."

The night broke apart around them in high-pitched bawls and neighs of terror. The drum of hoofs and the dust and the crush of a stampede pushing his horse back. An impossible force, a fast-moving current of horses and cows. The mare reared with terror, and he dug in his heels to control her.

Gage wrestled the mare through the mass of panicked animals, cutting diagonally through the deafening thunder of cattle and horses, gritting his teeth as a bull horn scraped his thigh.

He had to find Juan. He had to gather enough men to stop that fire, but the savage night fought him and there seemed no end to it. Already red glow stretched across his fence line, spreading lightning-fast through the tinder-dry grasses. Coming his way.

Toward the stables and the barns. Toward the house. With Lucy in it.

"Juan!" He cupped his hands.

A sting pierced his arm. He looked down and saw a bright crimson stain on his shirt, eerily lit by the glow of the rising flames. He'd been shot? Another crack boomed above the stampede and the greedy lick of the flames.

He felt the strength drain from his thighs. He was slipping to the left so he grabbed hold of the mare's thick mane. Held on as a cow slammed into the mare's hindquarters, spinning them against the fence, out of danger.

Before he could recover, a stinging pain skidded across his ribs. Another bullet. His fingers slipped and he slid in slow motion as the world tilted crazily in a swirl of red flames and thundering animals. He hit the ground with a teeth-rattling thud.

Hot blood wet his shirt as he came to rest in the grass. The mare sidestepped, ready to panic, her hooves striking the ground less than two inches from his chest.

He gritted he teeth, a growl tearing through him, and rolled away. The mare reared, churning the ground where his head had been.

"Look what I found, boys." Milt Owen seemed as tall as the sky with the old breech-loading Henry rifle braced in both hands.

Pointed at Gage's heart.

He acted without thinking. Grabbed the nose of the rifle and yanked it up and around. Almost had it.

Out of nowhere a rifle jammed against his chest and drove him into the ground.

"You ain't goin' nowhere, Gatlin." A boot caught him beneath the jaw.

Gage's head slammed into the ground. Stars flashed behind his eyes. He blinked, realizing there were four men towering over him. Guns gleamed darkly. His entire shirt was wet with blood.

"Who's the loser now?" The butt of Milt's rifle swung through the air and slammed into the side of Gage's face. Pain exploded in his jaw.

"Gonna call the sheriff? Looks like you can't get up. Too bad. I've got the upper hand now, boy. Now you'll know what it feels like when someone pushes you around.''

Gage didn't see the blow coming to his midsection, and the pain left him sick and dizzy. "I'm not your problem, Owens. You stole from me. I took back what was mine. Can't blame a man for that."

"Sure I can.'' Milt's boot slammed into Gage's head. "I needed them cattle. My family needed food on the table. I lost everything. Don't see why you can't join me."

Come on, Gatlin, you can get out of this. He thought of Lucy asleep in her bed. Of the grassfire speeding toward the house.

That was all the strength he needed. Gage knocked the Henry off his chest, felt the burn of smoke and fire as it went off. He lunged at Milt's knees, bringing him down with a heavy thud. The gun went flying as bullets fired, hitting the dirt around him. Milt's fist connected to his chest. Blood gushed from Gage's chest and he sputtered, fighting for breath.

"Gage!" It was Juan. Guns blazing, he appeared out of the thick smoke. He hit his target and one of Milt's hired men slumped to the ground.

Milt dove for cover, leaving Gage in the open. Bullets peppered the dirt all around him. He spotted a boulder, in the shelter of the creek bank, and ran for it. He dropped to his knees, safe from the gunfire. Trouble was, he had no gun.

"I sent my father to get Lucy out of the house." Juan slipped around the other side of the rock. Breathing hard. Bleeding harder. "I got shot but good. Those bastards crept through the grass. I didn't see 'em until it was too late. We're three against two."

"Don't like those odds, but I've had worse."

"Think we'll get out of this?" Juan emptied the bullets from his belt and handed over his revolver. "Needs loading. My hand's shaking too damn hard to do it."

"You're hurt pretty bad." Coughing, he pulled a handkerchief out of his trouser pocket and tied it around his face.

"I've still got some fight in me." Juan steadied the rifle on the boulder and sighted carefully. "They're taking time to surround us." He squeezed the trigger, the gun fired, and a bullet thudded into human flesh. "Winged him. Down, but not dead."

Gage squeezed off a shot. Knocked Milt's hat off his head and, judging by the cry of pain, skimmed his skull. "Guess Milt jumped the lookout."

"Wally took a bullet wound to the shoulder. Pretty bad, but he's going to make it. Seems Milt and his friends figured to steal some of your best breeding mares. They were a little short on cash." Juan stopped to squeeze off a couple shots. "Damn it. Missed. They started the fire to distract us when we had them surrounded."

"Tried to get away, did they?" Looked like it just might work. Gage caught sight of the wall of quick-moving flames that lashed at the sky. Tall now. Feasting greedily on the dead grasses, driven by the wind. Moving faster than a man could run. Moving directly toward them.

Bullets hammered into the creek bank two feet from his head. Fragments of clay and granite dove into his skin, and he shielded his face with one arm. Spotted a flash of movement against the orange wall of flames and sited it. Pulled the trigger. One of the hired men dropped to the ground. Didn't move.

"Two against two. Better odds." Gage tried to get a better view, but gunfire forced him back. "Take a look and see if they've gotten around us on your side. Hate to have one of those bastards shoot us in the back. Juan?"

Juan lay slumped against the boulder. "I'm bleeding bad, Gage. I can't hold the gun."

Chunks of the creek bank were breaking apart, exposing them more with each section that gave way under the gunfire.

It was only a matter of time before they could be taken from the side or behind.

"Hold on, buddy. We'll see if I can get us out of this." Gage took the Winchester.

He was ready. He could do this. With the rifle in one hand, the Peacemaker in the other, stumbled from behind the rock, already shooting. Hit Milt square in the chest. Owens tumbled forward, gun spitting fire.

Cold streaks shot through Gage's leg and chest. Bullets that knocked him backward. He stumbled, fighting for his balance. Where was the last gunman? Bullets peppered Gage from the side—there, heading for the creek and escape.

Fiery columns of flame hurled between them and Gage couldn't see anything but the fire approaching so fast, he couldn't get a clear shot.

It didn't matter. His knees were buckling. He tasted blood as the ground rose up to meet him. Lying there, he knew he thought about dying. About Sarah.

Sarah's kiss. Sarah's smile. Sarah's touch in the night.

He loved Sarah with all the depth of his being. And if he died here, she would never know it.

Blood choked him as he stumbled to his knees.

Caught Juan by the arm and crawled. Red embers rained down on him. His forearms blistered from the heat. It seemed like an eternity before he tumbled into the cool waters of the creek. Fire exploded behind him.

Gage pulled Juan onto the far bank and collapsed.

Chapter Sixteen

The town hadn't changed during the week she'd been away. So many things had changed in her life, that it seemed surprising. As if she could forget the past few weeks, and her memory could take her back to Gage. To the happy times she'd spent with him.

But it was too late, and she knew it as she walked through the door and into the doctor's office.

"Sarah." He looked up from his book and pushed back his spectacles. "I was just wondering about you. Heard you were out of town."

"I was looking for a new place to live. I need a change from Montana," she explained. It wasn't exactly a lie, but admitting the truth would hurt so much. She didn't want any reminders of Gage Gatlin. She had to move on.

"So, you'll be leaving us?"

"I'm not sure to where, yet, but my husband's cousin lives in Idaho Territory and owns a dress shop. I might have a part-time job with her. I'm still deciding. I'm here because I want to reassure you that I intend to continue making payments on Ella's bill."

"That's not necessary." He snapped his thick medical text closed. "Mr. Gatlin paid your account in full."

"He *what?*" She had to have misunderstood. "That was a lot of money. You mean he just walked in here and paid it?"

"Yep. You don't owe me a cent." The doctor took off his glasses and folded them. "Since you just came back to town, you might not have heard. There was a gunfight between Gage and your uncle. Milt's dead. Gage was hurt."

"How bad?"

"He's on his feet and back at the ranch. That foreman of his took a bad gunshot wound, but he's home, too." The doctor opened the door for her. "Thought maybe you should know. Seeing as how you nearly married the man."

She thanked the doctor. Halfway down the boardwalk she realized she was walking the wrong way. Not toward the boarding house, where Ella was waiting with Mrs. Flannery. Where she intended to start packing their belongings. But toward Gage's ranch.

It was finished between them. He didn't love her, she'd given back his ring and was planning a new future without him.

So why was she walking so fast? Why was Gage still trying to make her life better? He didn't have the right.

Gage tilted his hat to keep the sinking afternoon sun from his face. His shoulder screamed in protest. Working all day hadn't done his wounds any favors, but he wasn't about to sit around when there was rebuilding to do.

Besides, keeping busy kept him from thinking about Sarah. The woman he'd lost.

When he'd regained consciousness in the doctor's clinic, Gage had asked for her. Was told she'd left town the day before. Gone, just like that. When he was up and walking, he'd tried to hunt down Mary Flannery, but she had gone to Butte to visit her new grandbaby.

He'd had his chance and he'd blown it. He had no one to blame but himself. He sunk the shovel deep into the blackened earth and leaned on the handle.

He'd lost his outbuildings, his first hay crop, his well, his orchard, the new bunkhouse and the house in the fire. He'd lost all those things, but none of it compared to losing Sarah.

The bay filly nosed him, looking for more sugar. He rubbed her nose and was grateful he had good men working for him. And good neighbors. While he'd been laid up, others had rounded up his animals and corralled them. His hired men had started rebuilding fences and outbuildings. The house was next.

"Hey, Gatlin." Juan called out from his chair in the shade. "Looks like another one of those town ladies bringing you a cake or something."

"Great." The minute he'd been released from the doctor's care, the baskets and baking had started up again. It wasn't because of the fire or his injury. He hadn't married Sarah Redding, and was available again.

Not that he could ever marry anyone else.

He jammed his shovel into the earth, leaving it standing upright as he prepared to politely discourage yet another husband-hunting lady without hurting her feelings.

This time there was no fancy surrey rattling up his driveway. Only a slender woman walking along the dusty lane, her face shaded by a plain sunbonnet.

Sarah. She was too far away to see clearly, but he knew her in an instant. Was he dreaming? He blinked and she was still there, the wind shaping her calico dress around her soft, womanly curves. Curves he loved so well.

"The doc said you were injured. I'm glad you're up and around." She breezed to a halt in front of him, reserved, turning to study the prairie, as if that was what she had come for. "I'm relieved to see that you're all right."

"As right as rain."

Still, she refused to look at him. "You must have lost nearly everything."

"The livestock made it all right. Lucy rescued her new rag doll and the kittens from the barn. No lives were lost. We have what matters most, so I call that lucky."

"I'm glad Lucy is all right. Is she here?"

"She's in town at a birthday party."

"Oh. I wanted to say goodbye. I'm leaving tomorrow morning and I—" Then she saw the bruise beneath the brim of his hat, purple-red and as big as her fist. "So, you are hurt and you're just not admitting it. Look at that bruise."

"I'll be fine, Sarah. I'm the toughest horseman this side of the Rockies, remember?"

"I knew you were going to say that." It was like old times, she realized. She would laugh and Gage would take her into his arms and they'd be together. It was magic, this connection between them, and standing in his presence was all it took to make her hope for what could never be.

It was time to go, before she decided she'd take him any way she could have him. That his mutual regard was ten times more wonderful than another man's love.

But he didn't seem to want her.

"There's one more thing, Gage. I understand you paid Ella's medical bills."

"Guilty as charged. I wanted to help."

"I know, and it's generous of you. You're a generous man, and I'll always love you for it. But the last thing I want from you is money." She wanted what could not be. "I'm going to pay back every cent, and I need you to agree. My debts aren't your responsibility or your duty. I never want to be any man's duty."

"You handle the debt the way you want, Sarah. I didn't mean any harm."

Did he have to be so kind? It took all her willpower to turn away. "Goodbye, Gage."

"'Bye, Sarah."

She moved one foot forward. Then another. She *could* find the strength to walk away and leave him behind.

If only her other foot would move. It seemed glued to the earth and she couldn't lift it.

Maybe it wasn't her foot that wouldn't let her leave.

"Sarah. Before you go, I want to show you something." Gage held out his hand, palm up, a quiet invitation. "There's one thing that survived the fire, and I want you to see it."

She remembered all the times she'd placed her hand in his, skin to skin, palm to palm, his fingers twining through hers. If she touched him, then it would all come back. The way he'd brought love to her life. And what she would give up if she stayed.

She let him take her hand. He led her down the road and across the blackened yard where Ella and Lucy had once played. Across the steps where she'd sat in the evenings with Gage. To the blackened ashes that used to be the parlor, where the chimney towered above the ruins, blackened but not destroyed.

Gage released her hand and pulled out a corner brick to reveal a hollow. She couldn't see what was there, for the setting sun made the light thin and the shadows deep, but she knew.

"Your wedding ring." Gage held the gold band between two fingers, the diamonds sparkling like the joy he felt every time he looked at her. "This alone survived."

She couldn't believe it. The ring sparkled, rare and true, unharmed.

"I love you, Sarah Redding."

"You said you don't believe in love."

"I'm a poor, misguided, ignorant man, and I was wrong."

"That's absolutely true and I'm glad you realize it." She wiped tears from her eyes. "So now you believe love exists?"

"Absolutely, one hundred percent certain." He slid the ring onto her finger. "I've come to realize that I've never known love before you. Since I'm an ignorant, misguided fellow, I had the right to be scared."

"A big, tough lawman like you?"

She came into his arms soft as a breeze, and his love for her doubled as she rested her cheek against his chest. She felt so precious in his arms, and he was going to cherish her for the rest of his life. This woman who'd melted his heart of stone with her romantic love and dreams of forever.

And this would last forever, he knew. Because what mattered in this world could never be destroyed. Like brick and mortar, that's how strong their love was and would always be.

"Look at the sunset." Sarah pulled away from him, her skirts swirling around her slim ankles as she faced the west, where brilliant golds and purples lit the grand peaks of the Rocky Mountains. "I made a wish once, standing with you in the field."

"I remember." He joined her, feeling the changing light on his face, feeling the world transform around him. "What did you wish for?"

"That you would love me." She worried her bottom lip between her teeth, as if she were debating something important. "You told me once that you would say the words I wanted to hear, if that's what it took for me to marry you. Is that what you're doing? Because if it is, I can't be your wife. I can't be convenient and useful. I want to be cherished, just once. I want—"

He covered her mouth with his in a caress of lips and tongue. A tender, possessive kiss that made her toes curls and desire twist deep inside.

"This is no convenient kiss, is it?" He kissed her again, sucking her lip between his in a slow, sensual glide.

"It doesn't feel like one, no."

He folded her against him so they were breast to chest, hip to hip, thigh to thigh. So she could feel the hard ridge of his arousal against her stomach. "Does this feel like a useful hug to you? Or one that a man would give to the woman he cherishes?''

"You cherish me?'' It was too much to hope for, this happiness, this gift he was giving her.

"You are my first star of the night, Sarah, and my last star in the morning. All my hopes and all my dreams are right here. In what I feel for you. And if you don't believe me, look.''

The first star of the night. It glimmered pure and rare against the darkness.

"As long as that star burns, so will my love for you.'' His promise touched her deep in her heart. "Marry me, Sarah.''

"For love?''

"For love.''

How could she ask for more? The ring on her finger, the affection in Gage's touch as he pulled her close. Sarah knew she would love him for the rest of her life. "Look, Gage. The second star of the night. For as long as that star burns, I will love you.''

Sarah felt treasured as he held her close and led her through the ruins and down into the field, where the grass was fresh and green. Where wild roses scented the air. She welcomed her friend, her lover and her soon-to-be husband into her arms. They made love as the stars came out, one by one, and smiled down on them.

*   *   *   *   *

JILLIAN HART

grew up in rural Washington State where she learned how to climb trees, build tree houses and ride ponies. A perfect childhood for a historical romance author. She left home and went to college and has lived in cities ever since. But the warm memories from her childhood still linger in her heart, memories she incorporates into her stories. When Jillian is not hard at work on her next novel, she enjoys reading, flower gardening, hiking with her husband and trying to train her wiggly cocker spaniel puppy to sit. And failing.

Cravin' stories of love and adventure
set against the backdrop of the Wild West?
Then check out these thrilling tales from
Harlequin Historicals

ON SALE NOVEMBER 2002
RAFFERTY'S BRIDE
by **Mary Burton**
(West Texas, 1866)
*Will revenge evolve into a powerful attraction
between a life-hardened military man and
a bewitching nurse?*

BECKETT'S BIRTHRIGHT
by **Bronwyn Williams**
(North Carolina, 1890s)
Book #2 of *Beckett's Fortune* miniseries
*Watch for this prequel in the riveting new
cross-line series from Harlequin Historicals
and Silhouette Desire!*

ON SALE DECEMBER 2002
BOUNTY HUNTER'S BRIDE
by **Carol Finch**
(Arkansas and Texas, 1870s)
*Forbidden love ignites when a New Orleans
debutante weds a half-breed bounty hunter....*

BADLANDS HEART
by **Ruth Langan**
(Dakota Territory, 1888)
Book #3 of the *Badlands* series
*A feisty cowgirl falls head over heels
for a mysterious stranger!*

 Harlequin Historicals®
Historical Romantic Adventure!

Visit us at www.eHarlequin.com   HHWEST22

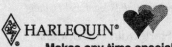
HINTBB

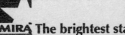

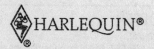

Free Gift Offer

With a Free Gift proof-of-purchase
from any Harlequin® book, you can receive
a beautiful cubic zirconia pendant.

This stunning marquise-shaped stone is a genuine cubic
zirconia—accented by an 18" gold tone necklace.
(Approximate retail value $19.95)

Send for yours today...
compliments of ✦ HARLEQUIN®

To receive your free gift, a cubic zirconia pendant, send us one original proof-of-purchase, photocopies not accepted, from the back of any Harlequin Romance®, Harlequin Presents®, Harlequin Temptation®, Harlequin Superromance®, Harlequin Intrigue®, Harlequin American Romance®, or Harlequin Historicals® title available at your favorite retail outlet, together with the Free Gift Certificate, plus a check or money order for $1.65 U.S./$2.15 CAN. (do not send cash) to cover postage and handling, payable to Harlequin Free Gift Offer. We will send you the specified gift. Allow 6 to 8 weeks for delivery. Offer good until December 31, 1997, or while quantities last. Offer valid in the U.S. and Canada only.

Free Gift Certificate

Name: _____

Address: _____

City: _____ State/Province: _____ Zip/Postal Code: _____

Mail this certificate, one proof-of-purchase and a check or money order for postage and handling to: HARLEQUIN FREE GIFT OFFER 1997. In the U.S.: 3010 Walden Avenue, P.O. Box 9071, Buffalo NY 14269-9057. In Canada: P.O. Box 604, Fort Erie, Ontario L2Z 5X3.

FREE GIFT OFFER   084-KEZ
ONE PROOF-OF-PURCHASE
To collect your fabulous FREE GIFT, a cubic zirconia pendant, you must include this original proof-of-purchase for each gift with the properly completed Free Gift Certificate.

084-KEZR

cupped her breasts, kneading and stroking until she bit her lip to keep from crying out.

"Seems to me you definitely like that." He plucked at her buttons again and slipped inside her dress. "Left your corset off, did you?"

"Hmm." It was all the speech she could manage. Pure bliss. She felt every muscle in her body relax. So good. So very good. She moaned when he withdrew his touch, leaving her breasts heavy and aching.

"I think we're officially alone." He helped her up, keeping her close at his side. "Let's find someplace more private."

"Not your bedroom. The thought of the girls right across the hall—"

"One day you're going to have to get used to that." His fingers curved around her nape, then trailed down her back in slow, sizzling strokes. "For now, I understand. We'll find a place to be alone, together."

"I'd love that."

"Good." His fingers stole into her gaping dress and caressed her. "I want you tonight, Sarah. I've never wanted anyone the way I want you."

His words knocked away the last of her disbelief. The doubt she'd been holding inside. The part of her that thought this was too good to be true, too incredible to be real. That Gage, heroic and strong and kind, would want her, Sarah Redding.

Because he did want her. His touch, his words, the tender brush of his lips against her temple. She wanted him, needed him, more than the earth at her feet.

As if he understood, he pulled her into the grasses. There was no need for words as he pulled the clothes from her until she was naked in the moonlight, shel-

face. Sarah couldn't ignore the flicker of want inside her that happened every time she looked at Gage.

The evening seemed to last forever. After supper Sarah ironed the curtains she'd finished hemming and Gage hung them in the dining room, according to the girls's instructions. Later, after bedtime stories and a lot of orders to quiet down, the girls seemed to be asleep, each tucked into their own bunk bed.

"Finally." Gage commented as he stole into the parlor. "It's only eleven."

"Are they actually asleep? And not faking?"

"I say we give them a few more minutes and we'll know for sure." He joined her on the front step and pulled her into the curve of his side. His arms held her tight as he nuzzled her ear. "I've been waiting for this all day. Couldn't think of much else."

"At least you didn't land in the sticker patch again."

"That's because I took a machete to it this morning. It's gone." His hands caressed the curve of her shoulders. "I didn't know if I could take another session of being doctored by you. I may have lost all control."

"What about now?"

"Close." He laved an extremely tender spot behind her ear.

Pleasure shivered through her and she leaned back against him. "That's nice."

"Nice? I don't want nice." He kissed lower, where her neck curved into her shoulder, while his hands circled around her waist. "I intend to ravish you, my sweet lady."

"I might like that." She arched her back as he